WINTER'S QUEEN

GIA
DAUGHTER

JENNIFER ALLIS PROVOST

C000075604

Giant's Daughter
Winter's Queen Trilogy Book Two

By Jennifer Allis Provost

Published by Bellatrix Press
Copyright 2021 Jennifer Allis Provost

All rights reserved

Publisher's Note
This is a work of fiction. Names, characters, places, and incidents either are the product of the author's imagination or are used fictitiously, and any resemblance to actual persons, living or dead, business establishments, events, or locales is entirely coincidental. The scanning, uploading and distribution of this book via the Internet or via any other means without the permission of the publisher is illegal and punishable by law. Please purchase only authorized electronic editions, and do not participate in or encourage electronic piracy of copyrighted materials. Your support of the author's rights is appreciated.

Electronic Edition, License Notes
This ebook is licensed for your personal enjoyment only. This ebook may not be re-sold or given away to other people. If you would like to share this book with another person, please purchase an additional copy for each person. If you're reading this book and did not purchase it, or it was not purchased for your use only, then please purchase your own copy. Thank you for respecting the hard work of this author.

Cover by Cover Villain

Chapter One
Anya

It was the second day of winter, and Christopher and I were standing in front of the old *shieling* with its courtyard of small, man-shaped stones at Glen Lyon. Today was the day we'd free my da, the giant called the Bodach, and my brothers from the stones they'd been imprisoned in for more than two hundred years. At least, we hoped we would free them.

We'd held off acting on our plan until after Samhain, in order to allow winter to begin and my new abilities as its queen time to fully manifest. Mum's theory was that since it had taken the full might of the Seelie King to imprison Da and the boys, it would likely take all of the Winter Queen's power to undo the curse. Never mind that when Mum was Queen of Winter she had attempted to free them time and again and nothing had happened, not even when she threw every spell and trick she knew at the stones. Still, even though my mother had reigned for thousands of years, and my reign had lasted mere days, I had an advantage she'd never have: my true father's blood.

No one, least of all myself, had suspected I'd been fathered by Udane, or anyone other than the Bodach. Udane had once been the counterpart to my mother as Elphame's Summer King. He was now known as Maelgwyn, the Unseelie King. This odd branch on my family tree meant I had inherited a portion of my father's power, which, along with what I'd gotten from Mum, meant I was more powerful that either of them.

It meant that I might actually be able to free my family.

A raw gust of air pummeled me, and I hunkered down into my coat; for all that I controlled winter I still felt the cold in every bone and sinew in my body. The sun shone brightly in spite of the frigid wind, and we were lucky it was as warm as it was. Sometimes, the countryside in and around Glen Lyon saw snow this early in the season.

Sometimes, I let myself get distracted by small things

like the weather to avoid doing what I'd set out to accomplish. Namely, reuniting my family once and for all.

And what if I could free them, and live among Da and my brothers as a complete family again? I'd wanted this for so long I could feel it. Needed it so much I could taste it.

Gods below, what if I fail?

I took a deep breath, and closed my eyes.

Don't worry, Da. I've almost got you.

I reached out not toward the stones, but to my right. Christopher, there as he always was, grasped my hand and squeezed.

"Are you ready?" he asked.

"Yes. Speaking of ready, do you have your phone?"

"I do."

Christopher held up his phone, revealing his sister's information queued up on the screen. We probably wouldn't need Karina's assistance, but Maelgwyn had pointed out that the stones may be portals, thus meaning Da and the rest might actually be imprisoned elsewhere in Scotland, or on an entirely different plane. If portals were involved, best to have Karina, the only living walker between worlds, on hand to deal with them.

"I doubt they're portals," Christopher said, sensing my thoughts as he always did. "When we freed Long Meg and her crew we took them directly out of their stones. I imagine it will be much the same here."

I nodded, and refocused my attention on the stones. When we'd retrieved Long Meg—yet another giant; my family was fair riddled with them—Christopher and I had walked widdershins around the stone that held her, thus undoing the knot of spells that held her fast. It was a brilliant spell, elegant in its simplicity. I hoped someday to be able to create such graceful and sophisticated spells myself.

I didn't sense the same type of spell around the *shieling* or its stones. This spell was simple, but it rather than the elegance that wove through Meg's spell true and fast, this was coarse, as if it had been thrown together in a rush and the caster had never bothered to revisit and fine-tune his work. If that wasn't an apt description of the Seelie King, throwing gobs of power at a problem and hoping for a speedy resolution, I didn't know what was.

Despite the sloppy spellwork, the prison had held these many years. Whatever was holding my family in the stones was an enchantment I was unfamiliar with, but I was certain it wasn't a web of knots.

"If not knots, then what?"

"What was that?" Christopher asked.

"Just thinking out loud."

I squinted at the stones, wondering if I could see evidence of whatever magic had been used. I'd never seen such things before, but I'd never been the Queen of Winter before, either. What this magic would look like, I couldn't guess. Sparkles, maybe? Just as I was about to ask Christopher to call his sister and ask if she had any ideas, I spied something near the largest stone's base.

"Could this be it?" I wondered, crouching down to have a closer look. Around the base of Da's stone weren't any sparkles or runes or other obvious signs of spell craft, but the area looked different. The colors of the grasses were more vibrant, and the air smelled of lightning.

"The spell is in the base," I said. "Whatever's holding them inside the stones, it's where the stones meet the ground."

Christopher crouched beside me. I wondered what he saw, this brilliant mortal who'd been touched by Elphame. "Does that mean if we tip the stones over, your family will be free? They can just climb on out?"

I blinked. It couldn't be that easy, could it?

"Only one way to find out." I got on my knees and heaved at Da's stone. I've always been strong; I used to think it was on account of being a giant's daughter. Now I know my strength comes from elsewhere, but it was the memory of the man that raised me I pulled on. Still, the stone, small though it was, did not budge.

"Maybe we need to rock it back and forth," Christopher suggested. "It's been here a while, right? Maybe it's just stuck."

"All right, then." We positioned ourselves on either side of the stone. "Toward me."

Christopher pushed, then I heaved it back toward him. After we did this a few times, the stone moved. It was the barest movement, but it was there.

"It's working," Christopher said. "Harder, now."

We kept rocking the stone back and forth, each push and pull loosening it ever so slightly. Then the stone moved of its own accord, trembled like a leaf in a gale, and flopped to the side. Underneath the stone was a deep, dark hole. I peered inside, and called, "Da?"

"Anya?"

"Da!"

I went down flat on my belly and thrust my hand as far into the hole as it would go. "Da, grab on!"

I felt a set of fingers, gritty from years in the ground, wrap around my wrist. Christopher latched onto my waist and together we hauled my Da, the legendary Bodach himself, up and out of his dark prison. As soon as he was fully out I threw myself into his arms.

"Easy now," Da said, patting my hair. "I've no wish to land back in that hole just yet."

"Da, I missed you so much," I said, my words muffled by his chest.

"As I missed you, my wee one. Och, it's bright up here," Da said, blinking in the sunlight.

"Have you really been down there in the dark this whole time?" I asked.

"Aye, lass, that I have." Da have me a squeeze that flattened my lungs and near cracked my spine. How I'd missed these squeezes! "Let me look at you."

I drew back, and got a good, full look at my father for the first time in more than two hundred years. Da was a giant and therefore capable of growing as tall as any mountain, but he'd kept himself human-sized. That meant he was tall and broad, with hands the size of hams and feet so big it took a full cowhide to make him a single pair of boots. He looked just the same as he always had, even if he was a bit dirtier. More than my glimpse of him, Da got a look at me.

"You're grown," Da said; I'd still been a girl hurtling barefoot over the fields when he'd gone away. "Anya, you are no longer my wee lass."

"Da," I said as sobs choked me. "I'm still her."

He ran his hand over my hair, and cupped my chin. "Bonnie like your mum, that you are." Da scanned the area around the *shieling*. "Where is she? And who is this?" he asked, his gaze landing on Christopher.

"Christopher Stewart." He stepped forward and stuck out his hand. Da looked down at him like he was a bug. "I am with Anya."

"I recognize your voice," Da said. "You've been here before. You spoke to us through the stones."

"Yes, sir, that's true."

"That was good of you." Da faced me. "And now you will tell me where my wife is."

"She couldn't be here," I began. "Oh, Da, so very much has changed. For starters, Mum's no longer the Queen of Winter. I am."

Da nodded, his dark brows low over his eyes. "Well, then. I supposed we'd best set about freeing the boys, and you can share the rest of the news with all of us at once. Christopher!"

"Here, sir."

"First of all, you can dispense with calling me sir. It's Bod, or Old Man, or whatever other names we devise while in our cups. Understand?"

"I do, Bod."

Da smiled. For all that he was a bruiser he valued a quick mind. "Good. Now then, I have a great many sons trapped under these rocks, and my back is weak and may give out at any time. Can I count on you to help me with these boulders?"

"Absolutely." Christopher pushed up his sleeves. "Which one should we start with?"

Chapter Two
Chris

For all of Bod's complaints about his about his sore back and waning strength, between him and Anya all of his boys were free in less than an hour. What really helped speed things up was that after the first few boys were back on the surface, they were eager to free the rest of their brothers and began tossing stones to the side as if they were weightless. It was like a deadly game of dodgeball where each team earned more players instead of points.

I have no idea how many brothers Anya had. We overturned ten stones, so logic would dictate ten brothers, right? Only there were more than ten. There may have been more than one hundred. Everywhere I looked I saw strapping Scottish lads climbing out of their prisons, clapping each other on the back, and a few were passing mugs of beer and congratulating each other on their recent freedom.

Where had the beers come from? I didn't know the answer to that, either.

"Christopher!"

Anya skipped toward me and grabbed my hands. "Isn't it wonderful? We haven't seen each other for so long and we're all just the same." She paused, glancing down at herself. "Well, I suppose I've changed a wee bit. But the boys and Da are exactly as I remember them."

"There certainly are a lot of them." The Bodach's sons all resembled him, with their broad shoulders, and dark hair and eyes. Not one of them resembled Beira in the slightest, except for Anya; then again, with her iridescent gray eyes and yellow blonde hair, she resembled Maelgwyn more than her mother.

I spied the tallest brother—and that's saying something in a family of giants—and a few others raising their mugs in yet another toast. "Are they magical? I mean, I know they're giants, but do they have other abilities, too?"

"Of course. We've all inherited a bit of Mum's magic, and…"

Anya's voice trailed off, and I felt like an idiot. In the

midst of what should have been a very happy day I reminded her that she hadn't inherited anything from Old Bod. All of her abilities came from Beira, and Maelgwyn.

Seeking to recover, I said, "Maybe we should think about getting them home."

Anya smiled, but it didn't reach her eyes. "Aye. I'll see to rounding them up."

***

Gathering up Bod and his sons didn't take long, and within half an hour all of us were standing in the Winter Palace's icy foyer. Now that Anya had fully come into her powers, she could teleport groups of people at once, much like Rina did with her portals. Even Bod was impressed when she moved her entire gaggle of siblings in one fell swoop.

Sarmi, an elf who was a combination of a trusted head servant and gruff aunt, stood at attention next to the entrance to the rest of the palace. According to Anya, Sarmi had overseen the daily operations of the Winter Palace since its creation. There was no aspect of the palace she didn't understand, and almost nothing she could accomplish. She also had a rather large crush on Bod.

"Master Bod, how delightful it is to have you back home," Sarmi greeted. "Anya shared with me that she was off to free you, but I didn't dare hope for her success."

"Free me she did, but what I am hoping for is a mug of your ale. I thought of it near every day I was gone," Bod said, and Sarmi blushed crimson. "Tell me you still make it just the same."

"Of course I do. I'll have a cask brought up directly."

Sarmi disappeared toward the kitchens, while the brothers wandered toward the living areas of the palace. As for Bod, he approached the stairway that led to the sleeping chambers.

"Beira," Bod bellowed up the stairs. "Beira, where are you, love? I have been dreaming of this night for nearly three centuries!"

"She's not here," Anya said. "Did I tell you we freed Long Meg? I'm sure she'll be by to say hello."

"Anya."

"Are you hungry?" Anya continued. "I'm sure you're all famished. I'll ask Sarmi to see about supper. After she's brought up the ale, of course."

"Anya!"

Bod's voice reverberated through the palace, cracking the walls and making the staircase list to the side.

"Have a care, Da." Anya raised her hand, and the cracks disappeared as the stairs righted themselves. Good to know we wouldn't end up suffocating underneath a collapsed glacier after every family squabble. "I cannot have you shouting until the walls come down. I just got this place to rights."

Bod regarded Anya for a moment, then he turned to me. "Where is my wife?"

"What?" I countered, panic squeezing my throat so I squeaked like a teenager. "Why ask me?"

"Because Anya is like her mum in that she believes that omitting the truth may spare a man's feelings," Bod replied. "But you would never lie to me, would you, Christopher? Not to the father of the woman you profess to love?"

Wonderful. His voice was strong enough to topple palaces *and* he was adept at emotional manipulation. "Beira is at the Unseelie Court."

"Why would she be there?" Bod asked, then he glanced at Anya. "Ah."

"Ah?" Anya repeated. "What does that mean?"

Bod narrowed his gaze, and countered, "Is Udane still playing at being Unseelie, rather than the Summer King?"

Anya drew back, eyes wide and mouth gaping. Beira had told us that Bod was aware of Anya's true parentage, but I don't think she expected him to be so free with the knowledge. I know I wasn't.

"He is," I said, when Anya remained silent. "Beira went there shortly after she lost her power."

"And there she has remained?"

I shrugged, spreading my hands wide. "She didn't really have a lot of options."

"Understandable." Bod smiled at Anya. "Lass, how did you take on Beira's mantle? I must admit that is something I'd not foreseen."

"Nor I," Anya said. "It was Mum's punishment. She tried kidnapping the gallowglass's bride in order to rescue you all, but everything went wrong."

"The gallowglass? You mean one of Nicnevin's assassins?" Bod asked. "What poor wretch is saddled with it now?"

"The same man, Robert Kirk, still holds the title," Anya replied. "I remember you speaking of him often, or at least whenever you got into a rant over the Seelie."

"You mean Robert is still around?" Bod shook his head. "That one was touch as old shoe leather. He would have made an excellent giant."

Anya nodded. "Aye, that he would have. Robert's bride—the one Mum kidnapped— is Christopher's sister."

Bod's gaze slid toward me. Apparently being somewhat related to the gallowglass improved my standing in his eyes. "Beira's lucky she survived against Robert. How did he strip her mantle?"

"It wasn't Robert," Anya replied. "It was Fionnlagh himself what punished Mum."

"Fionnlagh," Bod roared as chunks of ice fell from the ceiling and crashed around us. Anya glared at him, then she snapped her fingers and the ceiling reverted to its smooth, unmarred state. "That wee shite is still making trouble for all and sundry?"

"He can't, not now," Anya said in a rush. "He's been imprisoned in the glacier below the palace."

"Fionnlagh's trapped in ice?" Bod asked, and Anya and I nodded. "Well, now, that is a piece of good news. Anya, I will take you up on your offer to feed us a bit of supper. Afterward, we shall discuss what else has happened while the boys and I were away."

***

Sarmi worked her magic—maybe it was actual magic, who knows—and soon enough we were seated at a table long enough to fit all of the brothers, and a grand feast was laid out in the great hall. A few weeks ago Maelgwyn had assisted Anya in lifting the concealment wards from the palace, and now it bustled with servants; there were cooks, and chamberlains, and so many maids that dust and grime didn't stand a chance. We even had a liveried guard, and stables and mews out back. There weren't any horses or other animals on the grounds, and I thought that was for the best. Who knows what would happen if we filled the place up with polar bears and Arctic foxes.

Supper was a bit chaotic, but it went well. Anya took her place at the head of the table, with her father to her right while I sat at her left. On my left sat Angus, the eldest of the brothers and Bod's admitted co-conspirator. Angus's dark eyes tracked everything, from the servants as they moved about the room to what and how much each one of his brothers ate. Let me tell you, they ate a lot.

"Can I ask what it was like?" I asked him. "Under the stone, that is."

"What do you think it was like?" Angus countered. "It was cold, and dark, and boring." He pointed his dagger—did I mention that he was carving up his meat with an actual dagger and using the blade to shove it in his mouth?—at Anya. "How did you meet my sister?"

"My sister, Rina, and I used to teach at a university in New York," I began. "That's across the ocean, in the United States of America. Have you heard of it?"

"Have I heard of the ocean or America?" Angus countered. "The answer is yes to both. Giants aren't as stupid as the stories make us out to be."

Okay, then. "Anya was a student in Rina's class."

Angus's eyes narrowed. "Prowling among the schoolchildren, were you? You find a lot of your girls that way?"

"She wasn't really a student." I was not discussing my doomed relationship with my former student and ex-fiancée, Olivia, at the dinner table. Or ever again, if I could help it. "Beira sent Anya to watch over Rina."

"This sister of yours. She's special?"

"I like to think so."

"Karina is quite wonderful," Anya interjected. "I'll introduce you to her. I'll introduce all of you."

"But not until after we go to the Unseelie Court to visit Beira," Bod said.

Anya bit her lip, then she nodded. "Aye. We shall go

to the Unseelie Court first."

Bod shoved back from the table and stood. "Let's go now."

"But, what about your supper?" Anya asked, clearly panicked.

"I've eaten my fill."

"I haven't," Angus said, and the rest of the brothers agreed.

"The lot of them can remain here," Bod said. "Christopher will host you. You don't mind, do you, lad?"

"Not at all." Truth be told I didn't want to be anywhere near the Unseelie Court during Bod and Beira's reunion. My sense of self-preservation was too strong to allow that. "We'll have a great time."

"Very well," Anya said. "Da, before we go to the Unseelie Court I must see to something in the land. Will you meet me near the door to Elphame?"

"Aye, I can do that," Bod said. "Don't be long."

"I won't." Anya squeezed my hand, then she blinked out.

Bod shook his head. "Always in a rush, that one is. Christopher, can you not impress upon Anya the beauty of taking it slow?"

"Um. How exactly would I do that?"

Apparently that was a funny response, because Bod roared with laughter. "He doesn't ken how to slow her down," Bod yelled, and the brothers laughed and slapped the table so hard pieces of it broke off. I didn't know if I should be embarrassed or call for a carpenter. "What do you do when it's just the two of you?"

"Best go back to that American school, eh?" Angus said, elbowing my ribs. "Perhaps those schoolgirls can learn you a thing or three."

I smiled and concentrated on finishing my beer. Having Bod and the boys staying with us in the Winter Palace was going to be great. Just great.

Chapter Three
Anya

I blinked from the Winter Palace to Crail, trying my best to ignore the nagging feeling that I'd made a grave error leaving Christopher alone with my da and brothers. After all, he was only a human man, and historically lone humans among giants tended to not fare very well. However, my family was far from the first batch of supernatural creatures Christopher had encountered, and I doubted they would be the last.

Christopher is a strong, capable man, I told myself. *He's no stranger to Elphame's quirks and tricks. He will be fine.*

Just as I resolved to leave my worries behind, I recalled the time Da went to a croft in order to collect their promised tribute of bread and ale, but unbeknownst to Da a new minister had taken over the congregation. That minister instituted many so-called reforms, not the least of which was counseling the villagers against making any new offerings to the old ones. Da flew into a rage at the disrespect, plucked the mill stones from their place in the gristmill and threw them all the way to the top of a nearby mountain.

"Their punishment," Da had explained, "is to retrieve the mill stones before next year's tribute is due."

"But how will they make your bread without the stones?" I asked.

"They should have thought of that before they withheld my tribute."

When Da next returned to the village the minister was gone and the tribute was waiting for him, every single morsel of bread he was owed along with an extra cask of ale.

Now I stood outside the walker's modest home, but I didn't enter it. The workmen were still repairing the damage that had been done by the Seelie King's rampage, and they didn't need me appearing out of thin air and giving them the fright of their lives. Instead, images of Christopher in my mind, I went to the adjacent walled garden and found the wights. They were tiny sprites that spent most of their time tending gardens, but wights possessed two other fine qualities: they were fiercely loyal, and they could teleport just as well as I or Mum ever could.

A wight could instantly alert me to any mischief happening in the Winter Palace. Not that I was expecting mischief, but my brothers did bore easily.

"Mistress Anya," the wights' leader, Wyatt, said when he saw me. "What brings you to the garden today?"

"To see your flowers, which are as lovely as ever," I said; everyone knew that to gain a wight's assistance one must first complement their flowers. The unseasonably warm sunlight bathed the garden in a golden glow, and the blooms were heavy and bountiful. "Pretty as a picture, they are."

"Mistress, you are most kind," Wyatt said, his cheeks going rosy.

"I only speak the truth. Might I ask a wee boon of you?"

"Name it," he said.

"First, I have news," I began. "My da and brothers are free."

"Oh, mistress, that's wonderful," he said. "Shall I gather a bouquet to welcome them? A garland, perhaps? Will they be by for a celebration?"

"How kind of you. Actually, I've an errand I need to see to, and they've remained at the Winter Palace. Christopher is hosting them."

"You left a defenseless mortal alone with the Bodach," Wyatt said, aghast, his tiny fist clutched against his breast.

"Christopher is not alone," I said. "My brothers are there, too."

"Gods below." Wyatt flew to the far side of the garden and issued a few orders to the rest of the wights, then he returned to me. "Mistress, if it pleases you I would like to watch over Master Stewart until your return. That way if anything untoward were to happen, I could notify you in a trice."

I nodded. "Thank you, Wyatt. I owe you a favor."

Wyatt bowed his head, then he blinked away, I assumed to Christopher's side. I cast a glance toward the cottage, and resolved to check on the construction's progress another time, then I blinked from the mortal plane back to my home. Da was waiting for me in front of the door to Elphame. I was surprised he was already waiting, but he was anxious to see Mum.

"Shall we?" I asked.

Da opened the door and gestured for me to pass through. "We shall."

I stepped out of the palace and into Elphame proper. One of the first things Mum had done upon her exile to the Winter Palace was repair the path that led from it directly into the heart of Elphame. Since I'd moved in I also reestablished the path that led to the mortal realm, so Christopher needn't be dependent on me to come and go from Glasgow.

Da exited the palace behind me and closed the door. I wondered what was going to happen when we reached our destination. I noticed him staring at the charm bracelet on my left wrist.

"Do you like it?" I asked, giving my wrist a shake. "Mum made it for me."

"It resembles hers a great deal," Da said. "Does it have the same properties?"

"Mostly." I slid the bracelet off of my wrist and handed it to Da, and he proceeded to inspect the charms. There were five silver orbs, each of them a receptacle for a different bit of magic. Mum devised the charms long ago, so she could keep certain bit of magical assistance handy without needed to stop and cast a complex spell. When I'd explained the bracelet's purpose to Christopher he'd likened it to keeping spells fresh in Tupperware.

"Wise of you, to wear such a device," Da said as he handed me back my bracelet. "When you rise to a position of power challengers come from all directions. Soon enough, you may be challenged for your right to rule the cold."

"Let them come," I said as I donned the bracelet, the charms tinkling as I did so.

"That's my lass, brave down to her bones."

We followed a curve in the path that brought us past the Winter Palace's boundary, and into Elphame proper. The ground we waked on was packed dirt, and bramble thickets lined either sides of the path. As we got closer to the Unseelie lands, the brambles thinned out, but the wickedly sharp thorns remained.

"Have you ever been to the Unseelie Court?" I asked.

"Oh, yes. Many, many times," was Da's reply. "You handled your business in the mortal realm rather quickly."

"It was a small thing." I could never tell anyone, not even Da, I'd sent a wight to watch over Christopher. The teasing he and I would have to endure from my brothers would be relentless, and who knows what Da would do.

We reached a crossroads, and kept straight on. I almost asked Da if this was the same road he'd stomped down when he took out his anger over Mum's unfaithfulness on Maelgwyn. Gods below, for the second time in an hour I feared I was making a huge mistake. "You're not going to lose your temper in front of the Unseelie, are you?"

"I've never once lost my temper. I have always remembered exactly where I last set it down." I opened my mouth, but he continued, "I do, however, promise to do my best to not embarrass you."

I nodded, since that was the best I could hope for. "Thank you, Da."

"Anything for my best lass."

Soon enough the Unseelie Court rose above us, a foreboding black castle made of angles and spires that were precariously balanced on the edge of a crag. The whole of it cast a heavy shadow that was unaffected by the sun's position overhead. Once the sun set, the area around the crag was such a deep, dark black you'd be hard pressed to find your nose in front of your face.

We ascended the steps cut from the living rock; I could have blinked us directly into the throne room, but I wanted to give Mum and Maelgwyn plenty of time to see our approach and prepare themselves. No one appreciated it when the Bodach arrived out of the blue. At least he had remained man sized, though a giant approaching the court would have certainly tested the guards' courage.

The obsidian-armored guards greeted us, then Da and I entered Maelgwyn's throne room. The first time I came to the Unseelie Court the room was black as night, with only a single lamp left burning near the throne. Now the curtains were drawn back and the room was filled with light and color. I hoped it mirrored Maelgwyn's newfound happiness with my mother.

I glanced at Da. He frowned as he gazed about the room, no doubt noticing the same changes I had. I wondered if he attributed the differences to the passage of time, or if he recognized Mum's influence.

"Anya!"

I turned toward the voice, and saw my blood father striding across the room, his arms outstretched. At my side, Da grunted his displeasure, which didn't surprise me. I only hoped he would keep his opinions to himself for the time being.

Christopher thought Maelgwyn and I resembled each other enough to be twins. I thought I resembled Mum, but I couldn't deny how much my appearance favored my father. We had the same iridescent gray eyes, and were both tall and lean. His hair was such a light yellow it was nearly white, whereas mine was the same sunflower hue as Mum's. The biggest difference in our appearance was our skin, with Maelgwyn's being so pale it was almost sickly. I must remember to have Mum get him out in the gardens more often.

Maelgwyn saw Da beside me and halted, his head cocked to the side.

"Bod." Maelgwyn approached us cautiously, as one would a wild animal. That was wise of him. "I was not expecting you."

"I am certain you weren't," Da said. "Is my wife here?"

"Beira is in the courtyard," Maelgwyn replied. "I can take you—"

"I can make my own way," Da said, then he lumbered off in the direction Maelgwyn had indicated.

"I'm so sorry to appear unannounced like this," I said once Da was out of the room. I hoped he was out of earshot, too, but you never knew with him. "We only released him earlier today, and his first demand was to see Mum."

"Yes, I imagine it would be," Maelgwyn said. "Are your brothers free, as well?"

"They are," I replied. "As it turns out no portals were involved. The spell was lying right where the stones met the ground."

"And of course you divined it all, brilliant lass that you are." Maelgwyn gestured toward the windows that overlooked the courtyard. "Come. We can watch their reunion."

"Won't that be like spying?"

"Yes, it most definitely is spying. It will also be me watching over the two most volatile individuals present, and ensuring they don't destroy my home." Maelgwyn grimaced. "I do have some experience with Bod destroying my things." He leaned closer, and added, "Please don't take offense, but I won't be referring to you as daughter while he's near."

I smiled. "I won't be calling you Da, either."

"Look at us, co-conspirators in our own self-preservation."

Maelgwyn and I stood at the windows, and I immediately noticed Mum as she wandered among the hedgerows. She'd kept up her habit of wearing red, which before had marked her as an outsider in the Unseelie Court. Then the gardens had been a bleak sight of grays and browns, devoid of life or happiness.

Now the gardens were full of life, with rich greens and blues and vibrant yellows splashed across the landscape. Even the fountains look renewed, with sparkling clean water splashing into marble basins polished to a high sheen. I realized that despite the rainbow of hues Mum was the only living thing clad in red, and I wondered if that was by design.

"Why did you readily agree to tell Da where she is?" I asked.

"Beira is more than capable," Maelgwyn replied. "If she doesn't want to speak to Bod, she will make it known."

"I suppose she will."

We watched as Mum sat on a patch of grass. Amazingly, tiny purple flowers sprang up around her.

"Is she… Those flowers are growing because of her," I said.

"Yes," Maelgwyn agreed. "It's a most extraordinary thing. Now that Beira's command of the cold has left her, she's become quite adept at creating life. All the changes you see in the Unseelie lands are her doing."

I nodded, unsure if this new aspect of Mum was a good thing. Maelgwyn clearly thought it was, but he wasn't a good judge of anything Mum did. She could have installed a herd of elephants in the throne room and he would have thought it grand, and added a flock of pelicans to keep them company.

In the midst of my wonderings, Mum jumped to her feet. I followed her gaze; Da had entered the courtyard. Mum's eyes lit up, then she ran across the courtyard and leapt into Da's arms.

"They truly missed each other," I said.

"They did," Maelgwyn agreed. I glanced at him, saw him smiling.

"You don't mind them carrying on beneath your nose?"

"Not in the slightest. I have always understood that there is more than one aspect to Beira's nature, and that one person could never fulfill all of her needs. Bod's greatest failing was that he could not."

I watched Mum and Da as they held each other close, then at arm's length as they got a look at one another, and then close again. Maelgwyn was right. Da completed Mum in a different way that Maelgwyn did, and both ways were important to her.

"It's wonderful seeing them together again," I said.

"It truly is. Have you any news of Karina's bairn?"

"She's as brilliant as ever," I replied. Maelgwyn had taken an instant liking to Christopher's sister, and her daughter Faith. He'd even taken to sending the bairn gifts, and small toys his own children once played with. "Karina asked me to thank you for the silver rattle. It's Faith's favorite."

The Unseelie King grinned. "Mark my words, one day Faith Kirk will be a force to be reckoned with, especially with the Winter Queen to look up to."

I leaned on Maelgwyn's shoulder. As much as I adored my Da, Maelgwyn filled a void in my life I hadn't realized was there. "I'm glad you're my father."

"As am I. Let's not mention that to Bod, shall we?"

"It can be our secret."

Chapter Four
Chris

Despite his earlier protests about being hungry, as soon as Anya and Bod were gone, Angus put away his dagger and pushed back from the table. The rest of the brothers kept shoveling food into their mouths as if they hadn't eaten in a hundred years, and hardly looked up from their plates.

Actually, maybe they hadn't eaten in a hundred years.

"Did you have food while you were...Wherever you were?" I asked, since everyone but Angus was eating as if they wanted to make up for two hundred years of starvation.

"What do you think?" Angus sneered. I didn't reply, since I had no idea if a dirt hole of a prison provided three meals a day. I also ignored his attitude, but his abrasiveness was wearing on me.

Angus stood in the dining room's entrance and looked up and down the corridor. "What all goes on in this place?"

"Regular household activities, for the most part," I replied. "Didn't you live here, before?"

"No. This was always Ma's domain. My brothers and I kept to the real world, if you can call it that." He set off down the corridor. With a sigh, I followed. "The palace was always a bit fancier than I liked. I'm more of a man's man, you ken?"

"Sure," I said, even though I had no idea what that was supposed to mean. Angus made a hard left, and ended up at the Ninth Legion's indoor practice yard.

That part of the palace hadn't always been a practice yard. Back in its heyday the Winter Palace boasted three ballrooms, though why anyone would want to come dancing in the heart of a mountain made of ice was beyond me. Maybe Beira was secretly a party animal. Anyway, since we had three more ballrooms that we had use for, and the Ninth had remained under my command for the time being, we offered the largest of the rooms to the legion. They hadn't wasted any time repurposing it for their daily drills, and whatever else they required.

As for the other two ballrooms, they remained vacant.

You just never knew when you would have to throw together a dance for a few hundred of your closest friends.

"What's all this, then?" Angus asked. The Ninth was going through their standard afternoon maneuvers, also known as completing more exercise in a day I had in my entire life.

"This is the Ninth Legion," I replied. "I'm their standard bearer."

That's right, I was the proud member of a Roman legion. After the Ninth had gone missing in northern Britain around the second century they ended up in Elphame and became the Seelie Queen's personal army. Shortly before she'd been imprisoned by Fionnlagh, Nicnevin had sent me the legion's eagle standard, called an *Aquila*, and I summoned the entire lot of them during out epic battle against Fionnlagh. The legion had been understandably confused when I summoned them instead of Nicnevin, and was furious when they learned that Fionnlagh had imprisoned her. Without their help I don't know how the battle would have turned out.

Since Nicnevin had sent me the *aquila* I became the Ninth's new *aquilifer*, or standard bearer. The whole of the legion deferred to me, including their leader, the *legatus* Lucius Rufinus, and every one of them accepted me as Nicnevin's chosen replacement. It was simultaneously thrilling and unnerving to have one of the most well-trained armies in history under my command.

"Why is a Roman legion mucking about the in the Winter Palace, and with you of all people?" Angus asked.

"They were under Nicnevin's command, but in her absence they report to me."

"Do they? Wait, what do you mean about Nicnevin being absent? What happened to the old bird?"

"We don't really know," I replied. "She sent me the Ninth's standard, and shortly afterward Fionnlagh imprisoned her. She hasn't been seen since. We've no idea where she could be."

"Nicnevin's missing, then? Do us all a favor and don't look for her."

"Believe me, I don't want to find her." Truer words were never spoken. "Anya doesn't either, but if we don't find her who will look after the Seelie Court?"

"Does the court really need looking after?"

"I'd say so, what with the throne being vacant."

Angus frowned a bit. "Vacant, you say?"

Before I could respond to Angus's somewhat problematic question blue lightning shot before my eyes. When my heartbeat returned to normal, and I realized the lightning was actually a wight, I said, "Wyatt, how many times have I asked you to move a bit more slowly so as to not scare the crap out of me?"

"Apologies, Master Stewart." Wyatt settled on my shoulder and glared at Angus. "I thought you may be in need of my services, so I did make haste."

"Is that a wight?" Angus asked, as he regarded Wyatt like a bug in need of squashing.

"Yes, *he* is a wight," I replied. To Wyatt, I asked, "Did Anya send you here?"

"Certainly not," Wyatt huffed, his chin up and back straight as a pencil. "I came here of my own accord."

Angus leaned closer. Wyatt, unappreciative of his scrutiny, flew behind my back and alighted on my other shoulder. "How are you involved with both the Summer King's pets and Nicnevin's thugs?"

"Just lucky, I guess." The legion paused in its maneuvers, and Lucius hailed me as he approached us, thus saving me from responding to any more of Angus's boorish questions. "How goes it?" I asked the *legatus*.

"Well, as always," Lucius replied. He regarded at Angus over my shoulder.

"This is Anya's brother, Angus," I said, then I introduced Lucius to him. Neither seemed impressed by the other. "He, and Anya's father and the rest of her brothers, will be staying at the Winter Palace for a time." I paused, and asked Angus, "How many brothers are there, again?"

Angus showed his teeth. "As many as are needed."

"If any of you would like to join in the practice drills, just say the word," Lucius said to Angus, then he faced me. "Has there been any word of Domina?"

"Not so much as a whisper." Between Anya and Maelgwyn they'd sent spies across Elphame and into the mundane world searching for Nicnevin. She was either very well hidden, or in a third, as yet un-searched realm. Or she was playing us all for fools and in hiding, perhaps even spying on us from afar. I could just imagine her cackling as she watched us chase our tails searching for her.

A third option was that Fionnlagh had not only imprisoned Nicnevin but killed her as well, but I didn't believe that. Nicnevin wasn't just smart, she was a survivor. As much as I hated her, I could admit she had a shrewd mind and the ability to weasel her way out of any situation.

I would never share any of my opinions about the Seelie Queen with Lucius. To him, and the rest of the Ninth, Nicnevin was their commander, and a leader to be trusted. I didn't know the full extent of the Ninth's history with the Seelie, but Nincevin had won their respect long ago, and I respected Lucius too much to insult his leader.

"I will let you know the moment I hear anything," I promised.

"I've no doubt, Dominus." Lucius gave me a curt nod and returned to his men.

"If only he would call me Chris," I muttered.

"Dominus is a term of respect," Angus said. "They accept you as their leader. The least you can do to show your appreciation is accept a wee title."

Before I could reply Angus spun on his heel and stalked down the corridor. "Where are you going?"

"To visit a few of my old haunts."

"I thought you said you never spent much time here," I called, but his reply was lost as he turned a corner and disappeared from view. Wyatt hovered in front of me, arms folded and shaking his head.

"Giants," Wyatt said. "An unruly lot, even on the best of days."

"Angus is a little rough around the edges, but the rest aren't so bad," I said, thinking about the rest of the brothers. They may eat us out of house and home, but they'd been quite well behaved. "Have you known many giants in your time?"

"Oh, yes, many indeed." Wyatt glanced around, and asked, "Perchance, has Mistress Anya set up a garden I could have a look at?"

"You know, she hasn't." I extended my arm, and Wyatt perched near my elbow. "Let's have a look around, and you can tell me the best spot to install one. Perhaps it can be a surprise for Anya."

"What a thoughtful idea. You do think like a wight, Master Stewart."

I smiled at the compliment, and strode toward the courtyard. Better a wight than a giant, in my pinion.

Chapter Five
Anya

Da and Mum spent most of the afternoon together in the Unseelie gardens, with their every move tracked by Maelgwyn's watchful eye. I watched Maelgwyn watch them, simultaneously shocked and touched that he was allowing Da to reacquaint himself with Mum. What's more, he wasn't the slightest bit put out by the situation. Perhaps his great age had also lent him great wisdom; or, perhaps the wisdom was that he knew denying the Bodach was a fool's errand. I'd wager the latter had much to do with his easy acceptance.

The servants had no sooner laid out our afternoon tea when Da returned to the throne room and announced it was time for us to depart.

"Would you like to stay for tea?" Maelgwyn offered. "I've had cook prepare all Beira's favorites."

"Da, there's orange cakes," I said, attempting to sway him. Oranges were Da's favorite.

"Perhaps another time," Da said.

I glanced at Maelgwyn, but he only shrugged and wrapped a slice of chocolate cake in a napkin.

"Don't want you to be hungry," he said with a wink. I accepted the cake, and followed Da out of the Unseelie Court.

"Why isn't Mum coming with us?" I asked Da as we descended the palace steps. Maelgwyn's black-armored sentinels nodded at us deferentially, until Da growled at them. The sentinels were still as statues after that.

"She will," Da replied. "Give her time."

I found Da's newfound patience an odd if welcome development. We stepped onto the main road, and I placed my hand on his forearm.

"We should blink back to the Winter Palace," I said.

"Oh? Why is that, now? We walked here just as fine as can be."

I bit my lip, wondering how I should respond. The heart of my reticence was that very few were aware of my familial relationship with Maelgwyn, and for the time being both he and I—and certainly Mum—wished to keep it that way. The fewer individuals that knew of our closeness meant there were fewer who could exploit it. However, the last thing Da needed was yet another reminder of one of the most painful realizations of his life, and certainly not on this day of all days, when he was finally free.

Make that on the day he was finally free, and his wife was living in another man's home.

"There is much unrest among the Seelie," I said, which was the truth. "What with Nicnevin missing and Fionnlagh imprisoned, I've been limiting my time in the Seelie and Unseelie portions of Elphame. I don't wish to give any of our enemies a potential foothold."

"All right," he said. "If you think it's best. But, I would like to walk up the final path to the palace. It's been so long since I've seen it, and it is quite a sight."

"That's a wonderful plan." I set my hand on Da's shoulder. A moment later we blinked to the path that led to the Winter Palace.

"As smooth a trip as your mother ever made," Da said, then he turned toward the palace.

"Ah, now that's a sight for sore eyes," he said as gazed at the palace, and he was right. Mum's first throne and the original seat of winter had been atop the highest mountain in Scotland; she needed the height to not only keep an eye on those below, but to reach the clouds so she could seed them with frost and snow. In time her power grew, and when it could no longer be contained in the mortal realm she built herself a palace in between there and Elphame.

Much like the mountain that inspired it, the Winter Palace was so high it reached the clouds. It didn't resemble the dark crags of the Unseelie Palace, or the towers and spires of any mortal seat of power. Rather, the Winter Palace resembled a glacier, with blue and white panels of ice set at both lovely and precarious angles. It was a home, and a stronghold, and it embodied winter as thoroughly as Mum ever did. I only hoped to someday be worth of such a palace.

"Our home is lovely," was all I said to Da, having decided to leave my musings on worthiness for another time. "Ever since the power came to me, I cannot imagine being anyplace else."

"Winter is your birthright, never let anyone tell you

otherwise," Da said. "What you were saying, about the Seelie. No one has a clue where Nicnevin's holed up, is that right?"

I paused. "You think she'd hiding, and not imprisoned?"

"I do," Da said. "Nicnevin's a canny one, with a mind much sharper than Fionnlagh's ever was. She probably got tired of all the fuss of running the court and went on holiday, and then Fionnlagh, who's both lazy and opportunistic, likely spun a tale of her being imprisoned to explain away her absence. He does have a penchant for locking people away." We reached the palace's door, and Da held it open for me. "After you, lass."

I smiled as I stepped inside the palace. Then Da asked, "What with the Seelie Court vacant, who will mind the *sluagh na marbh*?"

"Do they need to be minded?" I asked. Mortals once referred to the *sluagh na marbh* as the host of unforgiven dead, but in reality they were any spirit who chose to remain tied to the earth instead of moving on after their natural life ended. As for where moving on would take them, it differed from culture to culture, and I certainly wasn't an expert on any of them. "It's not like they're children known for getting up to mischief."

"No, but the Wild Hunt will occur soon, will it not?"

My gaze slid toward Da. The Wild Hunt happened once every seven years, and he'd been stuck in a hole under Glen Lyon for over two hundred. "How can you be so certain of that?"

"I counted the days while I was gone," he replied. "It's not like I had much else to do."

"I suppose you didn't. The last Wild Hunt was led by Fionnlagh, along with the gallowglass. I suppose we could ask Robert what he thinks should be done about the coming hunt."

"I'm not surprised he's still fighting. That Robert Kirk is a man after my own spirit," Da said. "Do you ken where he's been holding up?"

"Oh, yes. He's staying in my flat in Glasgow with his wee family."

Da stopped walking and stared at me. It took quite a bit to shock the Bodach, and I must admit I was pleased I'd done so. "What on earth is the gallowglass doing in your flat?"

"Oh, it's quite the tale." We reached the ballroom the Ninth Legion had conscripted for themselves, and nearly bumped into Christopher.

"You're back." Christopher stepped close as if to kiss me, saw Da over my shoulder, and grasped my hand instead. "How were things?"

"Good," I replied. "Maelgwyn sends his regards."

"Beira was much pleased to see me," Da added, puffing up his chest like a bird showing off his plumage. Christopher looked as if he'd ask where Mum was, but I shook my head slightly.

"Has Angus given you any trouble?" I asked.

"Wyatt's been keeping an eye on him," Christopher replied. "Since that's what wights are good at. Watching grown men, that is."

"Where are my boys?" Da demanded. "Beira has given me a message for each and every one of them, and I mean to deliver them."

"They're out back, by the mews," Christopher replied. "Last I saw they were throwing logs around like footballs."

"Och, a game of catch. Can't miss that."

We watched Da lumber off. When he was out of sight, Christopher said, "So you sent Wyatt to babysit me."

"If you'd grown up with Angus you'd understand," I replied. "How long have they been out back?"

"Since they finished eating—by the way, there is probably no food left in Elphame after all that. I do have an entire legion protecting me."

"My brothers can outwit any legion. Why do you think Rome never gained a foothold in Scotland?"

"Fair enough." Christopher gathered me into his arms and gave me that kiss he'd been holding on to. "No Beira?"

"No. She wanted to stay with Maelgwyn, and Da seems fine with it."

"Interesting. Do you believe that?"

"Not for a moment." We parted, and walked down the corridor hand in hand. "I think we should visit your sister."

"What happened?"

"Perhaps nothing, but Da mentioned the Wild Hunt.

Have you ever heard of that?"

"Only in folklore. Wait, we live in a fairy tale."

"That we do. Anyway, it should be happening soon, but there's no Seelie King or Queen to lead it. I'd like to ask Robert what he thinks of the situation."

Christopher rolled his shoulders. "Think we can leave your siblings unsupervised for a few while we go visiting?"

I gazed at the palace I'd only recently gotten to rights. "It should be fine. They probably won't demolish the place in one day."

"Even if they do, we can always rebuild."

With that, we opened the door to Glasgow.

Chapter Six
Chris

I opened the door and held it while Anya went through ahead of me, then I stepped out of the Winter Palace and into Glasgow. Much like the door that led to Elphame, this was a way to leave the Winter Palace without needing to teleport. Since I was a mere mortal living amongst supernatural creatures, I appreciated this door a great deal. Unlike the door to Elphame, the door to Glasgow opened into a pub called Remy's Place, and that made me appreciate it just a little bit more.

And what a pub it was. In the recent past it had been a vacant bank right on Buchanan Street, and the new owners had preserved all of the fantastic Art Deco details. The building featured gorgeous leaded glass windows, highly polished woodwork on the walls and ceiling, and ornate columns that looked like they'd been designed by Charles Rennie Mackintosh himself. The new owners even kept the old vault intact, though now it led to the bathrooms instead of a hoard of cash.

Anya and I emerged from the back into the main room, which was awash in dancer and rainbow-colored stage lights. On the far side two patrons sang karaoke, badly, but the crowd didn't seem to mind. I couldn't wait to visit this place during Pride Month.

I followed Anya through the crush of people and saw one of the owners, a bear of a man named Remy and the place's namesake, behind the bar. I didn't know if Remy was his real name. Hell, I didn't even know if he was human, but every time he saw Anya and me he pulled out his best whisky and poured us two glasses, and refused our money. I wondered if the drinks were a modern Scot's tribute to the Queen of Winter.

"What's on the agenda today?" Remy asked as we accepted our drinks.

"Bit of visiting," Anya replied. "Family, you know it is."

"I certainly do. Be well, both of you." Remy tipped an

imaginary hat, then he moved on to his other customers. We finished our drinks and walked out into the bright sunshine and crisp early winter air.

"It's a beautiful day," I said. "Did you have anything to do with that?"

A coy smile. "Perhaps."

After a leisurely walk through Glasgow we knocked on the flat's door. Technically it was our home, but Rob, Rina, Faith, and Colleen had been staying there while they had work done on their house in Crail. As far as Anya and I were concerned they could stay in the flat for as long as they needed to.

Rob opened the door and smiled. "Come in, both o' ye."

"Good to see you." We stepped into the main living area of the flat, and I took in the many changes Rob and Rina had made over the past few months. For starters, the place was packed full of baby equipment. "How's Faith?"

"As bonnie as lass as there ever was," Rob replied with a grin. Fatherhood suited him much more than his prior life as Nicnevin's assassin. "Karina is just finishing her bath and puttin' her down for a nap. Karina love, Anya and Christopher are here," he called over his shoulder.

"Be right out," she called back.

We followed Rob into the living room. Anya trailed her fingertips across a stack of books on the coffee table. "Karina is still researching Norse traditions?"

I glanced at the books. The titles were *Nordic Traditions, Northern Magic,* and *Asatru for Beginners,* and on the side table were several reference books about Norse folklore. This research binge had come about after Nicnevin mentioned that our mother had been a volva, a type of Icelandic witch gifted with foresight. Granted, Nicnevin was the queen of lies, but she'd been right about Mom. Now Karina thought she'd inherited some of Mom's abilities, which made me wonder why Nicnevin had told us in the first place. That one never did or said anything except for her own personal gain.

"She is, for all that I wish she'd leave it be," Rob replied. "In my day witches of all sorts were persecuted. Sit, both o' ye, and I'll fetch some drinks. Tea, Anya?"

"Please." After we sat on the couch, Anya leaned close to me and said, "In all my days I never thought I'd have the gallowglass standing in my kitchen and making me a cup of tea."

"I heard that," Rob said from the kitchen.

"He hears everything," Rina said, joining us from the nursery. "He probably hears Faith's dreams."

"What do babies dream about?" I wondered.

Rina shrugged. "Bottles?" She turned to Anya, and said. "So. Today was the day?"

"It was, and it went perfectly," Anya said. "Da and all of my brothers are free."

"That's awesome," Rina said. "Did your dad see Beira? And does he know about Maelgwyn?"

"Yes, and yes," Anya replied. "I took Da to the Unseelie Court, and he and Mum had a nice visit."

"You brought Bod to the Unseelie Court?" Rob asked as he set a teapot and cups on the table. He poured the tea, then he returned to the kitchen and brought out two mugs of coffee for myself and Rina. "It's a wonder Elphame's still standing."

"Angus, Bod's eldest, is the bigger threat," I said, then I sipped my coffee. When I raised my eyes three people were staring back at me. "What?"

"My brother is not a threat," Anya said.

"But he is someone to watch," I said. "You should have seen how interested he was in the Ninth Legion."

"Of course he was interested," Anya said. "He was stuck in a hole for over two hundred years. After that anything is interesting."

I smiled. "True."

"What do you mean, your parents had a visit?" Rina asked, steering the conversation away from Angus, and my opinion of him. "Beira didn't go home with Bod?"

"She did not," Anya said. "She has elected to stay with Maelgwyn, for now."

Rina and Rob gave each other a look. "I do hope Maelgwyn kens what he's getting himself in to," Rob said. "What with the Seelie throne vacant we can no' have the Unseelie Court collapsin' into chaos."

"That's partly why we're here," Anya said. "Da

mentioned the Wild Hunt. It's coming up next month, correct?"

"Aye, so it is," Rob said. "Here I thought I'd never hear tell of it again, not since Karina rescued me from that life no' once, but twice." Rina smiled and leaned against his shoulder.

"I actually rescued you three times," she said.

"The last time was no' from Elphame."

"Still counts."

"Is the Wild Hunt really a parade of the soulless dead?" I asked.

"Yes and no," Rob replied. "Ye ken, no god can actually condemn a body to hell. Ye can be sent to one o' the hells, I am living proof o' that. But if an outside force sends ye, that means ye can always make your escape."

"Are you saying that some people send themselves to hell?"

"Oh, most definitely some, and possibly every resident o' the hells is theire ' their own doing. Guilt, shame, remorse… They're all powerful emotions. If a person truly believes themselves to be beyond redeemin', they will never move on as they should."

"Move on?" I repeated. "Move on to what, exactly?"

"Ah, well. That's another conversation entirely." Rob set down his teacup. "As for the Wild Hunt, 'tis a sad thing, really. Once every seven years Fionnlagh would set out on his stag, a beacon of light and hope if there ever was one. Those who'd damned themselves would see his light and assume their savior had at last come for them, but in reality Fionnlagh brought them to his court." Rob paused, studying his fingernails. "Some said those souls became the *fuath*, but we ken better than that, now don't we."

"I guess we do." I leaned back and considered Rob's tale of hells and redemptions. "What happens to these souls if no one rounds them up? Will they move on to wherever they're supposed to be on their own?"

"I suppose it's a possibility," Rob said.

"I don't think they do," Anya said. "If they did, there would be no need to collect them. It's not like Elphame has ever wanted for mortals; if anything too many mortals find their way underhill. No, there must be a reason why the Seelie desired these souls in the first place."

"Maybe Fionnlagh feeds them to the *fuath*," Rina suggested.

"Or Nicnevin," I added. "Beira never collected souls?"

Anya shook her head. "Never a one. Whatever would she do with them all?"

Before any of us could speculate what a winter deity would do with a surplus of souls, Wyatt appeared in the center of the coffee table. "Mistress Anya, please forgive me but your father is doing something unwise!"

Anya leapt to her feet. "What happened?"

"He and your brothers found where the kegs of ale are stored, and after they tapped them—"

"Where are they now?" Anya demanded.

"They are at the Unseelie Court, singing ballads to Mistress Beira," Wyatt replied. "The king is most displeased." Wyatt glanced at Rob, and added, "While I do not presume to offer you advice, you may wish to bring the gallowglass."

Anya looked at the clock on the wall and threw her hands up in the air. "Twelve hours! He hasn't been loose for twelve hours and already he's drunk and causing a ruckus!"

"It's all right," I said. "We can handle this." I looked between Anya and Rob. "Can't we?"

"If they're already drunk, most likely." Rob kissed Rina's cheek and stood, his armor materializing onto him as he did so. "Wyatt, please stay here with Karina. Come get me if I'm needed at home."

"Yes, Master Kirk."

"Be careful," Rina said. "All of you."

"I feel like I should have a weapon," I muttered.

"I am weapon enough," Anya said, then she teleported the three of us to the Unseelie Court.

Chapter Seven
Anya

Robert, Christopher, and I arrived on the plain below the Unseelie Court. From the look of things all was well, with the palace perched atop its crag as it always was, and the obsidian armored guards standing at proper attention in their proper places. For a moment I let myself breathe, and assumed Wyatt, nervous little creature that he was, had worried me for nothing.

Then I heard the singing.

"Och, that's dreadful," Robert said.

"It's like all the cats in the world are in heat at once," Christopher added.

"They certainly weren't practicing their singing these past years," I said, remembering the many drunken concerts my brothers had subjected me to as a wee bairn. I raised my chin and set my shoulders. "Let's round them up before they do something awful."

"This singing is awful enough," Christopher said, covering his ears with his hands. "Are you immune to it?"

Someone hit a particularly high note, so high I could feel the sound vibrate my molars and cut through my brain. "No."

I ascended the narrow steps up the mountainside and into the palace, Christopher and Robert following close behind me. I could have blinked us right into the thick of it, but I needed a few moments before I was confronted with my family's latest indiscretion. Twelve hours. Da and the rest couldn't even wait a full day before they were back to their old tricks. My gut instinct was to scream at the lot of them until they decided to behave themselves, but that was something the old Anya would have done.

I am the Queen of Winter now, and I needed to handle these matters accordingly.

The guards opened the front doors, and the full volume of the screeching hit me like a massive wall of sound. "Angus, I'll have your hide for this," I yelled, decorum be damned. As if I could ever embarrass myself more than this lot already had.

"You think this is Angus's fault?" Christopher asked. The singing paused, and for the barest moment I hoped they'd all passed out—then they started up again, this time a lament about a woman mourning her lover, who was long ago lost at sea.

"I certainly don't think he's innocent." I looked at Christopher, noted his pensive face. "You were right, earlier. Angus is the one to watch."

He nodded. "Then we'll watch him."

"After we silence him," Robert added.

We followed my brothers' off-key voices as they echoed along the corridors. The throne room was vacant, save for a few terrified servants. I wondered if any of them had been with Maelgwyn since his time as the Summer King, and if they remembered when Da had burst into the Summer Court and effectively destroyed it. Those poor souls must wonder if Da had returned to finish the job, and brought his sons along for good measure.

A footman caught sight of me and cringed, then he whispered to his companion that I was the Bodach's daughter. Some did remember, then.

"I'm not a threat to you and yours," I said to the footman. He turned white as a sheet. I shouldn't have said anything, since I had more pressing matters to deal with than a few nervous men. "I'm not the Bodach's daughter, not really, but he raised me all the same. I am going to him now, and I am going to fix this. No one will be harmed by him or the boys, on that you have my word."

"We thought you were Maelgwyn's child," the less terrified of the two sputtered, much to the footman's horror.

"Can I not be both?"

I turned away from the men and continued on toward the wailing, all the while thinking about what I'd said. Could I be the Summer King's child, a giant's daughter, and the Winter Queen? Were the parts of me so incompatible that I must choose one aspect of my nature and ignore the rest? And what of Da, was there still room for him in my life?

"What is that saying about parts and sums?" I asked Christopher.

"The whole is greater than the sum of its parts." He

paused, and asked, "Are you saying we need to divide and conquer your brothers?"

"That wasn't what I was thinking, but it is an excellent idea."

At last we reached the royal apartment's antechamber, and I didn't know if I wanted to laugh or cry. My brothers were spread about the area, as were mugs of ale and flagons of whisky, some fuller than others. Many of the boys were passed out cold while those that remained bellowed half-forgotten lyrics at the top of their lungs.

Gods below. It had only taken a handful of them to generate this soul-numbing wail. I must ask Sarmi to make the next batch of ale stronger, or perhaps she should add a sleeping draught to casks.

In the center of the noise and chaos stood a much harried Maelgwyn.

"Anya, I am so glad you're here," he said when he saw me.

"I'm sorry I wasn't here sooner," I said. "I hope you don't mind, but I brought reinforcements."

Maelgwyn nodded toward Robert and Christopher. "A wise choice. Normally I don't have such difficulties with drunkards and merely have them tossed out of the palace, but I though your brothers might be in need of a softer touch."

"And Da?" I asked, since certainly no one thought the Bodach needed anything soft.

Maelgwyn grimaced. "He is inside my private chambers, pleading his cause to Beira."

"Gods below," I muttered, then I turned to Christopher and Robert. "Could the two of you see to the boys? I'll handle Da."

Christopher cracked his knuckles. "Sure. It'll be just like when I was a resident advisor in college and broke up dorm parties."

Robert drew his sword. "University has changed much since I was a student."

"Is the sword really necessary?"

"We'll see."

I left them to it, and approached the closed chamber door. I debated opening it, but one of my brothers may take the opportunity to rush inside, thus further complicating the situation. Closing my eyes against whatever mess I may find within, I blinked past the door.

Once inside, I cracked a single eyelid. The room was quite jumbled up, but it wasn't as bad as I'd feared. I saw the library door abruptly close, but that wasn't where Da was. My da wasn't a man to avoid being noticed. If anything, he reveled in the attention.

"Da?"

"Is that my best lass?" he replied, then he started mumbling about families and obligations. I followed the sound of Da's voice and found him sprawled across the bed, soaked in ale and tears.

I sat next to him, and for all that I'd been furious a moment ago, seeing him in such a wretched state made my heart ache. "I see you found where we keep the ale."

"I built that alehouse," Da mumbled. "Built it with my own two hands, I did, back when the Winter Palace was naught but a twinkle in your mother's eye."

"Where did you live before the palace was built?" I asked, even though I'd heard the story a hundred times before.

"Why, on Beinn na Caillich," Da replied. "Times past it served as your mother's throne, so high up the mountain she was crowned with clouds." Da opened his bleary, bloodshot eyes. "I miss her something terrible."

"I believe you," I said. I cast my gaze around the room, and saw the library door open up a crack, and a flash of movement beyond. "Is that why you came back here, to see her again?"

"Aye. I thought if I could just prove how much I missed her, and how much I needed her..." Da shifted. "I do need her, you ken. I've a plan, a plan I've been thinking on for a long time. It will set our family up for the next few generations, should it all go well."

"A plan for what?" I demanded. "Da, you don't need to scheme and sneak, not in the name of helping the family. We're comfortable as we are."

"For now, yes, but we can always better our situation."

His voice trailed off. When I looked back at him, he was asleep. "Poor, sad man," I said, patting his hand. Then the snoring started up, every bit as loud and awful as his singing was. It was a wonder Mum hadn't gone deaf.

I pulled a blanket over Da, then I approached the library door. "He's asleep."

Mum opened it all the way and leaned on the doorframe. Her hair and gown were a mess, and her eyes were as red as Da's. "We should leave him be. He will be better when he wakes."

"Why are you hiding in the library?" Mum never once hidden from Da, not when he was drunk or in a rage. Often times they would rage together, going toe to toe until one of them gave in, or they both gave out.

"I am not hiding," Mum said, "but I'm also not as strong as I once was. I-I didn't... Bod doesn't understand how much weaker I am. Not yet."

Ah. Despite her protests she was hiding, and for a good reason. "Are you sure you want me to leave him here?"

"Yes," she replied. "He will be much more reasonable when he's sober."

"All right, then. I will get the rest home and out of your hair." I turned to go, and felt Mum's hand on my shoulder.

"Thank you, Anya."

"Of course."

"I mean it," she continued. "You shouldn't have to deal with this. This business between Bod and I... It's awkward."

"What's family if not messy?"

"Aye, and ours is a right slop."

"All the same, it's a slop I wouldn't trade for anything."

"Me neither."

I patted her hand, then I left the apartment in search of Maelgwyn. He had remained in the antechamber, which was now blissfully quiet. My brothers—those who hadn't passed out—were grouped together in the center of the room under Christopher's watchful gaze.

"Da is asleep," I told Maelgwyn. "Mum thought it best to leave him be."

"I trust Beira knows what she's doing," Maelgwyn said. "As for the rest, most seem able to make their way home."

"Wonderful," I said, then I realized who wasn't in the room. "Where's Robert?"

"I sent him to fetch the walker, so she can send them all home in one fell swoop," Maelgwyn replied. "I do hope they bring Faith when then return."

"You're quite taken with her." Maelgwyn had adored Faith from the moment he first set eyes on her. As a result the flat was packed with gifts from him, each more extravagant than the last.

"That I am," he agreed. "Karina said I'm like a fairy godfather. I tried explaining that I am not fae, but she insisted it's more of a title than a hard and fast description."

"Yes, and a good title at that." I left Maelgwyn to his grandfatherly musings and went to Christopher's side. "Were they any trouble?"

"They're happy drunks, so no," he replied. "The only troublemaker is one stone cold sober Angus."

I narrowed my eyes at my oldest brother. He stuck out his tongue. "Well, this has been an exciting first day with Da and the rest."

"It sure has." Christopher draped his arm around my shoulders. "I can't wait to see what tomorrow brings."

I thought about Da's mumblings of a plan, and decided not to mention it. After all, it was probably nothing but a drunk man's ramblings. Da couldn't have a scheme worked out again, not so soon after he gained his freedom.

Could he?

Chapter Eight
Chris

The next morning, I woke up in heaven. At least, it felt that way.

When Anya and I decided to move out of our flat and stay at the Winter Palace full time, I'd been supportive, if a bit skeptical of how us living in an oversized snow fort would play out. Rina and Rob's house in Crail had been all but destroyed by Fionnlagh—which was somewhat poetic, since he had given them the house in the first place—and Anya offered them the flat to stay in while their place was being rebuilt. Along with my sister and the gallowglass came baby Faith, of course, and Rina's best friend Colleen, who had come out for Rina's baby shower and never went home. Scotland had that effect on people.

The addition of three adults and a baby made our previously spacious flat seem like a tiny studio in the city, and being that Anya and I had an entire palace at our disposal we decided to relocate. As soon as we'd gotten Rina and the rest settled in, we moved a few things to the Winter Palace, and started fixing it up.

Being that the palace was primarily made of packed snow and ice, Anya did most of the remodeling. I'd worried that living in and around all of that ice would be cold, but the palace was always pleasantly warm. What's more, after we'd started dragging the furniture out from storage and into their proper rooms, and airing out the linens and rehanging the tapestries, the palace started to feel like home. No portion of the palace was cozier than our bedroom.

It wasn't really a bedroom so much as a series of rooms for Anya's and my private use, tucked away in a wing on the second floor. There was a parlor, two dressing rooms, a solarium, and a library in our suite. All of those rooms led to our quiet sleeping chamber, fitted with heavy oak doors that locked out the sounds and problems of rest of the world. Beyond that door was a truly enormous bed bedecked in soft sheets, pillows like so many marshmallows, and an actual white fur coverlet. Every morning I woke up feeling like I'd slept on a cloud, then I rolled over and saw the most beautiful woman in the world sleeping next to me.

With mornings like this who needs heaven?

On that morning she was sleeping late, which wasn't surprising. The prior day's adventures of setting her family free, only to round them up again at the Unseelie Court, left both of us exhausted. At least Anya could let herself rest now. For a long time, she couldn't.

When Anya first became the Queen of Winter a combination of anxiety and poisoned tea meant she hardly slept at all, but the closer we got to winter, and the more her powers settled, the more relaxed she became. Finding out who was poisoning her and having him removed from the picture also helped.

Now Anya was like a cat, always ready to stretch out in a sunbeam and take a nap. I wondered if her body was making up for her lack of sleep a few months ago, or if she just naturally needed more rest to balance out her new abilities. Either reason was fine with me. I just wanted her to be happy.

I moved closer to Anya and tucked a length of her buttercup yellow hair behind her ear. She stirred, but didn't open her eyes. Deciding to leave her to it, I moved to rise. Shortly after we moved into the palace, and I realized there was no place for me to plug in my laptop, I brought over a typewriter and few reams of paper. My next book's deadline was drawing near, and I had plenty of work left to do. Might as well get to it.

"Where do you think you're going?"

I glanced over my shoulder. Anya was smiling at me.

"I thought you were sleeping," I said as I put down my notebook. Work could wait.

"Can't sleep all the time." She stretched, arching her back as the coverlet fell back and bared her to her waist. I slid back under the blankets and kissed her. A moment later she was underneath me, my erection pressing into her belly.

"Now?"

"Not yet."

That was fine with me. I kissed her again as my hands roamed across her body, one cupping her bottom while the other tangled in her impossibly soft hair. Anya broke the kiss, grinned, and flipped me onto my back.

"Now," she said as she slid down my cock. Yeah, heaven can wait.

Afterward we lay together, Anya's head on my chest while I ran my fingers through her hair. "You know, I was going to get some writing done."

"I was thinking about the souls of the damned."

"During sex?"

She pushed herself up so we could look each other in the eye. "Not during, but before. And now. Why do you think Fionnlagh was collecting the souls?"

"Honestly, I have no idea." I noted the wrinkle between her eyebrows. That wrinkle always meant she was thinking hard on a problem. "Why?"

"That's just it. Why do it at all? Why not just leave them to wander?" She fluffed a pillow and set it against the headboard. "The Wild Hunt is an enormous undertaking. It's why it's only done once every seven years. Fionnlagh must have somehow benefitted from collecting the souls. Otherwise, why would he even bother with such an event?"

"Maybe the souls are the ones that benefitted," I said. "What if he, evil though he is, was actually doing them a service? Just because he was an awful person doesn't mean everything he did was bad."

Anya's forehead wrinkle deepened. "I hadn't considered that."

"What brought all this on?" I asked. "You said Beira never collected souls, so you don't have to either. Right?"

"That's correct. But, should they be collected? Is the world better off without the Wild Hunt, or is it worse?"

"I… don't know." I scowled at my typewriter; never had I so acutely felt the lack of an internet connection, and the information I could call up with a few keystrokes. My gaze traveled to our closed doors, and I remembered what lay beyond.

"What kind of books are in the palace's library?" I asked. "And are any of them in English?"

"They're in a range of languages and subjects. Why?"

"Maybe some have to do with the Wild Hunt, or souls. Maybe there's an encyclopedia or dictionary sitting on a shelf that will tell us exactly what you're supposed to do with a collected soul, damned or otherwise."

"Are you proposing a research session?"

"I'm a teacher. It's what I do best."

Anya leaned close and kissed me. "You have many other talents, beloved," she said against my mouth. "And the vast majority of those talents are much, much more fun than research."

My face warmed all the way down to my neck. "Which talents are these?"

"Let me show you my favorites."

***

By the time we made it downstairs for breakfast it was closer to brunch. I'd wanted to begin going through the library right away, but Anya had insisted we eat first. In addition to us needing sustenance, she also reminded me that the library was not only vast in the number of volumes it held, this volumes were written in many different languages. Since I could only read English and Latin, she suggested we have one of Sarmi's people go through the inventory and separate out all the books in English, so we would have a solid starting point. Naturally, I agreed with my brilliant girlfriend.

Anya delivered our requests to Sarmi, then we finally headed downstairs. Seated at the head of the dining room table was Rina, with Faith snug in a carrier against her chest.

"Good morning, winter rulers," Rina said cheerfully. I noted the coffee service and tray of pastries on the table. Knowing my sister she'd charmed the staff and they were now preparing a three course breakfast featuring all of her favorite foods.

"Good morning to you," I said. "How long have you been here?"

"Not long. I've only had one cup of coffee so far." Rina loosened the carrier and handed Faith off to Anya.

"My darling snowflake," Anya cooed to Faith. "Have you been good?"

"Anya gets to hold her first?"

Rina shrugged. "What can I say, she's a queen."

I poured myself some coffee while Anya fussed over the baby. "Where's Rob?"

"He is overseeing the reconstruction of our house. And before you ask, Colleen is having a day to herself in the city, so it was the perfect time for Faith and I to visit." She glanced around the room. "I thought there would be a few dozen brothers hanging around. Did you kick them all out after yesterday?"

"Oh, they're here," Anya said. "Knowing that lot they'll be sleeping it off for a good while, yet."

A parade of servants entered the room bearing platters of pancakes, bacon, and a tureen of scrambled eggs. Anya watched them set out the food, confusion plain on her face. Then Sarmi placed a crystal pitcher of maple syrup next to Rina's plate.

"Here we are, Mistress Karina, just as you requested," Sarmi said. "Are you sure we can't prepare anything for the bairn?"

"She's good," Rina replied. "This all looks wonderful. Thank you so much."

"It was our pleasure, Mistress," Sarmi said, then the servants bowed and left. Anya watched them leave, then said, "They didn't even ask if I wanted anything. It's like I'm the queen of nothing around here"

"That's the Rina effect." I grabbed Anya's plate and started filling it. "She can charm anyone at any time."

"I shall remember that," Anya said. "I am glad you requested a hearty breakfast. I'm starved."

Rina smirked at me. "I bet."

"Anyway, younger sibling," I began. While I knew Rina wouldn't tease Anya, unfortunately she considered me fair game. "I'm sure you didn't stop by just for breakfast."

"You would be correct," Rina said, then she picked up out mother's cane and laid it on the table.

Only, it wasn't really a cane. Mom had carried it everywhere with her, which is why Rina and I assumed it was a cane. Clues that it wasn't were Mom's total lack of mobility issues, and that this "cane" was over four feet long, was decorated with beads and feathers, and had runic symbols carved into it. That, and our recent knowledge that Mom was a volva told us that what we'd assumed was a cane was in actuality a wand.

"Your mother's wand?" Anya asked, and Rina

affirmed it was.

"Why did you bring it all the way here?" I asked.

"I was thinking about Mom's diary," Rina began, "and her predictions about you. Anya, want some syrup?"

"Yes, please."

While Anya and Rina drowned their plates in syrup I thought about the premonitions Mom had written about in her diary. Scrawled across the pages were the words "she will kill him and I won't be able to help." Apparently I was the one doomed to die, but whoever was going to kill me remained a mystery.

"I don't suppose you've figured out who my potential murderer is?" I asked.

"I haven't, but I don't think we have to figure it out on our own. Have you ever heard of the Norns?"

"The what?" I asked, as Anya said, "Of course."

I glanced between my girlfriend and my sister. "Go ahead," Rina said, nodding toward Anya. "I'm sure you know way more about them than I do."

Anya swallowed her bite of pancakes, and adjusted Faith in her lap. "They're seers, and live at the base of the world tree, Yggdrasil," Anya began. "There are three of them, I believe, and they're said to be the first giants that came to this realm from Jotunheim."

"Jotunheim?" I repeated. "Isn't that from Norse mythology, like Thor and Odin?"

"Neither Thor nor Odin are giants," Anya replied. "Well, not that I'm aware of. I suppose it's a possibility."

"If we've met Greek gods and fairies I suppose it's only natural that Norse gods are real live people," I muttered to my eggs. "Are unicorns real, too?"

"I hope so," Rina said. "Faith would love a pony."

I pinched the bridge of my nose. It didn't help. "Okay. So. Norns. How can they help me?"

"Mom had foresight, and they're the three queens of foresight," Rina replied. "They keep a well filled with magic water."

"The well's purpose is to water Yggdrasil," Anya said. "The Norns care for the tree, which in turn cares for the world."

"But why would they help me?" I pressed. "It sounds

like they already have a lot on their plates. I'm sure they don't want some random mortal poking around their business."

"You are not a random mortal," Anya said. "Your mother was a volva, therefore she, and all three of you, are their kin. While the Norns aren't ones to try and change a man's fate, I see no reason why they wouldn't answer a few questions."

"See that?" Rina grinned. "Norns are our only hope."

"Norns it is. When should we set out?"

"After breakfast is cool with me."

"What about Faith?" She was sleeping against Anya's shoulder like a tiny angel. "We can't bring her."

"Why not?" Rina countered. "Faith is descended from volvas, too. I feel like this is a strength in numbers mission."

"I do agree," Anya said. "The Norse take family very seriously. If your mother was close to the Norns meeting her granddaughter will greatly please them."

"You think my mother hung around with a group of legendary giants who can see the future? I find that a little far-fetched."

"Says the guy who sleeps with the Queen of Winter," Rina said.

I blew out a breath. "All right, the Stewarts are going to Yggsdrasil. I assume you're coming too," I said to Anya, then I stopped.

"Because I'm a giant's daughter?" she finished. "As we're all now aware, I'm not."

"Anya, I—"

"It's all right." She handed Faith off to Rina and refilled her teacup. "Normally I would enjoy such a trip, but I think it's best I stay close to home and keep an eye on our own sleeping giants, at least for the time being."

"Good point," Rina said.

"Da hasn't even come home yet," Anya continued. "Who knows what sort of a state he will be in?"

"How did you used to handle him when he was out carousing?" Rina asked.

"I did no handling of the sort. I was quite young at the time," Anya said to Rina. "Mum, however, ruled him and the boys with an iron fist. I remember Da complaining of how his head ached after a night of drinking and her freezing his hair to his head."

I shuddered, remembering when Anya had almost frozen me to death. It had been an accident, and I had fully recovered, but it was a horrible experience. "Did he get frozen often?"

"Not often enough to teach him a lesson," Anya replied. "And Mum never froze any of my brothers. Instead she would lay smooth ice onto the floor and watch their drunk arses slide all over the place."

Rina laughed. "I might need you to do that once Faith's a teenager."

***

After we finished breakfast, Rina portaled herself, Faith, and me from the Winter Palace's dining room to a forest filled with tall, slender evergreens. The air was humid but not uncomfortable, and the ground was thick with ferns and mosses, and a gentle fog lent the scene just the right amount of spooky. Golden sunlight slanted down through the branches, making the forest seem more otherworldly than any part of Elphame I'd ever seen.

"I thought it would be colder."

"This region's technically a temperate rainforest," Rina replied. I took that to mean the weather in this area tended toward warm and moist, and left it at that. I could have asked for clarification, but knowing Rina that would have started a two-hour lecture on dendrology and microclimates.

"Which way is Yggsdrasil?" I asked, since all I saw were trees in all directions.

Rina cocked her head to the side, then pointed to her right. "That way, maybe a quarter of a kilometer. East, I think?"

I turned my face upward. The canopy was too dense for me to know where the sun was. "Why didn't you portal us directly to the tree?"

She shrugged. "I don't know if the Norns like surprises, and I'd rather not find out the hard way."

"Can they still be surprised if they can see the future?"

"Maybe. Who knows."

We set off through the eerily quiet forest, Rina leading

the way. Throughout it all Faith slept in her carrier, and I didn't know if that was for best, or of something was keeping her asleep. Images of the Pied Piper rose in the back of my head.

"Are you sure it's okay for Faith to be here?"

"If anything goes sideways I'll portal us away in a hot second." She smiled over her shoulder, and added, "You, too."

A bird screeched overhead. "Thanks." I heard a flapping sound, but I couldn't see the bird, if it even was a bird I was hearing and not a product of my overactive imagination. "Is that bird supposed to be following us?"

Rina held up Mom's cane as if it was a sword. "Don't worry. I'll protect you from the mean forest creatures."

"What if they're guarding the tree?" I asked. "What if their purpose is to stop us, or trick us, or—"

I stopped talking. Rina was laughing so hard she couldn't hear me, anyway.

The trees thinned out, and I could finally see the bird circling above the branches. It seemed to be an eagle, though at that distance I couldn't be sure. At least it wasn't a vulture. The ferns and other plants thinned out, too, and the ground became uneven. I looked down and realized we were no longer walking across the pine needle-carpeted forest floor. Instead, we were on top of a vast network of tree roots.

Rina paused, then said over her shoulder, "We're almost there."

"How do you know?"

"Whenever I decide to portal to a location, I can sense where it is. It's like I have built in GPS."

She had never mentioned that before. "Have you always been able to do that?"

"No. This walker gig is constantly changing the rules."

The roots swelled in size, getting wider and more robust until Rina and I could walk along the top of one with relative surefootedness. We followed the root's curve, and it led us to a tree so massive I couldn't see around the trunk.

"Is this Yggsdrasil?" I asked.

"I guess." Rina approached the trunk and laid her hand against the bark. "It's warm. Come say hello."

At any other time I would have thought Rina was nuts for asking me to say hello to a tree, but if this was indeed Yggsdrasil respect was due. I placed my hand next to hers on the rough bark. She was right, it was warm.

"Does the warmth mean it likes us?"

"Let's hope so." Rina nodded toward the base of the tree. Below us was a spring bubbling up through the smaller roots, and it was surrounded by three women.

"They must be the Norns," I said. "Why don't you do the honors?"

"Sure thing. Hello," Rina called. The women looked up as one. "Would you mind if we came down to talk to you?"

"Not at all," replied the central woman.

Rina touched my elbow, and a moment later we were standing next to the spring. Up close I saw that the women were similar, but appeared to be different ages. One appeared to be a teenager, the central woman who'd hailed us was about my age, and the third woman was more mature. They all wore similar cream-colored robes, elegant n their simplicity, and were barefoot. Since the tree's roots were as warm as its trunk, shoes were unnecessary.

Rina put on her thousand-watt smile and began the introductions.

"Thank you. I'm Karina Stewart, this is my brother, Chris," I waved hello, "and this little one is my daughter, Faith. Chris and I believe you knew our mother."

"Oh?" said the middle woman. The other two Norns remained silent, but observant. "How would an American woman have crossed our paths?"

"She wasn't American," I said. "She was Icelandic, and her name was Elisabét Lund."

Rina held out Mom's cane. "This was hers. Do you recognize it?" Rina's voice cracked, then she asked, "Do you remember her?"

The women stilled, and while their mouths didn't move I heard whispering. "We remember Elisabét," the central woman admitted.

"She lives no longer," the eldest said. "I cut her thread long ago."

I blinked away the sudden pressure behind my eyes.

"That's true. Both of our parents are dead."

"They died together," Rina added. "We know our mother was a volva. I think I inherited some of her abilities."

The youngest Norn approached Rina and peered into her face. "No, you didn't. You, however," she rounded on me, "did."

"What? No." I held up my hands and backed away from her. "That's not right. Rina's a walker. I-I'm just an English teacher."

"So?" she countered. "As a rule, volvas don't create portals."

"But I can't see the future," I protested.

The Norn laughed. "Do you think that foresight is the only trait a volva possesses?"

I looked at Rina. She shook her head slightly. "I... I guess I don't know the answer to that."

"Our mother saw the future," Rina said. "She wrote her visons down in a diary. The last one said that a woman was going to kill Chris." Faith squirmed in her carrier, and Rina paused to soothe her. "Is there any way you can help us figure out what or who she meant? We've already lost most of our family. I don't want to lose my brother, too."

"You will risk angering Fortune to do so?" the eldest asked. "Altering the path of time is not wise."

"Wait, we could mess things up if we play with time?" I asked, and she nodded. "Is that what happened to our mother? Was she punished for having foresight?"

"She was not," she replied. "Elisabét was born with foresight, therefore the gift was hers to use as she saw fit. You, however," she continued, fixing Rina in her gaze, "give me the impression you want to know the future so you may alter it."

"If I can change it so no one murders my brother, I will," Rina said.

"Think of the family you're making," the elder said, gesturing toward Faith. "You would take such a risk?"

"Yes," Rina replied, adamant. "It won't be much of a family without Chris."

The Norns huddled together, and his time I could hear them whispering to each other along with the whispers in the leaves. I got the feeling that there was far more to the Norns than the three women in front of me.

"Very well," the elder announced. "You both seek us, but for very different reasons, and yet none of the questions you raise are the questions you should be asking. We are amenable to offering help, but until you understand what it is you seek, you must find answers on your own.

"You," she continued, facing me. "You want to know about your mother, which requires looking behind. However, instead of seeking answers from a woman long dead, should you not be seeking a woman that still lives?"

I blinked, the realization of whom they were referring to hitting me hard. "Are you saying Nicnevin's alive, and I should concentrate on finding her instead of the woman who's going to kill me?" The Norn raised an eyebrow, and remained silent. As she said, these answers were for me to discover.

"And you, young one," she continued as she faced Rina. "You learned your mother was volva, and you sought to learn more about your heritage, which is admirable. Elisabét was strong, and intelligent, and fierce. I see much of her in you, but your gift for traveling comes from elsewhere. Perhaps you should consider where this gift will take you, and your child."

Rina nodded, tears streaming down her cheeks. "Okay. I will. Thank you."

"We have gifts to help you on your journeys," the youngest said. She withdrew two glass bottles from the folds of her dress. "These bottles contain water from our well, the Urdabrunnr. When you drink the water touch one of these stones." She indicated three stones circling the neck of each bottle. "Blue is past, yellow is today, and purple is what's yet to be."

"The water will give us foresight?" I asked. "Or hindsight?"

She smiled. "It will, but you must be careful. You already have a touch of the sight, though it doesn't normally point toward tomorrow. Drink too much at once and there's no telling what you might see."

I closed my hand around the bottle. "I'll be careful."

She nodded, and handed Rina an identical bottle. "As for you, I don't know of a walker ever drinking from the well. If you decide to partake, will you come back and tell us what happened?"

Rina's hand trembled as she accepted the bottle. "Won't you already know?"

She smiled. "Eventually, yes, but thousands of threads are woven and cut every day. It will be faster if you tell us yourself."

"Okay." Rina tucked the bottle into the carrier next to Faith. "I promise I'll tell you all about it."

"So it is agreed," the central Norn said. "We will speak soon."

A heartbeat later and we were inside our Glaswegian flat. "Did you do that?" I asked.

"No."

Rina sat on the couch, then she undid the carrier that held Faith. "Here, I'll take her," I said when I saw Rina's hands were still trembling. "I don't know what I was expecting, but it wasn't that."

"Every time I try to get closer to Mom, I end up farther away." She covered her face with her hands and hunched down over her knees. "I've always, always wanted to be like Mom. I tried drawing like she used to, but I can't do that. I tried dressing like her, but I'm not elegant and well put together like she was. When I found out she was a volva, I figured that since I'm a walker I finally had something in common with her. That I was a volva like her." Rina snuffled and grabbed a box of tissues from the coffee table. "And now I'm not even that."

"You are so much like Mom," I said. "You talk like her, you think fast like she did, and you would do anything for your family. Even your questionable sibling," I added.

"Yeah, well." She put her bottle of Urdabrunnr water on the table. "What should we do with our magic water?"

"Right now? Nothing." I felt warmth against my chest. I checked Faith, but the warmth wasn't due to anything she'd done. "Let's have a good, long think before we do anything with it. I'd hate for us to end up as a Nordic cautionary tale."

"Good idea." Rina's brows pinched. "Your chest is wiggling."

"What?" I handed off Faith and reached inside my coat pocket. I'd stashed the miniaturized version of the Ninth Legion's *aquila* there. Now it was heating up and vibrating.

"I… I think Lucius is trying to get my attention."
Rina blew out a breath. "That can't be good."

Chapter Nine
Anya

After Christopher and Karina left to meet with the Norns at Yggsdrasil—gods below, that was an amazing situation to be involved with, even for me—I spent some time in the dining hall alone with my thoughts. The hall was a beautiful room, with the shining ice white walls bedecked with red and gold tapestries, and the ceiling painted in the pale blues and yellows of a cold winter sunrise. It was a room I could see myself spending much time in over the coming weeks and months as I considered winter and all of her cold glory. But before I could settle in to the dining hall or any other part of the palace, there was the matter of the land to attend to. Or rather, the land's weather.

I blinked from my seat in front of the breakfast dishes to the stony, snowy peak of Beinn na Caillich. Mum had many thrones scattered across Scotland, but this one had always been her favorite. Now it was my favorite, as well. Perhaps it was because it was on the Isle of Skye and therefore near to our summer cottage, or perhaps it was due to the fine views to be had in all directions. Of course, Mum hadn't set foot in our summer cottage since before Da and my brothers were imprisoned. Now that she was hiding at the Unseelie Court I didn't see any family vacations happening in my future. I suppose the views were what had drawn me here after all.

With a wave of my hand the Winter Queen's throne rose from the ground. It was an ancient seat, made of stacked stone and held together by Mum's—and now my—will. I settled onto the frosted seat, glad I'd worn jeans and a sweater instead of the filmy gowns Mum had always favored, and surveyed the land spread below me.

It was still early in the season, so there was no need for Scotland to be too cold as of yet. At least, I didn't think it needed to be any colder than it already was. Mum could remember the weather patterns from every winter since her reign commenced, right down to the number of snowflakes that had fallen in Dumfries a decade ago, and the average wind gusts in Galloway over the past century, but I'd yet to build such a store of knowledge. What I did have was an almanac that had been given to me by Christopher's brilliant scientist of a sister, Karina.

"What's this?" I'd asked when she handed it to me.

"It's an almanac," she'd replied. "It gives you phases of the moon, planting calendars, and it has historical weather patterns. Scientists often use them when planning the right time for field work. Don't want to set up a dig and end up fighting a blizzard," she added.

"No, I imagine not." I flipped through the pages, noted the average temperature per day on the calendar, along with the times for sunrise and sunset. "Mum never used anything like this."

"Maybe she should have. Tolls are there to make our work easier, you know?"

She was right, and I had found the almanac quite useful. Now, I opened the book and flipped to the weather for this date last year, and made certain the exact same conditions were in effect. Were they the ideal conditions for this date? I didn't know the answer to that, either, but I was keeping a close eye on things. If anything untoward occurred I could fix it in a trice. I hoped.

The weather was behaving as planed across the island, until I noticed a pocket of warmer air hovering over the eastern coast of Fife. Assuming I'd made an error, I pushed the cold toward Fife. When nothing changed, I pushed a bit harder. The warmth not only remained, it resisted me.

"Hmm."

I thought about Fife, and what sort of anomalies that region may contain. It was an ancient kingdom, bound by the Firth of Tay and the Firth of Forth's watery borders, but historically its weather wasn't anything out of the ordinary. Of course, nestled within Fife was Crail, where the gallowglass and the walker owned a home that had been fair created from Elphame's magic. As Christopher would say, almost nothing good ever came out of Elphame.

Neither Robert nor Karina had ever mentioned the cottage having any magic associated with it, weather-based or otherwise. What's more I'd been inside the cottage several times and had never detected anything remarkable about it.

Whatever was happening in Fife was either a new event, possibly a spell Fionnlagh had cast and designed to appear at a later time, or the region was a bit warmer than the surrounding area for perfectly natural reasons. I'd just made up my mind to ask Mum if she'd ever noticed a similar anomaly when Angus appeared at my elbow.

"Gods below, you scared the life out of me," I said. "Is that what it's like when I blink into a room?"

"Oh, no. When you do it it's much worse." Angus kicked over a sizeable boulder and sat on it.

"Can the rest of our brothers blink?" I asked, imagining the entire hoard of them turning up in the midst of a pub or football game and causing a ruckus.

"Not sure," he replied. "You and I are the only ones that ever go off on our own. The rest are like a pack of wolves, and only follow the leader."

I recalled the wolves that flocked to Mum's side whenever she set foot outside the palace. "Then we all inherited the trait from Mum."

"Who else would we have gotten it from?" When I didn't respond, Angus said, "I take it the cat's out of the bag about Maelgwyn."

"Aye. That it is. And would you like to know the oddest part about it? Just as I didn't know who he was to me, neither did he. We found out about each other at the same time."

"That must have been quite the revelation."

"It surely was." I glanced at Angus. "The rest of you always knew?"

"When you were born with those eyes," Angus jerked his chin toward my face, indicating my iridescent gray eyes that were a perfect match to Maelgwyn's, "we had our suspicions. When Da stomped off to the Summer Court and beat its king half to death, we were rather certain."

"I bet you were. The rest are all Da's, then?"

"As far as I'm aware, yes." He scooped up a handful of pebbles and flung them down the mountainside, one after the other. "Why are you asking such questions? Looking for more relations to rescue?"

"I'm looking to understand myself," I snapped. "While I adore the stinking lot of you, I am starting to wonder if bringing you out of imprisonment earlier than planned was the best idea. What were you all thinking, drinking yourselves silly and singing to Mum?"

"We weren't thinking much, that's for certain. Did you have to set the gallowglass on us?"

"You're lucky Robert's all I sent after you. From now on if you get any brilliant ieas, run them past me first."

"I suppose we could, but you forget that our worst ideas come from Da himself. For instance, yesterday's concert was all his notion, as it was when Da tried to take over the Seelie Court and all of us daft fools went along with it." Angus flung the next few pebbles with a bit more force. "Still can't believe we did that. Strength in numbers we had, but what we were sorely missing was strength in brains."

I laughed. "What even gave Da the notion to try such a thing? He must have known that awful plan was doomed from the outset. Really, not one of you tried to talk some sense into him?"

"Now sister, you ken well we have little sense between us," Angus replied. "Da got it in his head that Fionnlagh's crown—the antlered deal he hauls out for special occasions—was the focus of his power. Our plan, lame though it was, was to steal it and thus take that power for ourselves."

"Da really thought that by plunking Fionnlagh's crown on his head he would suddenly rule the whole of the Seelie?" I gave my brother a look. "You're right. The lot of you are daft."

"Hey now, there are plenty of instances of magical objects lending power. The countryside is littered with holy relics that bestow all sorts of fortune on those lucky enough to find them."

Angus had a point. If one was lucky enough to stumble on a holy relic—a real one, not just a bit of bone someone claimed was a saint's remains—true power was at their fingertips. The crown in question, however, was not such an object.

"Despite your careful research—by which I mean your total lack of research whatsoever—I can say with certainty that the crown is not at all magical," I said. "Maelgwyn retrieved it after we sent Fionnlagh into ice, and it's been sitting in his library ever since. It's nothing more than rather homely family heirloom."

Angus grunted. "Be that as it may, the Seelie power flows from somewhere. If we'd had more time at the court we would have found the source of it."

"What do you mean, the source? Are you saying that Fionnlagh's power isn't his own?"

"Think on it. Maelgwyn, back when he was still Udane, was the Summer King, as was his father before him. All the power goes to the firstborn in that family, with nothing left over for the rest. Fionnlagh was a lesser son and so powerless he was unable to conjure up a fart at a feast, then Maelgwyn goes down and Fionnlagh suddenly has his own court?" Angus shook his head. "Makes no sense. Fionnlagh couldn't have gotten the power from Maelgwyn, because Maelgwyn still has his power. Therefore, how did he become the Seelie King?"

"I… I have no idea." I thought about the Seelie Court, and the many tales of Fionnlagh's vast strength, both physical and magical. I'd seen that strength demonstrated with my own eyes, more than once. "If what you say is true—"

"Which it is."

"Fionnlagh owes someone a great debt for all of that power." I met Angus's gaze. "Someone, or something."

Angus nodded sagely. "That is exactly what we wanted to find out, and maybe nick a bit of it for ourselves."

"Gods below. What in the world have you done with all that power? Don't answer that," I added when Angus opened his mouth. Some questions were better left unanswered.

"More importantly, where would Fionnlagh have gotten that kind of power? And since he didn't have any wealth or influence until after he was Seelie, how did he pay for it?" I stood and dusted off my jeans. "Fancy a quick trip to the Seelie Court?"

"What for?" Angus asked.

"I'd like to have a look around."

Chapter Ten
Chris

Rina sent me from the flat's living room directly to the Winter Palace's empty dining hall. The breakfast dishes and table linens had been cleared away, and someone, probably Sarmi, has polished the long table until it shone. Knowing Sarmi's meticulous standards every surface in this hall was clean enough to eat off of, including the floor. Bing that the hall was empty, these freshly scrubbed surfaces gleamed for my eyes alone.

I'd expected Anya's brothers to be having a late breakfast of their own, but they were either still asleep or otherwise indisposed. How long did it take for a giant to sleep off a hangover? They'd been out for at least ten hours, maybe more. Apparently, increased size did not equal increased alcohol tolerance.

A tremor rocked the palace. I grabbed onto the table, and wished I could call Rina. She would know if northern Scotland known for earthquakes. Then again, the Winter Palace didn't exist strictly in the mortal realm. For all I knew this area was prone to earthquakes, volcanoes, and the occasional monsoon.

The *aquila* quivered in my chest pocket a bit faster than before, and I got the sinking feeling that whatever this shaking was, it was not a natural disaster. Shit, the brothers must be awake. What were they up to now?

I burst out of the dining hall and ran toward the ballroom where the Ninth Legion usually hung out during the day. A barracks had been constructed at the rear of the hall, and thanks to a healthy dose of Anya's magic they'd created their own Roman outpost inside the Winter Palace. I rode out another aftershock as I saw Lucius striding toward me.

"Is this you?" I asked, holding up the miniature standard. It had gone from quivering to buzzing, and was almost too hot to hold on to.

"Forgive me, but I had no other way to contact you."

"It's fine. Do you know what's causing these tremors?"

Lucius frowned. "These are no tremors. Come with me, if you will."

I followed Lucius through the palace and to the throne room. In the center of the room, in front of the grand double staircase and directly below a chandelier made of ice so clear it shone like diamonds, was the Bodach. He was sprawled out face down on the floor, one arm bent under his forehead while his other arm stretched in front of him. I noted his clenched fist, and the cracks in the floor radiating from it.

"Is he dead?" I asked. As if to answer, Bod raised his arm and punched the floor so hard the palace's foundations shook.

So that's why everything was shaking. I would have much preferred an earthquake. Or a volcano.

"Is Anya here?" I asked. "Or Angus?"

"They have both left," Lucius replied. "Shortly after they took their leave the Bodach returned. He was in quite a state, though I know not why. After he raged about the ale house and then the kitchens for a time, he entered this room and started beating the floor apart."

"He never said why he's mad?"

"He does not seem mad, so much as distraught."

"Huh."

I regarded Bod, and realized Lucius was right. Bod's face was streaked with tears and dust, and for all the tremors he was causing he was only halfheartedly beating the floor. I had no doubt that if he wanted to he could reduce the entire palace to rubble.

I cautiously approached the giant. "Hey, old man," I began. "What happened?" When he remained silent, I sat on the floor near him, but out of reach. "I can't help if you don't talk to me."

"And what help would you be offering?" he wailed. "What can you do to fix things?"

"Nothing, if you don't tell me what's broken."

Bod raised his fist and let it fall to the floor. The entire room shook, and part of the stair railing collapsed. "Not only will she not come home with me, she won't even see me. She won't even talk to me."

"She?"

"My wife."

I sighed in relief. Relationship trouble was something I could commiserate on. "Maybe Beira just needs some time."

"Time?" he demanded. "All we've had is time apart, time to think. All this blessedly endless time has done is made her remember the bad, and never the good. And I know whose fault it is."

"And, whose fault would that be?" I asked, desperately hoping Bod blamed himself for this situation.

"You know who's behind this mess!" Bod reared up on his knees with his fists clenched overhead, moving far faster than a creature of his size should be able to. "He is!"

Bod locked his fists together and slammed them onto the floor. The shockwave sent cracks moving lightning fast across the floor in all directions and snaking up the walls. I heard a mad tinkling overhead; the chandelier was shaking like a leaf in a windstorm.

"Bod, why are you taking your anger out on the floor?" I asked, keeping my gaze on the chandelier. "Destroying it won't get you your wife back."

"But it will get me him." Bod slammed the floor again, and I remembered who was imprisoned beneath the Winter Palace: Fionnlagh.

Shit, I'd thought Bod meant Maelgwyn was the guilty party in Beira leaving him, but Bod blamed everything on Fionnlagh.

Bod raised his fists again. He was ready to beat his anger out on Fionnlagh, and was prepared to destroy the palace to reach him.

"Lucius!" I stood and withdrew the *aquila*.

"Here, Dominus." Instantly, Lucius and a dozen legionnaires in full armor were in the room.

"We need to get Bod out of here!"

Lucius barked a few commands, and the legionnaires surrounded Bod. He ignored them, and kept on beating the floor into smaller and smaller pieces.

"Shields up," Lucius ordered. The legionnaires raised their rectangular *scutums*. "Close in!"

Step by step the legionnaires closed in on Bod. When their shields were less than an arm's length from the giant, they moved as one and forced Bod first to his feet, then to back away from the hole he'd created.

Bod roared.

A legionnaire lost his footing on the broken floor and went down. Those on either side closed the gap.

"You will not keep me from my quarry," Bod yelled.

"I can't let you destroy Anya's house," I said. I helped the fallen legionnaire to his feet. "You okay?"

"Yes," he replied, then he shoved me aside. A moment later Bod's meaty fist connected with the legionnaire's breastplate. I landed on my ass as the legionnaire was flung across the room.

Bod had tried to hit me with his full strength. Anya's da had tried to kill me.

The chandelier finally had enough, and crashed to the floor. I rolled out of the way, barely avoiding the scatter of razor sharp ice. When the dust cleared eight of the twelve legionnaires were down, and Bod was gone.

"Sarmi," I yelled. "Sarmi, we need medical attention!"

Sarmi poked her head into the room, then disappeared. She reappeared a moment later with an army of servants in tow, each of them bearing bandages, bowls of water, and trays filled with herbs and salves, and whatever else they could find.

Lucius offered me a hand up. "He got away."

"Yes he did." I surveyed the damage Bod had caused. Worst of all were the wounded men; red stained the frozen floor, and Sarmi had already ordered the removal of three of the legionnaires to the palace infirmary. Along with the human loss the entire room was trashed; the stairs that led to the throne listed to the side, what was left of the walls sagged, and the floor looked as if it would cave in at any moment. I knew Anya could fix the structure, but what would happen to the legionnaires? How would she feel when she realized Bod was responsible for all of this destruction?

"I'm so sorry, Lucius," I said. "I never meant for your men to get hurt."

"They're soldiers," Lucius said. "We all understood the risks when we signed on."

"Still. I'm sure none of you thought you'd be facing a giant."

Lucius shrugged. "Rome was always beset by its share of monsters, and the creatures grew more strange the farther north we ranged. Why should our present assignment be any different?"

"Why, indeed."

I followed Bod's escape path from the throne room and through the palace. Instead of footprints his giant feet had left craters in the floor. Convenient, that. The path led me out of the throne room, up the stairs and toward the dormitories where we'd put his sons. A broken window told me Bod had jumped to freedom. I peeked through the shattered glass. There was no body on the ground below, and no sight or sound of Bod in the courtyard.

"Crazy giant could be anywhere," I muttered. I pushed open the dormitory's door. All of Anya's brothers slumbered away, with the exception of one empty bed: the one that belonged to Angus.

"How is he involved here?" Angus was the only one of the brothers that hadn't been drunk at the Unseelie Court, and he was conspicuously absent now. From what Anya had told me her brothers operated with one mind, and all of them did whatever Bod, or Angus, asked of them. What made Angus different than the rest?

I eased the door shut and returned to the throne room. The wounded legionnaires had been relocated, and Sarmi's crew was busy mopping up what was left of the floor. Lucius surveyed it all, his arms crossed over his chest.

"He's gone." I mimicked Lucius's posture, but I didn't think anyone would mistake me for military any time soon. My affect was more of a stern lunch lady's. "Jumped out of a second floor window."

"Odd for him to bother with such theatrics. The door was closer." Lucius frowned. "Do you suspect the giant of trying to distract us from something else in play?"

"I don't think he was trying to distract us. If anything, he's heartbroken." Lucius grunted. "Ever have a broken heart?"

"Once you enlist in the legion wives are forbidden," he replied. "Women are a distraction like none other."

"What about men?"

Lucius grunted, then looked away. "Best to avoid entanglements and focus on the job at hand."

"You will accomplish more than way." I didn't press

the matter, but I was curious. Lucius had led the Ninth Legion for thousands of years. Had he really been alone that entire time?

"Would you like me to send a search party after the Bodach?"

"It would be a wasted effort. With the amount of destruction he leaves in his wake we'll know where he is soon enough." I frowned at the heaps of rubble. Anya had been so proud of how she'd rebuilt the palace, and especially this room. Bod had all but destroyed it in a few short minutes. "For better or worse, we all will."

Chapter Eleven
Anya

Angus and I blinked from Benn na Caillich to just inside the boundary of the Seelie Court, and what a spectacle that court was. Whereas Maelgwyn's palace sat atop a dark and dreary crag surrounded by a darker and drearier landscape, the Seelie had surrounded their home with acres of well-tended lawns and finely manicured hedgerows. Statues and water features were placed at regular intervals, lending an overall sense of serenity and grandeur to the area. If I hadn't known better I would have thought I was on a European garden tour visiting the castles of empires long since fallen.

The Seelie palace itself sat in the center of the gardens, and it resembled nothing so much as a massive vanilla frosted cake. It was again the opposite of the Unseelie Court; where the former was all dark stone and tall spires, the Seelie's home was low and squat, with white columns and decorative frills carved from fine white marble crammed onto every surface. Little did the Seelie's subjects know that this grand and lovely exterior housed a set of murderous rulers with rot in their hearts. I considered the scene before me, and decided I much preferred the honest darkness of the Unseelie Court, and the icy clarity of the Winter Palace.

While I ruminated on the beautiful if somewhat deceptive home of the Seelie, I was struck at how well-tended the castle and gardens were. Everything was in full bloom, and there wasn't a stray leaf or twig in sight. Even the grass appeared to be freshly trimmed.

"With Fionnlagh and Nicnevin gone, who is looking after the place?" I cupped a handful of lilac blossoms from a nearby shrub and inhaled deeply. They'd always been my favorite. "Lilacs! Can you believe it? In winter, no less."

"It's always been like this, so perfect it's ugly," Angus replied. "Give me an old field strewn with boulders any day. As for the gardens, maybe one of your wight friends works here."

I dropped the flowers and faced my brother. "You've been here before."

"Aye. Many times. Before Da got in in his head to take over the Seelie, Ma brought us to court often. We all hated it, even Ma. No idea why we kept coming back."

"I wonder why." Mum had never once brought me to the Seelie Court, and with good reason. Maelgwyn and I were so much alike anyone acquainted with him would have instantly placed me as his daughter, and thus a potential heir to the Seelie throne. If there was anything Fionnlagh hadn't liked, it was potential heirs. Now all of that was out in the open, or at least no one was denying who had fathered whom. It also meant that my potential albeit weak upon the Seelie Court was common knowledge. I wasn't quite sure how I felt about that.

Add to all of that the fact that Mum never did anything unintentionally, and always thought ten steps ahead of her current situation. I wondered what plans she'd set in motion back then, and if any were still in play.

"Where are you headed?" I asked Angus. He was stomping down the main garden path with purpose, as if the way was familiar to him.

"There's a treasury in the eastern wing," Angus replied. "It's as good a place as any to start looking for answers."

"How do you know where the treasury is? Wait, don't answer that," I added, as visions of my brothers fair swimming in Seelie gold filled my mind's eye.

He shrugged. "What can I say, we got bored often enough and did some exploring. As far as I know Fionnlagh was none the wiser."

"Still, I don't think it's wise to just waltz into the treasury. I imagine the guards will have something to say about that."

Angus turned to face me and spread his arm wide. "What guards? This place is deserted."

He was right. We'd crossed the entire garden and were almost at the palace walls, yet we hadn't seen another soul. Even so, Fionnlagh was a sneaky bastard, and I didn't want to inadvertently trigger one of his traps.

I spied a darkened corner of the gardens. From that corner came the sound of running water. "Let's go over here for a moment," I said, and I made my way toward the grotto.

A stacked stone wall marked the boundary of the grotto, and the many vines that climbed the wall absorbed the mist kicked up from a small waterfall. The water emptied into a pool, and thick branches overhead blocked out most of the light.

"Wait," Angus called. "Anya, stop! You don't want to go there!"

His warnings told me what I suspected about the grotto was true. I stood at the edge of the pool and looked at my reflection in the rippling waters, wondering if Christopher was doing the same at Yggdrasil's base. I couldn't wait to hear about his adventure with the Norns.

"Have you word of her?" came a raspy voice from behind me; the water spirit inhabiting this grotto was one of the *fuath*, the water demons that were also Fionnlagh's children, and this child of the Seelie had come to talk. Before I could reply my noble brother crashed into the grotto, intent on rescuing me.

"Anya get back!" Angus flailed about like a fish on dry land, tearing down vines and knocking aside the carefully arranged stonework. Being that the *fuath* was made entirely of black mist, Angus passed right through the creature and, with a mighty splash, landed in the pool.

"Angus, you daft idiot," I said. "The *fuath* are our friends." I regarded at the ephemeral beast. "We are friends, aren't we?"

"We like friends," the *fuath* replied. Not the answer I was looking for, but good enough for the moment. "Have you word for us?"

"Word of what?" Angus demanded as he climbed out of the pool.

"Nicnevin," I replied. "The *fuath* have been helping us search for her." Angus opened his mouth, glanced at the *fuath*, and closed it. My brother isn't totally devoid of brains, then.

"I'm sorry, but we have no new information about her," I said. "We are still searching for her. My entire court, and the Unseelie, are devoting resources to the search. We will find your stepmother." The *fuath* shrank in on itself, and my heart went out to the beast. The *fuath* may be Fionnlagh's children, but he'd made them into monsters. Their stepmother, Nicnevin, was the only one who'd ever cared for them, and she was missing.

"Nicnevin's your ma?" Angus asked. "I never kent that."

"There's much that goes on behind these walls that never sees the light of day," the *fuath* hissed.

"May I ask you about one of those events?" When the beast remained silent, I continued, "It may help us understand Fionnlagh a bit better, and help us find Nicnevin."

The *fuath* nodded. "Ask."

"Did you ever accompany Fionnlagh on the Wild Hunt?"

"Yes," he replied; I was certain the creature before me was male, because Fionnlagh had murdered all of his daughters at birth. And we called the *fuath* monsters. "We were the ones who snatched the souls, and we were the ones who sent them to their due."

"Their due? Do you mean you sent them to be punished?"

"Not punishment. Payment. We brought them to the island to the west, and sent them through the altar stone." The *fuath's* smoky form went still. "They come."

"Who does?" I turned around, and saw the Conall, the leader of an ancient group of Picts who were also yet another band of Seelie mercenaries, approaching.

"Have the Picts been bothering you?" I asked the *fuath*. Silence. When I turned back, the *fuath* was gone.

"All hail the queen," Conall called. "How can we help you, your majesty?"

"All alone? I didn't think you set foot out of doors without your band of merry men to protect you."

"This is my home," Conall said. "What would I need protection from?" Conall narrowed his eyes. "Why are you here?"

Angus stood beside me and glowered at Conall. "Have a care how you speak to the Queen of Winter."

Conall's eyes flashed, but he didn't have a quick retort for Angus. It was amazing how quickly his courage waned when his men weren't behind him. "What can I do for you?"

"We were wondering about the *sluagh*," I said, using the Gaelic word for the host of unforgiven dead. "Who will collect them this year?"

"No one can collect them save my king," Conall replied.

"That won't be happening," I replied. "Why was he collecting them?"

"So many questions," Conall said. "It seems to me you should have thought to ask all of these before you froze my king solid. Why don't you thaw him out and ask him what you will."

"This is pointless," Angus said. "His brain's as tiny as his cock. Come on, let's find someone who kens a thing or two."

"Good plan." I put my hand on Angus's elbow and blinked us to the edge of the Seelie Court. Even at that distance we could hear Conall yelling about our sudden departure.

"What a pathetic little man," I began, then the *fuath* from the grotto materialized in front of us.

"Hello again," I said. "I take it you don't like Conall either?"

He growled a reply. Even though I couldn't make out the words, I understood him just fine. "There is more, about the *sluagh*," he said, much more clearerly.

"What about them?"

"Father owed them as payment for his court, his land, for everything Even us. He could not have done this," he gestured to his smoky form, "without the *sluagh*."

"Was he using the host to transform you into…into this?" I asked.

"He traded the souls for power."

So it was a debt. "Who did he owe?"

"An ancient, evil creature, one who many thought was banished long ago. Papa owed his debt to Crom Cruach."

I grasped Angus's arm, shocked that even Fionnlagh would sink to such a level. Crom Cruach had been known the world over as evil incarnate, and tales of his awful deeds were still told around campfires and to frighten children.

"These souls, why does Crom want them?" I asked. "Is he hoarding power? Does he mean to return to this realm?"

"Papa never told us," the *fuath* replied. "But what else would he need the souls for?"

The creature dissipated. Angus and I looked at each other. "Now what do we do?" I demanded.

"Bollocks if I ken."

Chapter Twelve
Chris

Sarmi and her staff did everything they could for the throne room, but no amount of cleaning or polishing could cover up the holes Bod had punched into the floor, or repair the shattered balustrade and stairs. As for the chandelier, that was the most lost cause in the history of lost causes. Since none of us knew how to repair a room made of ice and snow we'd just swept up the debris and shut the door. The room would just have to remain off limits until Anya returned to take care of the heavy lifting.

It bothered me that Anya was going to return home to this mess. She'd been so excited to see Bod and her brothers again, and on his first night back Bod had gotten drunk and caused a scene at the Unseelie Court. Anya had been appalled by his behavior, but not surprised. In fact, no one had been surprised, either here or at the Unseelie palace. Bod getting hammered and causing a ruckus seemed to be the natural order of things.

Speaking of the Unseelie, Maelgwyn and Beira had borne the brunt of Bod's antics for centuries. I wondered if they would be willing to make some of the repairs to the Winter Palace to help out Anya. I'd just shut the throne room's doors and resolved to contact the Unseelie when I heard Anya and Angus return.

"Christopher?" she called.

"Here." A moment later I saw them round the corner into the corridor.

"Hello, love," Anya greeted. She saw the closed doors behind me and frowned. "What happened?"

"What makes you think something happened?"

"These doors have never once been shut, not when I was a wee bairn, and not since I've been back." I stepped aside, and Anya approached the doors and shoved them open. She gasped, covering her mouth with her hand as she took in the damage.

"Bod was trying to get to Fionnlagh," I said. "The Ninth got him out of the room, then he ran off. Fionnlagh's still where he's supposed to be."

"Ran off where?" Angus demanded. "Where did Da go?"

"No idea," I replied. "He jumped out a window and was gone."

"I'll rally the rest and track him down," Angus said, then he put his hand on Anya's shoulder. "It's just a floor and some walls. We can fix it."

Anya nodded. "Aye. That we can."

Angus squeezed her shoulder. "There's a lass."

I watched him walk down the corridor and turn toward the stairs that led to the brothers' dormitory. "Think they can find him?"

"I can't believe he did this." Anya took a step into the throne room. "My own Da did this to my home."

I came up beside her and snaked my arm around her waist. She molded herself to my side, but didn't look away from the destruction. "He did. No one else was involved, just Bod."

"You're not going to make excuses for him? Tell me I should look kindly upon him because he's my da?"

"No. I'm not." I cupped her face with my hands. After a moment, she met my gaze. "What Bod did was awful, and I'm not going to apologize for him. That's for him to do. But Angus was right. There's nothing broken in here that isn't fixable."

She pulled me against her, and for a few minutes we held each other. Anya's breathing was ragged and her shoulders trembled, but I didn't call her on it. She needed time to process what had happened, not my half-assed advice.

"You're right," she said. "You're always right."

"I have many former students who would dispute that." Anya laughed, and I felt a surge of happiness. I loved making her happy. "How can I help clean this room up?"

"For now I think it's best to leave it be." We separated, and after Anya gave the mess one last look, we left the throne room. As Anya shut and bolted the doors, she said, "Pity about the chandelier. I have no idea how Mum created it in the first place."

"We can always go modern, and install some electric lights."

Anya smiled, but it didn't reach her eyes. "How were things with the Norns?"

"Confusing," I replied, then I told her everything that had transpired with Rina and me around the roots of Yggsdrasil. By the time the story was complete we had relocated to the library, and Anya was holding the bottle of well water.

"Fascinating," she said, as she turned the bottle from side to side. "Have you had any of the water yet?"

"Hell no. Having a drink of this water is probably a once in a lifetime opportunity, like three wishes from a genie. I don't want to squander it."

"Caution is probably best." She set the bottle on the table. "While you were at Yggsdrasil, Angus and I went to the Seelie Court and spoke to a *fuath*. The beast claims that Fionnlagh led the Wild Hunt and collected souls in order to make offerings to Crom Cruach."

"That sounds pretty sketchy. Who's this Crom guy?"

"He's a fertility god from the old days," she replied. "All the tales claim he was an awful beast, right down to his core. Even so, his followers were a devoted lot. They made offerings to him of milk, grain, and flesh."

I swallowed the lump in my throat. "Flesh?"

"Aye. Many of the old ones took human sacrifice. Not Mum," she added. "The changing seasons were what fed her power. My power."

I recalled the party Demeter had thrown for her followers, a regular bacchanal in the heart of New York. "Then I assume accepting human sacrifices was a quick power boost for Crom."

"Oh, most definitely."

I tapped the table. "Do we want him to be powerful?"

"What do you mean?"

"If we don't complete the Wild Hunt, and therefore don't feed Crom any souls, he would therefore be less powerful. Assuming, of course, the souls are his primary means of obtaining power." I leaned back in my chair. "There's also the question of what happens to these souls after they get handed off to Crom. What if they end up in a hell dimension? If they do, do we really want to be part of that?"

"Absolutely not," Anya said. "I'll not have the first year of my reign marred by damning mortal souls." She bit her lip, and added, "If they really were damned. What if Crom somehow uplifts them?"

"You mean he might send them to Crom heaven?" I asked, and she smiled again. That time it reached her eyes, and lit up her entire face. "All right, we have a new mission. How can we find out what happens to these souls?"

"I supposed I can ask Maelgwyn, and Mum," Anya said. "Being that they're both old ones, they may know something of Crom. Would you like to accompany me?"

"I'd like to, but should really talk to Rina," I said. "She was pretty upset when the Norns told us that I was more like our mother than she is."

"It's hard to live up to the memory of one's parent. I am an expert on such emotions." Anya stood and smoothed her shirt down over her waist. "Very well. I shall bring you to the flat, then I will speak with Maelgwyn."

"Anyone ever tell you you're one hot taxi driver?"

"Now there's a summer occupation I hadn't considered."

Chapter Thirteen
Anya

I blinked Christopher to the hallway outside our flat's front door, and after we said our goodbyes I went directly to the Unseelie Court. While I went out of my way to not arrive unexpectedly in the middle of Karina and Robert's home, I did not afford the same courtesy to Maelgwyn. Our relationship was no secret—in fact, it was becoming less secret by the day—but I tried to limit how often I was seen walking in and out of his court because I did not want to see overly familiar with my blood father. There were always those willing to exploit such familial ties, and I would rather not deal with any of that. I'm sure he didn't, either.

To that end I arrived in the corridor outside the main receiving room, which was devoid of servants and other onlookers. Thank the gods for that bit of fortune. After I wandered about the palace looking for the king and his consort, one of the footmen informed me that Maelgwyn had been in his library for the better part of the day, with strict instructions that he not be disturbed. He had no news about Mum's whereabouts, and based on his face he preferred it that way.

"Thank you," I said to the footman, then I turned on my heel and made straight for the library in question. Was it presumptuous of me to assume Maelgwyn would welcome my presence above all others? Most definitely, but I was confident that once I asked him about Fionnlagh's connection to Crom Cruach, he would understand my brash behavior. Whether he appreciated it or not remained to be seen.

As I walked down the corridor my attention was drawn to the rich tapestries that lined the walls. They were exquisitely woven, the detail so fine I recognized Maelgwyn in a scene; he was standing in a summer meadow, surrounded by dancing children. The next tapestry was him in winter, gazing toward a woman atop a mountain; the woman and the terrain were both garbed in white. Mum. When I saw the third tapestry, which featured him and the same woman locked in combat, I realized that the tapestries told the story of

Maelgwyn, from the time he was the Summer King, to when he had whatever he'd had with Mum, and to today. It was his legacy, and mine, too.

I noticed many more tapestries upon the walls, but instead of seeing what stories were woven into them I went back to the second tapestry, the one where Maelgwyn watched Mum from afar. I wondered if he'd fallen in love with her first, or if Mum had pursued him. Either way she had such a profound impact on his life, and he on hers. And now that they were finally together again I'd gone and thrown Da between them.

Well, what else was I supposed to do? I couldn't let Da and the boys languish in those holes under Glen Lyon any longer, not when I had the power to free them. To be honest I really thought that once Da was free, Mum would leave the Unseelie Court behind and we would be a family again. The events of yesterday had proven what a naïve hope that had been.

Forgoing the library for the moment, I slipped down a side passage and made my way toward the royal apartment. If I knew Mum she was having her midafternoon tea. When I entered the room I saw her seated in front of the garden windows, cup in hand.

"Anya, how lovely," Mum said. "What brings you by today? Wait, don't tell me Bod and the boys are up to mischief again so soon."

"They aren't. Well, perhaps they are, but that's not why I'm here."

Mum poured me a cup of tea, and pushed a tray of cakes toward me. "Then tell me why my sweet lass has come to visit."

I took two pieces of cake. Conversations such as these required ballast, the more the better. "Why were you hiding from Da?"

She plucked at her skirt. "I wasn't."

"Then why did you shut yourself inside the library while he raged about the bedroom?"

Mum looked toward the library door, then quickly away. Her gaze skated around the room, landing on bookcases and tables and even the rug on the floor, but never once did it land on me. "Anya, you have to understand, things aren't as they were," she said at last. "Your Da is one of the strongest men that's ever lived, and I'm... Am I strong now? I fear the answer is plain."

"You're still powerful," I said, recalling the many spells I'd watched her cast since being exiled.

"But am I strong enough for him?" she said. "I used to be as strong as Bod, if not more so. I used to match him blow for blow."

"Then you hid because you worried he would hurt you," I deduced. She remained silent. "Don't you think this is something you should talk to him about?"

Mum smiled sadly. "Bod's never been much for talking. Perhaps I'm not, either."

"Still, you're going to have to deal with him eventually. Da's so upset he nearly destroyed the throne room. He beat that lovely smooth floor to bits." I eyed Mum, and added, "The chandelier has been shattered to bits."

"What? It took me an entire season to craft that piece! It's older than Angus! Doesn't he understand how difficult it is to maintain such clear ice?" Mum got up and stalked around the room, muttering away about Da and his big, clumsy fists. I leaned back in my chair, satisfied. Mum and Da would come together again, if for other reason than to talk to have one of their epic ragers. I was sure of it.

Maelgwyn burst into the room, and I felt a pang of guilt. Should I be wishing for my mother to reunite with Da when she seemed so happy here? When Maelgwyn seemed to finally be happy, too?

"Anya, how long have you been here?" I took in Maelgwyn's searching eyes and frazzled appearance, and shelved my guilt. He hadn't been so unkempt wen a score of my brothers were drunk on his doorstep.

"What's wrong?" I demanded.

"The crown," he replied, then he went to the far side of the chamber and began searching through the book cases. Mum approached him and laid her hand on his back.

"Your father's crown?" I prompted.

"Yes, my father's crown. The one I reclaimed from Fionnlagh." He faced me. "It's missing."

Chapter Fourteen
Chris

After Anya kissed me goodbye, I knocked on the flat's entrance. A few moments later Rina flung the door open.

"You knock on the door of your own house?" she asked.

"It's polite." I stepped inside. Faith was laying on her back in the middle of the living room floor underneath what I'm sure was a very educational toy, batting at a few colorful balls that dangled from an equally colorful arch above her. I didn't see Mom's cane anywhere. "You all alone here?"

"Yep. It's just us." She gestured to the couch. "What happened now?"

"What makes you think something happened?"

"Something always happens. It's our way."

"You're right about that." I watched her for a moment. Her cheeks were ruddy and her nose was stuffy. Rina had been crying. "About what the Norns told us."

"I've been thinking about that," she said. "They were definitely right about you."

I blinked. "They were?"

"Absolutely." Rina grabbed a notebook from the table. "According to my research volvs—boy volvas are called volvs, you know—don't just see the future. They also have a tremendous insight into the past, and that's something you've always had. Every article about your books goes on about your uncanny intuitions about the Elizabethan era, and all that."

"You read articles about me?"

"I like to look for my name." She flipped through the notebook's pages. "So yeah, you're the volv around here, but whereas Mom had foresight you seem to have hindsight."

"Huh." Trust me to have the least useful magical attribute in history. "So what good is that?"

"I am not sure," she admitted. "Do you just understand the past really well, or could you interact with the past?"

"Like time travel?"

"No, silly. Like, can you immerse yourself in the facts and details of a particular time perios and come to an understanding as to why things happened the way they did, like you do when you're writing about Shakespeare and his friends. Maybe you could immerse yourself in the time when Mom had her visions about you and try to figure out who she was writing about." Rina leaned over and adjusted Faith's contraption. "Or maybe you could figure out where Nicnevin went."

I laughed through my nose. "Because finding her is on the top of my to-do list."

We heard keys in the front door. A moment later Colleen entered.

"Hey, all." Colleen dropped a few shopping bags next to the door. "Chris, good to see you. How are things in the land of ice and magic?"

"Absolutely insane," I replied.

"Nothing new, then." Colleen sat on the sofa and grabbed the remote. "Mind if I turn on the news?"

"Go for it," Rina said. "I'd like to think about something else for a while."

Colleen glanced at me. I shrugged, so she clicked on Channel 4. There were the usual headlines about politics and the weather, then the anchor announced some breaking news from Ireland.

"That's unusual," Colleen said. "They usually only report on Northern Ireland."

"Must be some news," I said. On the screen was an image of a boulder. There were a few lines carved into the top of the stone, and it was in a display case in a museum. "Hey, Rina, this story is about rocks."

"Irish rocks are fun." Rina leaned toward the television as Colleen turned up the volume.

"Reports indicate that the museum has never before been a target for violence," the anchor said. Another image of the boulder was presented. It had been smashed to bits. "The item in question has no monetary value, its sole significance to the local culture and historical societies. Other treasures in the museum, some of which are quite valuable, were left untouched."

"Someone broke into a museum and beat up a

boulder?" Colleen said. "That's just weird."

"It's not just weird, it's inhuman," Rina said, her eyes tracking the information crawl at the bottom of the screen. "That boulder was originally solid granite, and more than six feet tall. It must have weighed a few tons. What in the world could have destroyed it?"

I observed the pile of gravel that had recently been a boulder, and my stomach sank. "A giant."

"What giant? You mean the Bodach?" Rina asked.

"Wait, Anya's dad?" Colleen added. "I guess he'd be capable of destroying a boulder, but why?"

I pointed at the screen. "Look."

The anchor continued, "A second stone, which is an admittedly poor replica of the stone housed in the museum, was also destroyed. While authorities are hesitant to draw a connection between the two events, it is odd that two stones dedicated to the pre-Christian deity Crom Cruach were targeted in the same six hour period."

The anchor moved on to the next headline. Colleen shut off the television and we stared at the blank screen in silence.

"It was Bod," I said. "Had to be."

"I agree, but we still don't know why," Rina said.

"Is he trying to impress Beira?" Colleen asked. Before Rina or I could reply, Anya appeared in front of the door. After the shock of the destroyed bounders we didn't even flinch at her sudden arrival.

"Apologies," she said. "I meant to arrive out in the hallway."

"What's wrong? Are you okay?" I demanded. I'd teleported with Anya many times and she had never once missed her target, not even by a centimeter.

"I'm fine," she replied. "Maelgwyn's crown has been stolen."

"The crown he took from Fionnlagh?" I asked, and she nodded.

"It was their father's crown," she said. "He was the Summer King of old. The crown should have passed directly to Maelgwyn, but Fionnlagh stole it from their father's deathbed."

"And now it's gone again." I took Anya's hand, and

said, "We were just watching a news report from Ireland. No one knows how it happened, but two boulders dedicated to Crom Cruach were destroyed earlier today." When Anya's eyes widened, I added, "They were reduced to gravel."

"Gods below." Anya looked past me to Rina. "Forgive me, but we need to go."

"I get it," Rina said. "Yell if you need help."

"I am certain we will." Anya grabbed my other hand, and we blinked out.

Chapter Fifteen
Anya

We appeared in Maelgwyn's throne room amid a flurry of servants hurrying this way and that. So intent they were on their duties they hardly noticed our arrival. I dislike being ignored, and stepped in front of a steward, halting her. She startled when she recognized me.

"Your Highness," she said, bobbing a curtsey. "Forgive me, we weren't expecting you."

"Tell me about this uproar."

"Himself, he isn't pleased," she replied.

"Maelgwyn's angry?"

"Oh, no. My lord is never angry. Never raised a hand to any of us. But," she leaned closer, "he's in such a state even your mam has taken leave of him."

Mum was avoiding everything and everyone lately. "You may go," I said, and she scurried off. "My mother is hiding and my father is raging."

"Divide and conquer it is," Christopher said. "I'll find Maelgwyn while you handle Beira."

"Are you certain? If he really is angered you might get hurt."

"You yourself said I'm almost as resilient as you are." Christopher brought my hand to his mouth and kissed my knuckles. "I'll see if I can help him. If I can't, I'll distract him by telling him all about Yggsdrasil. Besides," he added, "I remember what Beira's like when she's mad. I'll take my chances with Maelgwyn."

"Wise choice. I'll come find you in an hour," I said. I watched Christopher as he walked toward the windows that overlooked the courtyard, and then as he questioned a few servants. He was such a brilliant, capable man, and I kept coddling him as if he was no more than a bairn. Mum had once coddled me, and her actions caused me to leave home for decades while I lived in hot regions near the equator, places I'd specifically chosen because they were never cold and had no real winter. Places that were far beyond her reach.

I was not my mother, not by any stretch of the

imagination. Nor was Christopher a helpless child, just as I hadn't been when Mum's actions had driven me away from home for so long. I needed to loosen my grip on Christopher before I smothered him, and he found himself a less stifling place to call home.

Having resolved to do just that, I set aside those emotions and slipped inside the apartment Mum shared with Maelgwyn. I don't know why I felt the need to be secretive. It's not as if any of the servants would challenge my right to be there. As I looked around the room, I was struck by the different feel and appearance of these rooms from the rest of the palace, differences I'd failed to notice during my earlier visits. Whereas the Unseelie Court as a whole tended toward blacks and grays, these rooms were reminiscent of a summer's day. The ceiling was painted a bright, glorious blue, and rounded glass sconces served as clouds and light sources. The eastern side of the room was made up of windows with an excellent view of the gardens, and all of them were flung open with their jewel-toned draperies fluttering in the breeze. The scent of flowers wafted toward me. It seemed that the Seelie Court wasn't the only place where flowers bloomed when they chose to.

When I'd mentioned that lately flowers sprung up wherever Mum walked, Maelgwyn claimed that she had become adept at creating life. Were these summery, colorful rooms thus due to her newfound talents? Or, had Mum been a life bringer all along, but had endured her talents being frozen and unrecognizable beneath her icy surface?

Regardless of the answer to those questions, my mother was nowhere to be found. After I'd completed an exhaustive search of the bed chambers, library, and courtyards later, I still hadn't found Mum. *First Nicnevin, now Mum.* It seemed that the women of Elphame were going missing, one after the other. Perhaps I would be next.

I stopped, dead in my tracks as Karina would say. What if Mum wasn't hiding, but she really was missing? What if she'd been kidnapped? The Beira of a year ago couldn't have been harmed by any but the strongest of creatures, and even then only in the height of summer. During winter my mother had been the strongest being in existence. Now, that title fell to me.

Mum's days of incredible strength were over, and I needed to accept that my mother was more vulnerable now than she'd ever been. I'd wasted so much time looking after and coddling Christopher, when I should have been looking after Mum.

Panic squeezed my heart. I closed my eyes and took slow, even breaths. First off, I had no evidence that anything untoward had happened to Mum. Her lack of presence in a few areas meant only that she was somewhere else, nothing more. Second, even though she was weaker now than she'd ever been, my mother was far from powerless. If some fool had captured her, they would regret it soon enough.

I opened my eyes, and let the sight of the green courtyard calm my frayed nerves. If I let these baseless thoughts spiral out of control I would be the one who needed watching, and who knew what would happen to the weather if I ended up in such a state. I turned to reenter the palace when another realization hit me as surely as if I'd run into a wall. I knew of one man both strong enough to carry Mum off, and thick-headed enough to believe it was a truly good idea. What's worse, he had a small army of co-conspirators, all of them loyal to him unto death. That daft man was my da, the Bodach.

"Gods below, he wouldn't," I muttered. "Would he?"

"What wouldn't he do?"

I turned around and saw Mum sitting on the edge of the fountain, which was the one bloody place I hadn't looked. I took another deep breath and willed my heartbeat to slow. I also admonished myself for jumping to conclusions, and not bothering to check the entire garden before dissolving into madness.

"I was looking for you, and when I couldn't find you I wondered if Da had come back carried you off," I said, coming to sit beside her.

Mum sniffed. "If you're ever wondering what Bod is up to, just think of the most reckless, foolhardy plan you can devise. Odds are he's already done it, gotten his arse handed to him, and moved on to the next scheme."

"About his plans. Has Da ever mentioned Crom Cruach?"

"Crom Cruach," Mum repeated. "There's a name I

haven't heard in an age. He was a strong one in his day, but he went underground more than a thousand years ago. Why are you asking about him?"

"There are—were—stones dedicated to Crom. They were in a museum. Someone destroyed them, reduced the boulders to pebbles."

Mum sighed and covered her face with her hands. "That certainly sounds like Bod's work. The question remains, though, what is he after?"

"Do you know?"

"I don't, but I'll wager it's nothing good."

Chapter Sixteen
Chris

After conferring with a few of the servants, I found
Maelgwyn in a grand hall near the rear of the palace. He was
plainly looking for something—most likely the missing
crown—hadn't noticed my arrival. While I considered how
best to approach him, I considered the room we were in.

I'd never been in this room before, and it was a place
like none other in the court. The walls were covered with a
rich green wallpaper—I believe the color was called "arsenic
green" in Victorian times—decorated with vining flowers,
and the woodwork was gilded. Heavy dark wood furniture
filled up the room, the centerpiece of which was a long dining
table.

I looked toward the ceiling, and saw a chandelier
centered above the table. It was an exact copy of the one Bod
had destroyed in the Winter Palace, although this one was
made of glass instead of ice. The floral walls and delicate
glasswork were at odds with the rest of the room. Had
Maelgwyn started redecorating this room for Beira? If that
was the case, it meant either Beira or Maelgwyn, or maybe
both of them, were planning on remaining a couple. If that
was the case, someone needed to distract Bod before he
destroyed the rest of the Winter Palace, and the Unseelie
Court, too.

I cleared my throat. Maelgwyn raised his head from
the bookcase he was ransacking. "Christopher. Is Anya here
as well?"

"She is. She went to speak with Beira." I approached
the Unseelie King, but I didn't get too close. I'd never seen
Maelgwyn lash out in anger, but if he did I'm certain I
wouldn't last long, inherited volv-ness or no. "Anya told me
that your crown is missing."

"And how could it be missing?" Maelgwyn mused.
"Hardly anyone knew it was here. And even if someone did
know of its whereabouts, who could have entered my court
and taken it unawares?" Maelgwyn turned away and resumed
tearing apart the shelves. "It is supposed to be in this room,"

he roared, as books and other objects went flying. "It must be here!"

I took a breath. "Have you considered Angus?"

Maelgwyn went perfectly still. I heard a horrible noise like metal scraping metal. In Maelgwyn's hand was a bronze vase, crumpled like so much paper. I hadn't even seen him pick it up, yet he'd crushed it like a piece of newsprint.

"You have reason to believe Angus absconded with my father's crown?" Maelgwyn asked softly.

"I have no evidence either for or against, but he is capable of it," I replied.

"Agreed. Why would he do such a thing?"

"Bod wants to impress Beira. Perhaps Angus is trying, in his own misguided way, to help reunite his parents."

Maelgwyn set the destroyed vase down and faced me. "A logical assumption. Where would he have put it?"

"Angus, if he did steal the crown, would have brought it to Bod. About Bod." I took in the mangled metal in his hand, which was left of the vase, and decided to take a step back. "We think he is currently in Ireland."

"Ireland. It's a lovely land, one I am quite fond of. Is Bod in hiding?"

Maelgwyn's calm demeanor was far more unsettling than his anger. "We saw a news report about some sacred stones being destroyed in Ireland. The stones were huge, and it stands to reason than only a giant could have done so."

"And Bod is a lunatic and a giant, so you naturally thought of him," Maelgwyn deduced. He wasn't wrong. "Whom were these stones sacred to?"

"Crom Cruach."

"Oh. No matter. Crom's followers died out centuries ago."

"Does Crom need followers?"

"For strength, and power, yes," he replied. "All of the old gods do."

"Forgive my asking, but do you have followers?"

"A sound inquiry," Maelgwyn said, a rare note of approval in his voice. "My strength is familial. Being that I, and my fathers before me, ruled the warm half of the year we derived our strength from the seasons."

"Much like how Beira, and now Anya, draw strength

from the cold," I surmised, and Maelgwyn nodded. "But Fionnlagh didn't draw his power from the seasons, did he?"

"No. It remains a mystery as to how he was able to create a court at all."

"Actually, we know how he did it. He was collecting souls and giving them to Crom in exchange for power."

If Maelgwyn was calm before, now he went still as a statue. "My little brother did what?"

"The Wild Hunt," I began. "We—Anya and I—have been doing a bit of investigating. We couldn't figure out why Fionnlagh bothered with the hunt, since it was arduous and—"

"What did he do with the souls?" Maelgwyn demanded.

"He used them as payment to Crom," I replied. "That's where he got his power, all those eons ago, and that's why he kept up the Wild Hunt. Every seven years he owes Crom a new batch of souls."

"How did you learn of this?"

"One of the *fuath* told Anya. Angus was there when she learned of it."

"And you believe the *fuath*," Maelgwyn began, then he paused. "Where would Fionn have obtained his first payment?"

"The first batch of souls?" I spread my hands. "I don't know. Maybe Anya can talk to the *fuath* again, and find out."

My words trailed off as Maelgwyn stalked out of the room and down the corridor like a man possessed. I raced to catch up to him; I had no idea where he was headed or what he was planning, but his anger had suddenly given way to something resembling desperation. A desperate man was capable of many things. A desperate Unseelie King even more so.

Maelgwyn crossed the entire palace complex and the courtyard without raising his eyes or saying a word. He finally halted at the far end of the gardens in front of a stone mausoleum. He paused at the entrance, his head bowed, then he entered the mausoleum, Not knowing what else to do, I followed.

The interior was meticulously clean, and the stone surfaces shone. There were many inscriptions carved into the marble walls, and while I couldn't read them I didn't have to. It was set up like a family crypt, and based on Maelgwyn's actions that's exactly what it was. Maelgwyn touched the inscriptions one by one, and dropped to his knees to touch the last, smallest memorial.

"She was only a baby," he said.

"What was her name?"

"Daisy." He laughed softly. "She probably wouldn't have kept that name, but it was her mother's favorite flower. She loved daisies, and we loved our Daisy."

"She sounds beautiful." I looked around the mausoleum. All of the memorials seemed to have the same amount of weathering, which means they were installed at about the same time. Either a lot of people had died at once, or the memorial had been built after the fact. "Are all of these memorials for your family?"

"My children," Maelgwyn replied. "After Bod beat me near to death, Fionnlagh hunted down and murdered every one of my children. I'd always assumed he was removing potential heirs to his new throne. Even so, I could never feel their essence. It was as if he had obliterated them from existence."

I sat heavily on a nearby stone bench. "That's…that's awful. I am so sorry."

"Don't be sorry, Christopher. Be glad. You have finally solved a mystery. For Fionn to have entered into such an agreement with Crom the first payment of souls would have to have been richer than a standard installment, to sweeten the pot as it were. Crom wouldn't have wanted mortal souls, not entirely. He would have wanted those who had some sort of power."

"What are you saying?"

"Fionn must have stolen my children's souls and delivered them to Crom. It's the only explanation as to why I've never found them. And now that I know where they are, I mean to get them back."

Chapter Seventeen
Anya

Maelgywn and Christopher found Mum and me sitting on the edge of the fountain, and proceeded to explain their wild new theory: Fionnlagh had offered the souls of Maelgwyn's children to Crom, which was how he had initially obtained enough power to establish the Seelie Court.

Maelgwyn's children. My siblings. How my heart ached for those poor bairns I'd never known!

Most of their theory was based in fact. Apparently Fionnlagh had done away with all of Maelgwyn's children long ago… Though as Maelgwyn spoke I realized that he only assumed he knew what happened. He claimed to have searched for his missing children high and low, but to no avail. Gods below, with such a lack of information the children could be anywhere. They could even still be alive.

But if they were alive, where have they been all this time? I glanced at Mum. Her uneasy face and tense posture told me that she too had concerns.

I took a step toward Maelgwyn. "You're certain the bairns are with Crom?"

"They must be," he said. "Once I regained my strength I searched everywhere for them. Everywhere! I found nothing, not even their bones. Not even the barest shred of their essences." He grabbed my hands. "Now I know why. Now, I can save them!"

He was gripping my hands so tightly I could feel my bones grind. "Maelgwyn. Father. What if they're not with Crom?" I extricated one of my hands and placed it atop his. "What if they're someplace else?"

"They must be with Crom. I've looked everywhere…" He cupped my cheek with his hand. "Of course, you're right. They may not be with him at all, and honestly that would be a blessing, too, in its own way. But I have to look. I need to keep looking for them."

I nodded. If I understood anything, it was the drive to protect my family. "Then look for them we shall."

"We'll need help," Mum said. "And a lot of it, if

Crom is half the devil the stories have made him out to be."

"You think I can't handle a weak entity with no followers?" Maelgwyn asked.

"Consider what we know," Mum began. "Fionnlagh grew to be more powerful than you, and Crom would have only given Fionn a portion of his power. Now that Crom's been fed who knows how many souls all these eons, he could be capable of anything."

"Are we so sure he doesn't have any followers?" Christopher asked. "Anya and I encountered a Greek deity who was rather powerful, and it turned out that she had followers even in present day America. If she can have followers two thousand years after she was popular, so can Crom."

"Power is like an addiction," I said, remembering the trouble Demeter had caused in New York. "Once you have a taste, you want more. The fact that Crom kept demanding souls speaks to his lust for power, as well as Fionnlagh's."

Christopher clapped his hands together. "Great, then we can start by finding Crom's people. They probably congregate near the stones that Bod destroyed."

"If he destroyed them," I added. Perhaps it was the wee lass in me, but someone needed to think the best of Da.

"Are you going to go door to door and ask people if they have heard of Crom?" Mum asked.

"If people are holding gathering in Crom's name, someone will have heard about them," Christopher replied. "These days, when anything out of the ordinary happens it ends up on social media within a few days, or hours. It should be easy enough to run an internet search. I can handle that."

I nodded. "While you do that, I will locate Da and Angus."

***

As it turned out, locating Da was rather easy. Mum merely closed her eyes, waited a few moments, and then rattled off Da's exact location in Ireland. I wondered if she could instantly locate her children as well, or Maelgwyn. Based on Maelgwyn's shocked face he'd had no idea Mum possessed such a skill.

After Christopher left to make his way back to Glasgow, Maelgwyn and I blinked to Ireland. We found Da just where Mum said he would be, sitting on the bank of a river skipping stones across the water's surface. I wondered if those stones were all that was left of the boulders he'd decimated earlier.

"Da," I called out as we approached him, He looked up and smiled at me, though it turned to a grimace when he noticed Maelgwyn behind me. "We heard that you're breaking boulders across the countryside."

"Ah, well." He tossed in the last of the stones and got to his feet. "Those won't be the first or last set of bounders I've broken, eh?"

"What do you know of my children?" Maelgwyn demanded.

"Other than the one who should have been mine?" Da countered. "Nothing."

Maelgwyn's eyes flashed. I stepped in front of him, and said to Da, "We think Crom Cruach may have them. Their souls, at least."

"Any why in the world would you think that?" Da asked.

"Fionnlagh obtained the bulk of his power from Crom," I explained. "We suspect that his first offering was Maelgwyn's children."

"How would he get his hands on your—" Da began, then understanding lit his face. "Ah."

"Ah, indeed," Maelgwyn said. "You left me too weak to care for myself or anyone else, and as a result my children were taken by my murderous brother."

Da shook his head. "I know nothing about any little ones, but while I was in the ground I heard whispers about Crom, and about his domain. I fear any souls given over to him may be lost for good."

Maelgwyn made a cutting motion with his hand. "I refuse to believe that. I must look for them," he said, then he grabbed Da's collar. Amazingly, Da let him. "Don't you understand? I must see for myself."

"Aye, that I do," Da said. "When I went after you I only wanted my wife back. I never meant for any harm to come to your family."

"I appreciate that, Bod," Maelgwyn said. "I do know what it's like to lose Beira. I can imagine how you must have hurt."

"Hurt I did, and hurt I do again. Still, my wounded pride isn't the point, not any longer. I will help you find the little ones."

Maelgwyn released Da's collar, then he grabbed his hands. "Thank you, Bod," he said. "Thank you so very much."

As I watched the man who'd fathered me come to an agreement with the man who'd raised me, I felt contentment the like of which I'd never experienced before. I'd been so concerned with keeping the two of them away from each other, I hadn't considered how wonderful it would be for them to work together.

"Thank you, Da," I said, and he looped his big arm around my neck. "We'll need you for this."

"And I shall need my crown," Maelgwyn said. "If you wouldn't mind returning it."

"I ken nothing about a crown," Da said. Maelgwyn and I both drew back.

"You don't have it?" Maelgwyn asked, while I said, "We thought Angus gave it to you."

"I haven't seen Angus since before I drank all your whisky," Da said. "Are you referring to the *dahm coroin*?" he asked, using the crown's formal Irish moniker.

"Yes," Maelgwyn replied. "It's gone missing from my home. We have reason to suspect your eldest stole it."

"Ah, well. That does sound like something Angus would do." Da drew himself up and cracked his knuckles. "What say we deal with Crom first, then we'll track down that boy of mine and see about getting your property returned safe and sound?"

Maelgwyn nodded. "We have an accord. Where do we find this Crom?"

***

"I feel a bit foolish about the first stone I destroyed," Da said. We were standing at what was left of the roadside replica of Crom's stone. "I came across this one first, and while it didn't seem authentic I thought best to smash it anyway."

"Better safe than sorry, I suppose." I nudged a few of the remaining pebbles with the toe of my boot. Shrines to powerful beings had a different feel about them, a sensation that changed even the soil they rested upon. There was certainly nothing special about this site. I had a feeling Da had smashed the stone solely for the sake of smashing it, which was a very giant thing to do.

"What of the stone in the museum?" I asked. Since it was daylight and the museum was filled with innocent mortals, we were hesitant to enter the structure and possibly put them at risk. "Did it seem authentic?"

"Most certainly, but the essence of him was old. Worn away, even." Da's gaze swept across the landscape. "I have no doubt that the stone in the museum was once the way to Crom, but that door's long since closed."

"If memory serves, Crom's altar was destroyed more than a thousand years ago," Maelgwyn said. "Sacrifices were made to him on a nearby plain. Perhaps that is where the gateway to his world remains."

Maelgwyn set off, Da and I close behind. Since he seemed to know the way, I caught up to him and asked, "Are you from Ireland?"

"From? No," Maelgwyn replied. "But I am very familiar with the landscape. In my youth this region was mostly seafaring tribes, and when you have a sound vessel the distance across the water becomes less than the same distance across the land. Our islands have much shared history, and customs."

"So they do. What was it like, when you were young?"

"The air was cleaner, for a start."

"Aye, that it was," Da chimed in. "The mortals' Industrial Revolution did nothing so much as pump dirt into the air."

"There was also less war," Maelgwyn continued, "though battles then were bloodier, and victories celebrated in song and poem."

"And revels," Da roared, clapping Maelgwyn on the back. "You can't have forgotten the revels!"

Maelgwyn narrowed his eyes at Da, but I saw the hint of a smile. "I do recall revels."

We reached a meadow Maelgwyn referred to as *Magh Slécht,* which rather appropriately meant "plain of the monument". It was where Crom's stone—the real one from the museum, not the roadside imposter—had once stood for many centuries before it had been dug up and carted off to a museum.

"As I recall the stone was here," Maelgwyn said, halting on a patch of grass that looked the same as all of the other grass. "It was destroyed by Ireland's saint more than a millennia ago. That saint, now he had true power. With one blow he drove Crom out of Ireland and out of this dimension."

"Do we know which dimension he ended up in?" I asked.

Maelgwyn shook his head. "I don't, but I know who we can ask." He closed his eyes, then he turned in a slow circle. "The disciples remain in place."

"Whose disciples?"

"Crom's, of course. While he was in power he employed a group of twelve to do his bidding, much how Fionn uses the *fuath* when he'd rather not dirty his hands. When the saint struck down Crom, the disciples sank into the earth, and there they have remained."

"You're certain they're still here?" I asked.

"We shall know soon enough." Eyes remaining closed, Maelgwyn extended his arms on either side. "Rise, and tell me where your master lies."

Power coursed through the ground, along with a silent tremor that shook not the material world, but ether around us. Slowly, silently, a circle of twelve stones rose from the earth.

Beneath, hummed the stones. *Follow the water.*

"And now we ken the way," Da said.

"All they told us was to follow water," I pointed out.

"Aye, but after the saint destroyed the idol he went and founded a well, and I happen to know just where it lies."

***

Maelgwyn and I followed Da as he stomped across

meadows and over hills until we reached a crumbling old graveyard. Sights such as this weren't uncommon in this part of the world, what with many graveyards and their associated churches having long since lost their roofs, and, one would assume, their congregations. It was certainly what had happened here. But these places were frequently built upon places of old power—Karina liked to call them *nemetons*—and that power kept the stones and mortar of the walls intact despite being pummeled by the elements for scores or even hundreds of years. It was hard evidence that anyone who thumbed their nose at the older deities was woefully ignorant, and outright asking for trouble.

Da pushed his way past the rusted gate and navigated around the monuments and stones toward the rear of the graveyard. That was where the holy well was located, the sunken entrance lined with smooth granite slabs. Next to the pool was a stairway that descended into what I assumed was a crypt, or perhaps a storage vault. No one had left offerings near the sacred waters in the recent past, though the steps that wound down into the earth next to the well were swept clean of debris.

"Someone is caring for this site," I said. I noticed a torch in a metal holder, with a flint set under a nearby overhang for igniting the pitch-soaked rags. "Perhaps a priest is still assigned to this area."

Maelgwyn removed the torch from its holder. It ignited in his hand. Nice to know we wouldn't want for light while we explored the crypt. "Perhaps, indeed." He pointed the torch so it illuminated the stairs. "They told us to go beneath."

Da stepped onto the stairs. "We have fire and we have ice, and, most importantly, we have my strength. We are well equipped to learn what else awaits us in Crom's lair."

While Maelgwyn held the torch aloft we descended below the graves, but to my surprise we did not enter a parallel plane of existence. The dirt above us was the same soil we'd just trod upon, with the tree roots and the undersides of coffins clearly visible; amazingly, all of those coffins and roots stayed put, a clue to the massive amount of power at play in this subterranean room. As for the rest of the chamber, the walls and floor were made of dressed stone similar to a crypt beneath a church.

"What is this place?" I wondered, stopping to examine a wall niche. Instead of a statue or font, it held a pile of bones. "Are these human?"

Da peeked over my shoulder. "Aye. Looks like they were someone's fingers."

I glanced up at the coffins. "I wonder if the priest has been raiding the burials."

"Or if the god himself steals the dead," Maelgwyn said. We reached the far end of the chamber, and the way beyond was blocked by a wrought iron gate. Maelgwyn thrust the torch between the iron bars, illuminating a storage room.

"What could be in those boxes?" I wondered.

"They're not boxes." Maelgwyn crushed the lock with his bare hand and pushed the gate open. We entered the room, and once the torchlight revealed the contents I understood. Stacked up along each wall and up to the ceiling were more coffins. Some of the coffins were stone, and some were wood, and some were little more than bundles of bones caught up in linen shrouds.

And some didn't seem very old at all.

"Are… Are people still being sacrificed to this creature?" I demanded, aghast. "Who would be making sacrifices in this day and age?"

Da and Maelgwyn shared a glance. "Och, lass, at times I forget how young you truly are," Da said. "Times past sacrifice was the order of the day. The common folk thought it best to keep the blood flowing, as it were. Thought it kept them safe from the likes of us."

"Did it?" I asked.

"Yes and no," Da replied. "Now, no one ever sacrificed a human in my name, at least not that I'm aware of, but I was given plenty of tribute. The crofts that took the best care of me were the ones I spared when I, ah, went out into the world."

I remembered when Da regularly went out among mortals, drinking and carousing and toppling mountains in Mum's name. "And you?" I asked Maelgwyn.

"I never demanded blood, but it was given to me more often than not," he replied. "I appreciated the tributes left for me, and did my best to look after the people. I strived to be the custodian of the land, rather than its overlord."

"And see where that got you," Da muttered.

"Say the man who spent the last two hundred years in a hole in the ground," Maelgwyn retorted.

I left my fathers bickering behind and moved further into the room. A second stairwell was at the far end, and it promised to take me even deeper into the earth. Since we were told to go beneath, down I went. A greenish glow emanated from the base of the stairs, bright enough to guide me but not for me to truly discern what I was looking at.

At the bottom of the stairs was water. It was shallow, not even reaching the first step, but it was stagnant and smelled awful. Along with the stench and the glow came the faint sound of keening.

"Da," I called over my shoulder. "There's something alive down here."

I heard Da's heavy footsteps, saw Maelgwyn's accompanying torchlight flickering behind me. Da plunged into the dark, still water, heedless of the stench or whatever beasties may be lurking in its depths. He was a giant, after all, and had trekked through many swamps and bogs in his day. Maelgwyn and I waited on the stairs. It wasn't long before Da called out from the recesses of the crypt.

"Udane," Da bellowed, using Maelgwyn's old name. "You'll want to see this with your own two eyes."

We moved forward, and I was grateful that the water remained shallow. Along the left side of the flooded chamber was an archway closed off with yet more iron bars. Da stood in front of it, pointing at a symbol at the apex of the arch. Carved into the granite was an image of a stag in front of an oak tree.

"The tree and the stag," Maelgwyn murmured. "It was my symbol, before."

"What is it doing here," I said, peering beyond the bars.

Maelgwyn's torch guttered and went out. "So much for light," he muttered as he tossed the extinguished torch aside.

I touched Maelgwyn's arm. "The keening, it comes from within."

Da grasped two of the bars and ripped them from their

places. "Onward we go," he said, as he stepped into the room. With no other options, Maelgwyn and I followed.

Chapter Eighteen
Chris

After I passed through Remy's Place, and downed my complimentary shot of whisky, I took my time walking through Glasgow. The lights were up on Buchanan Street, and the way was filled with tourists and locals alike seeking a good time. Despite the crush of people, I felt safe. In fact, I'd always felt safe in Glasgow. Being that I'd grown up in New York, and now lived primarily in Elphame, there was nothing in Glasgow that scared me. At least, nothing in the present time scared me. Who knew what tomorrow would bring?

Actually, tomorrow didn't matter. Whatever happens, bad, good, or indifferent, Anya and I will handle it.

I found myself walking along the banks of the River Clyde, a romantic stroll that I wished Anya was sharing with me. I thought about her and Maelgwyn, who were in Ireland trying to locate Bod, and, with any luck, Maelgwyn's missing children. I couldn't imagine how Maelgwyn felt, first with the shocking loss of his children, and now with the spark of hope that he might learn their fates. To be that devastated, then to only have all of that pain brought back to the surface years later...

I shook my head, the thoughts having been too much for me. I'd known my share of loss, but losing a child must be unbearable, and Maelgwyn had lost all of his children at once. How he'd survived without going mad was beyond me... or maybe he had gone mad, if only for a short time. I recalled how he'd been ransacking the Unseelie Court as he searched for his crown. Maybe he was still mad.

An image of Faith flashed behind my eyes, along with the memory of her burbling laugh. Rina said most of her smiles and laughs were due to gas, but I knew better. Faith loved her Uncle Chris, and she made sure to laugh at all of my jokes. I also knew that if anything ever happened to her I would move heaven and earth to help her.

I stopped walking, and gazed at the brightly lit Clyde Arc where it spanned the river. Despite all the relationships I've had I'd never really thought about having children, not until I moved to Scotland with Anya. She was so generous and caring, and I couldn't help but imagine her and I with a house filled with children... But was that wise? After learning what had befallen Maelgwyn's children, not to mention the horrible fates of other residents of Elphame, I wondered if it was a good idea to bring more children into this world. Maybe I should just take my happiness with Anya, and be grateful for that. Then again, it would be nice to give Faith a playmate.

When I finally got to the flat, everyone was asleep. Not surprising, since it was the middle of the night; with me spending so much time in the Winter Palace time tended to get away from me. Anya claimed that all those folk tales about time passing differently in Elphame were nothing but fiction, but I can attest that when you take a modern man and stick him in a place without clocks or phones it's hard to keep track of the hours. That, and I kept forgetting to wear my watch.

I opened my laptop, and was promptly confronted with a packed inbox with messages from my agent, publisher, and other literary folks. Right, I'm supposed to be working on a novel. I loved writing, but putting out another book didn't seem as important as it once had. The way things were going meant that it might never seem important again.

Since I was well acquainted with regret, I wrote myself a note to review these emails in the morning, then I plugged in my phone. While it charged I went into the kitchen to make some tea. I'd just filled the kettle when Rob came out of the study to see what all the noise was about.

"Sorry I didn't call first," I said, but he only shrugged.

"'Tis your home," he said as he found a mug for himself. "Be in it whenever ye like."

"I'm surprised Rina's not up." My sister had been a night owl since birth, much to my parents' chagrin.

"She claimed exhaustion, and went to be shortly after she put Faith down for the night," Rob replied. "I thought it best to let them rest."

I almost asked Rob if Rina told him about what we learned from the Norns, but didn't. She had probably already told him, but what if she hadn't? Everything we'd learned about our mother had left her rather shaken, and she might need time to come to terms with everything.

"Rina said you were at the cottage earlier," I said, instead. "Is the construction coming along well?"

"The work is being done well, but slowly." Rob paused, and said, "'Tis beyond strange, but while I have no doubt of the craftsmen's skill, they get hardly any work done in a day. 'Tis as if someone has bespelled them to move as slowly as possible."

I froze, mug in hand. "Do you think something supernatural is involved?"

"Truly, I have no notion. And why would anyone wish to lay a hex on me home?" I gave Rob a look. "I attribute that foolish question to the late hour. How goes things at the Winter Palace?"

"Interesting," I said. "Bod had a tantrum and nearly destroyed Anya's throne room, and we think Angus stole Maelgwyn's crown."

"Is that why you're here? To hide out from the boys?"

"No, but them not being here is a definite plus." The kettle whistled, and I filled our mugs. We were having tea American style, with tea bags. Rina's corruption of Rob was complete.

"Does Maelgwyn ken Angus took the crown?" Rob asked.

"We're not certain that Angus did it, but he is our prime suspect," I replied. "Maelgwyn's more worried about finding his children."

Rob set his mug down on the counter. "What children?"

"The children he had while he was the Summer King. You know how Fionnlagh turned out to be a madman," I began, and Rob nodded. "Well, this whole business with the Wild Hunt was apparently Fionnlagh's way to gain enough power to become the Seelie King. It's why he collected souls."

Rob crossed his arms over his chest. "Ye are incorrect. Those souls were collected by Fionnlagh, yes, but they were given a new life in Elphame for as long as they consented to be his servants."

I could have sworn the floor fell out from underneath my feet. "What?"

"Later. Why is Maelgwyn searching for children that long since passed?"

"He was told that Fionnlagh killed them, and gave their souls to Crom," I replied.

"Crom?" Rob yelled. "Are ye referrin' to Crom Cruach, as close to a devil as ever existed in this land?"

"Um, yeah. One of the *fuath* told Anya—"

"The *fuath*," Rob scoffed. "Did it no' occur to any o' ye that the *fuath* are evil? Liars and murderers is what they are."

"But why would they—" Realization smacked me hard in the face. "They sent Anya and Maelgwyn after Crom so he would kill them."

Rob's sword materialized in his hand. "Where are they now?"

"They went to Ireland," I replied. "We saw a news report about some boulders that were consecrated to Crom. They'd been smashed to pieces, and we though the Bodach was responsible."

Rob pinched the bridge of his nose. "Did it no' occur to any of ye before ye ran off half-cocked that if Crom seeks retribution against the Seelie corner o' Elphame for having been unjustly accused by the *fuath* and who knows who else, that corner may collapse?"

"What may collapse? The court?"

"No. Elphame itself."

"Maybe we should let it collapse," I said. "Nothing good comes from that place."

Rob squeezed his eyes shut, his spine straight and fists clenched. I got the impression he was trying not to hit me. "Evidently ye do no' understand the whole of what Elphame is," he ground out. "'Tis no' just the Seelie and their lot playing at tricks and games. There are people, as well."

"People? Like captives?"

"Families," Rob said. "Just as people pair off and raise their bairns here on this plane, the same happens in Elphame. If the plane collapses, ye are dooming them all."

I sucked in my breath. "Families, like farmers, craftsmen? Schoolchildren?"

"Aye," Rob said. "Hundreds if no' thousands of innocent lives."

I swallowed hard. "All right. We need to fix this. Should I call up the Ninth?"

"No' yet, but keep the *aquila* close. We may yet have need of it."

Chapter Nineteen
Anya

The further we went into the crypt, the stranger things became.

For one, the caskets and other bundles of bones that were so abundant near the entrance to this underworld had dwindled down to almost nothing. It made me wonder if those remains had once been parishioners of the ruined church above, rather than sacrifices to Crom. Perhaps their graves had needed to be moved, or perhaps they couldn't be interred close to their time of death for one reason or another, and their bones had been forgotten. There were many reasons to leave a body unburied.

However, I could think of no rational explanation for the passage through which we now walked. The dressed stone and columns of the crypt were gone, and the water had long since dried out, revealing a shining black tile floor. It was a welcome reprieve to not have to slog through the standing muck, but soon after the water's departure the walls and ceiling went from masonry to packed earth, and then to the interior of a cave. Throughout it all the tile floor remained, along with the eerie green glow.

"Why would someone tile a cave floor," I said.

"To make it level," Da suggested, but he didn't sound convinced. If the Bodach thought the state of things in the cave was odd, that meant they were odd, indeed.

"We are walking to the center of the earth," Maelgwyn said. "We are entering Crom's lair."

"You're certain that's where we're headed?" Da asked. Maelgwyn's head swiveled on his neck like and owl's, his eyes that were so like mine reflecting the green light toward Da. Gods below, I hoped my eyes never did that. Perhaps I'd invest in a pair of dark glasses, just in case.

"Yes," Maelgwyn said. "I am certain."

I pulled one of the charm off my bracelet and cracked it open, and felt the protection spell settle around us. It wasn't the most powerful way to keep us safe from whatever we may encounter, but it was all I had to work with.

"Don't waste your magic," Da growled. "It's not wise to waste what we cannot replenish."

"Is any of this wise?" I countered. "What if this Crom doesn't care to be disturbed?"

"I imagine he doesn't," Da began. "A being who chooses to reside in such a place as this dank hole doesn't do it in order to receive a great and many visitors."

"I must look for my children," Maelgwyn said. "We press on."

I peeked at Da. He didn't look pleased about pressing onward, but nor did he argue.

"Maelgwyn," I began. "How did you lose your children?" He stopped moving and turned toward me, his face twisted in fury, and I glimpsed the terrifying visage of the Unseelie King of legend. "I only wish to understand what happened, so we have a better chance at finding them," I added.

Maelgwyn's scowl faded and his shoulders relaxed, followed by my own. Good. I hadn't wanted to feel the full brunt of the Unseelie wrath whilst trapped in an underground crypt, or anywhere else for that matter. "After *he* beat me near to death," Maelgwyn began, pausing to glare at Da, "I retreated to my family's home to commence healing, since that is where my power is strongest. While there I fell into a stupor, what some might call a healing trance but truth be told, I was little more than a breathing corpse. After I emerged, I learned that my children had been taken by Fionnlagh."

"Taken," I repeated. "But you don't know if they were... If they're still alive?"

"If they are alive why haven't I found them yet?" Maelgwyn demanded, desperation plain on his face.

"I don't know," I said. "Hopefully, here, we can learn something about their fates."

Maelgwyn nodded, his mouth a slash across his face. Before he could speak, Da beckoned us forward.

"He's through there," Da said. He pointed toward a dark shaft that was little more than a hole in the ground. Not even the green glow of the crypt cut through the heavy darkness. With no other options, we entered the shaft.

"Are you certain?" I asked as I felt my way through

the near total blackness.

"They say he rests at the bottom of a shaft, black as the darkest night, deep in the earth," Da replied.

"Who says?"

"The whispers," he replied. "In the ground."

"Did you learn many things whilst in the ground?" I asked.

"Yes and no," Da replied. "I heard many rumors and odd bits of gossip, though it was some time before I thought to pay attention to any of it. I often wonder what useful information I simply ignored."

"I'm surprised you heard anything at all."

"So was I. In the beginning I could only discern the wails of the departed, or the cries from the occasional mortal who'd plunged beneath. Once my ears learned how to tune out the noise, and tune in to what I wished to hear, I heard the old ones speak."

"Crom was one of these old ones?"

"Aye, that he was. Gods rise and fall, much like empires do, and many of the old ones went to ground waiting for the right time to reemerge." Da paused, and added, "Perhaps this Crom grew tired of waiting and decided to make his own fortune, and that was how he fell in with Fionnlagh."

"More like my brother was unsatisfied with his place in the world, and sought to steal that which wasn't his," Maelgwyn muttered, then he cocked his head to the side, his outstretched arm keeping Da and me from advancing. "Do you hear that?"

"I don't hear anything," I began, then I realized what he meant. "The keening. It's gone."

"Quiet as the tomb now," Da said. "Stand aside, Udane. I want to know who lays their head in such a desolate place."

The ground rumbled. "When did Ireland last suffer a quake?" I demanded.

"The earth shakes all the time," Da said. "Most don't notice."

A fourth voice rumbled, "But you do?"

The question emanated from all around us, pulsing through the rock cut walls and coursing up our legs from the ground. I glanced at Maelgwyn; his shocked face told me he knew as much about what was happening as I did.

"Are you Crom Cruach?" I asked the void.

"Crom Cruach?" the voice repeated. The cavern shook. "What do you think you know of Crom Cruach?"

The cavern went from a gentle tremble to nearly a full quake, as the walls shook and the tile floor rippled beneath out feet. Pebbles and sand rained down from the ceiling, and for a single heart-stopping moment I feared this cavern would also be our crypt. Then a being raised himself up at the far end of the cavern, and I truly felt fear.

The being was made of mud and stone, and its form was vaguely in the shape of a man. His head was like a boulder with a chasm that served as a mouth, and the deep pockets of his eyes were lit by the same sickly green light that had illuminated the watery crypt. He was taller and broader than Da, and something told me he was stronger, too. Any being that could best the Bodach in combat, fair or otherwise, belonged in a dark hole in the earth, banished from everyone and everything he could hurt.

"Crom," Maelgwyn said. Apparently this monster was indeed the one we'd come to find. "It has been a long time."

"Summer King," Crom growled. "Why have you disturbed my rest?"

"You haven't been resting long, have you?" I asked. "Seven years, or thereabouts?"

The creature fixed me in its gaze. "Who questions me?"

Remembering every lesson Mum had given me about behaving like a queen even when I didn't feel like one, I lifted my chin. "I am the Queen of Winter."

"Are you, now," Crom said, looking me over as one would a horse at market. "I remember you having nicer tits."

Frost bloomed in my clenched fist. "I am not Beira."

Crom grunted. "Did you kill her?"

I narrowed my eyes. "What if I had?"

"When did you last see my brother?" Maelgwyn demanded.

Crom didn't take his gaze from me. "I did not know you had a brother. Is he as stupid as you are?"

"Fionnlagh didn't bring you souls in exchange for

power?" I asked. "You didn't help him become the Seelie King?"

"Who accuses me of such?" Crom demanded. "I need not beg for souls! My tributes of flesh and spirit come willingly!"

"Of that I have no doubt." I stepped closer to Da, and said, "We've been lied to."

"So it appears, lass," Da said. "Get behind me."

"Da, I can—"

"Get behind me," Da roared. No sooner had he put himself in front of me when Crom raised his rocky fists over his head, then he doubled over to strike the floor.

No longer pebbles and sand, rocks and boulders now rained down onto us.

Maelgwyn threw his magic above us, creating an umbrella that shielded us from the bulk of the debris. "Run! Now!"

I threw a handful of cold at Crom's feet, freezing him to the floor, then I grabbed Da's hand. "We go together!"

"Aye," Da yelled, then he threw Maelgwyn over his shoulder and we ran as if there was fire at our backs. We splashed through the swampy water, slipping and sliding on the tile and uttering every curse we knew, none us cursing as loudly as Maelgwyn.

When we'd made it across the water and reached the church's basement, and Da set Maelgwyn on his feet.

"How—How *dare* you," Maelgwyn spluttered. "To haul me—me!—off like a sack of potatoes!"

"You're not as fast as me, or my lass," Da said. "If I hadn't grabbed you Crom would have snapped your skinny back in two."

"I have my magic to protect me."

"Is it stronger than Crom's?" When Maelgwyn didn't answer, Da continued, "That's right, we have no idea which of you is stronger. I've precious few allies in the world, and I'm not about to let one of them end up as Crom's toothpicks."

Maelgwyn looked down his nose, and asked, "You consider me an ally?"

"You fathered my lass, therefore you're kin," Da began, then the cave erupted behind us. Crom came up through the floor and smashed the ceiling, causing the crypt to collapse onto us. Big hands pushed me forward, and Maelgwyn and I sprawled onto the floor. Caskets and bones tumbled from their shelves, covering us in bones and old rotted wood. I pulled on the protection spell I'd cast earlier and formed it into a magic bubble. It saved us from being buried by the dead, with the dead.

The dust and bones settled, and I dropped the bubble. "Are you all right?" Maelgwyn asked.

"I am," I replied, then I realized that only Maelgwyn and I were on the crypt's floor.

"Da," I called. "Da!"

I jumped up and picked my way through the rubble toward the mouth of the cave. The passage to the cavern was blocked by a boulder the size of a cottage. I sent forth a tendril of magic, seeking answers about what lay beyond the boulder. My magic told me that the entire cavern had collapsed in on itself.

"Da." I slumped to my knees, my hands on the stone that had crushed my Da. My sweet, noble, big-hearted Da.

"He saved us." Maelgwyn stood beside me, his hand on my shoulder. "His last act was caring for you."

The earth shook again, but this tremor was localized to the rubble from the collapsed ceiling. With a mighty yell Da stood up from underneath the massive stones and pushed them off and behind him. He'd only just dropped the last of them when I flung myself into his arms.

"I am stronger," Da said over my shoulder. "Faster than you, Udane, and stronger than that stone beast."

"Don't ever do that again," I said into his neck.

"Don't do what? Save you?" Da patted my back. "I thought you kent by now that the most important mission in my life is to keep my lass safe."

I gave him a final squeeze, then I stepped back. "We should go before Crom demands a rematch."

"Aye, and we need to ask Angus what he's been up to," Da said.

"Agreed," Maelgwyn said, then he indicated Da should go first. "Strength before wisdom, Bod."

"Aye, and don't you be forgettin' it."

Chapter Twenty
Chris

After Rob explained to me how many regular families occupied the Seelie portion of Elphame, he and I were of one mind: we needed to stop Crom Cruach before any innocents were hurt. Figuring out his ultimate objective could wait until after Elphame's residents were safe.

Rob went into the bedroom to wake Rina, and ask her to send us to Ireland so we could track down Anya. He reemerged a moment later, frowning.

"What's wrong?" I asked. "Is it the baby?"

"Faith is well," Rob replied. "Your sister, however, has taken a turn for the worse."

I walked past Rob into the bedroom, and saw Rina lying flat on her back in bed, her arms outstretched to either side. Her skin was ashen and she had a fever, evidenced by the sweat-soaked hair plastered against her forehead and cheek. I remembered her stuffy nose from earlier, and realized she hadn't been crying. She was sick.

"It's the flu, or something like the flu," I said, remembering the many times I'd taken care of Rina when we were younger. It always started with a headache, and ended with her in bed for a few days. "It always hits her hard and fast, but never lasts longer than a day or two."

"Chris?" Rina asked, her voice weak. "This sucks."

"I know it does. I'll get a cool washcloth for you."

I went into the bathroom, and dampened a washcloth. When I returned Rob was sitting on the bed next to Rina, holding her hand. He took the washcloth from me and dabbed at her cheeks.

"The feared walker, felled by a humble sickness," Rob said.

"I don't think anyone fears me," Rina mumbled.

"Then they have no' seen ye angry," Rob said, and she laughed a bit. "As ye can see, Christopher, I am no' going anywhere."

"Go, I'll be fine," Rina said, then she started coughing.

"She does this, too," I said. "Claims she's fine, then she refuses to stay in bed and get better."

Rina threw a tissue at me. It fluttered menacingly before landing on top of the blankets. "Stop telling Robert all my secrets."

"Get some rest, and I will." I turned to Rob, and said, "I'll head back to the Winter Palace. Come by when everyone's healthy."

"I shall. Godspeed, Christopher."

***

As I walked back to the gate to Elphame, I thought about what Rob had told me. There were people in Elphame. Families. I have to admit he was right; I'd never thought of Elphame as anything other than a land of trickster fairies, and while there were plenty of those there were also regular folks living their lives. Now that I knew there were families, I understood why Rob insisted we fight for the Seelie Court. Hell, if there's just one family, or even one single innocent person, that's enough to fight for.

I also wondered what else my prejudices were blinding me to about Elphame. Granted, my first experience with the realm had been horrific, but so many good things had happened to me since then. There was Anya, the single best person I have ever met, and I really don't know if I ever would have spoken to her if it wasn't for Elphame. When Nicnevin had enthralled me to her, I'd gotten the side effect of being able to see through glamours. Fast forward a few months to Rina's Geology 101 class, and I instantly noticed the fae girl among the students. A beautiful, mesmerizing fae girl, and despite the fact she was fae I needed to learn everything about her. I'm so glad I did.

I now know that Anya isn't fae, and that Beira had sent Anya to watch over Rina in New York. That in itself was suspect, because Beira never did anything without having an ulterior motive or three. Evil mothers in law aside, I decided to set aside some time and reexamine my stance on Elphame. These prejudices would only end up hurting me, and Anya, which meant I needed to deal with my issues sooner rather than later.

I turned onto Buchanan Street and stepped inside Remy's Place. Despite the very late hour, it was packed as always. The titular bartender winked at me, filled a glass half full with absinthe and set it below the countertop water reservoir. A moment later he balanced a pierced silver spoon across the top of the glass, added a sugar cube, and opened the fountain's spigot to a slow drip. As the clear, cold water dissolved the sugar cube and dripped into the acid green liquor, I found myself wondering if the water was melted snow.

"Here you are, m'lord," Remy said as set the finished drink on the bar. The glass and spoon had the delicate feel of antiques, the former so thin I worried I'd break it.

"I'm no lord. Thanks for the drink." Once, I asked Remy why he poured whisky when we arrived from the Winter Palace, but switched to absinthe for the return trip. He'd claimed a good bartender never gave up his secrets, and I hadn't asked again. I don't need a liquor-related curse following me around this world or Elphame. I took the glass and headed toward the back room, when the bartender called after me.

"Sir," Remy called. I guessed that was better than lord. I turned around, and saw him holding up the ornate silver absinthe spoon. "Don't forget your spoon."

"Why?" I asked as I accepted the spoon. "Is it magical, like a key?"

He grinned. "Not in the least, but they do clang around the bottom of the dishwasher. I like to keep 'em where they're needed, you ken?"

"I ken. Thanks again." I stuck the spoon in my jacket pocket, then I headed toward the beaded curtain in the back. I downed the absinthe, pushed the beads aside, then I stepped out of Glasgow and into the Winter Palace.

"Whoa." I set the absinthe glass in a niche carved into the ice wall, and grabbed the shot of whisky that someone had thoughtfully placed inside. I didn't know if I'd ever get used to the trip from the bar to the palace, and vice versa. It wasn't a smooth transition like traveling via Rina's portals, not that I was ever going to bring that up to Anya. Some things were best left unsaid.

I wandered through the palace, all the while fingering

the *aquila* in my pocket. It was too soon to summon the Ninth for help against Crom Cruach, mainly because we didn't have a battle to point them toward. Legionnaires without an upcoming battle were just a bunch of guys standing around looking for a fight, and I didn't need them accidentally tangling with Anya's brothers. I'd just decided to track down Lucius and tell him what I'd learned about Crom and ask his advice when I heard the Bodach's rumbling voice, followed by a string of curses from Anya.

Great. I hoped Bod wasn't destroying the rest of the palace. We did need someplace to sleep. I followed the voices, and found the two of them and Maelgwyn standing in the corridor adjacent to the throne room.

"Hey, everyone," I greeted. They turned toward me, and every one of them seemed miserable. They were covered in dust and debris, and Bod had bits of stone in his beard. He hadn't been so filthy when we'd pulled him out of the ground at Glen Lyon. "I take it things didn't go so well in Ireland."

"Crom almost buried us alive," Anya replied. "If not for Da—"

She looked at Maelgwyn, but he seemed unaffected by Anya referring to Bod as her father. "If not for Da he would have succeeded," she finished.

"Are you all right?" I asked.

"I am. We all are."

My heart was in my throat. Anya was nearly invincible, especially in winter, but she almost hadn't come back to me. "Thank you," I said to Bod, then I approached Anya. "What do you need from me?"

"What I need is to find the *fuath* that lied to me, make his body corporeal, freeze him solid and bury him in ice," she snapped. "Fionnlagh was never in league with Crom! That creature wanted Crom to finish us off!"

"Rob mentioned as much," I said. "I guess we should have talked to him first. What happened with the children?"

Anya glanced at Maelgwyn. "They were not in Crom's lair."

"I guess that's a good thing, in its own way. What do we do next?"

"I for one shall locate Angus, and find out what he knows about the missing *dahm coroin*," Bod said. "We'll get your property returned to you, Udane, safe and sound."

Maelgwyn nodded, then Bod lumbered off toward the kitchens. I imagined a giant must need to ingest a large amount of food. His sons certainly did.

"He didn't even apologize for what he did to the throne room," I said, not mentioning how Bod had almost killed me and injured members of the Ninth Legion.

"Don't hold your breath waiting for one." Anya kicked off her shoes and scowled at the chunks of mud that came off with them. "Sarmi will have my head for this mess. I'm off to a bath."

Anya squeezed my hand, and I watched her walk toward the stairs. That left me alone in the corridor with the Unseelie King. I realized then that he hadn't said a word since I arrived, and when I faced him I understood why; his face was drawn and his shoulders slumped. He was devastated. He'd pinned all of his hopes on finding his children with Crom and bringing them home, and that hadn't happened.

"Let's sit for a bit," I said, and Maelgwyn followed me into the first floor study. It was set up like a Victorian men's club, complete with oak paneled walls lined with bookcases, a fireplace, and rich leather furniture. Anya had indulged my whims in many parts of the palace, but this room was by far my favorite. The cabinet Sarmi kept stocked with single malt whisky and writing materials only increased my good opinion of the study.

Maelgwyn sat in front of the now-cold fireplace, and I poured us two glasses of whisky. I handed one to him, and said, "I'm sorry you didn't find them."

"Ah, well." He downed the whisky. "It was a foolish hope."

"It wasn't." I refilled his glass, and claimed the opposite chair. "What if they had been there? You had to find out, one way or the other."

"And I almost got my sole living child killed in the process."

"But, you didn't. And now you know of another place where they aren't." I fingered the edge of my glass. "If you ever want to look for them someplace else, I will help you. If you want me to."

"Anya tells me you are the one who takes after your

mother, the volva. Do you have a touch of foresight?"

"Not exactly. My sister thinks I understand the past, rather than the future."

"Karina is a dear heart. How is the child?"

"Faith is good." I almost mentioned Karina's flu, but Maelgwyn was already in a delicate place. Hearing that Rina was less than one hundred percent healthy might push him over the edge. "Anyway, since Rina's the smartest person I know and usually right about everything, I've been thinking about understanding the past. I can't find out where your children are now, but maybe, once I get a handle on this volv business, I'll be able to see where they've been. That should point us in the right direction."

"You would do that for me?"

"Of course."

Maelgwyn set down his glass and took both of my hands in his. "Christopher, thank you. That you would help me locate my missing children means everything to me." He paused, and added, "Even if what I fear most is true and they no longer live, my heart rests easier knowing that Anya has chosen you."

As Maelgwyn made his declaration I felt something, a sensation deep in my chest; it was pride, and I hadn't been proud of myself for a long time. I could help find Maelgwyn's missing children. I would tap into whatever ability Mom had given me, find out who had taken them, and where they are today. I was certain of it.

And if I could do that, I could do anything.

Chapter Twenty One
Anya

I stomped up the stairs and into my chambers intent on that bath, and began shedding my dusty clothes as soon as the door was closed behind me. By the time I reached the bathing chamber I was fully nude, and only then did it occur to me I'd never requested a bath. My time in the mortal realm had accustomed me to the luxuries humans favored, such as hot and cold running water piped directly into their homes. I wondered if we could have water pipes installed here in the palace, and perhaps a radiator or two. For all that I embody winter I do prefer a bit of warmth.

No matter how many luxuries beckoned me from the mortal realm, the Winter Palace possessed one advantage the humans would never have: Sarmi. She must have overheard my desire for a bath, and had somehow gotten the tub filled with steaming water before I made it upstairs. As I sank into the water up to my chin I wondered what I ever did to deserve her.

My bath was quiet, and solitary, and the water was the perfect temperature, all of it due to Sarmi's exquisite ability to transform my every want and desire into reality. Despite all of that I emerged from the bath as agitated as when I'd trudged into the room covered in dust and dirt like a filthy beggar. That lying, scheming *fuath* had almost gotten us killed, Nicnevin was still missing, and the Seelie Court remained vacant, and therefore vulnerable. As if that wasn't enough we had disturbed Crom for no good reason, and he wasn't likely to forget the affront any time soon.

Add this latest problem to the ever-growing list, and it was almost too much to contemplate.

I dried myself off and put on a pale blue silk robe, all while my mind filled itself with images of Crom; Crom raising himself from the muck, rearing back to strike at us, and how his rocky slab of a face had twisted as he bellowed his anger. I'd seen many beasts and beastly creatures in my time, but Crom Cruach was truly terrifying. That, coupled with his amazing strength meant he was more than a worthy foe. He was entirely capable of destroying us and claiming the whole of Elphame as his.

I paused, my comb halfway through my hair. What if Crom had been after the Seelie portion of Elphame all along, and we'd played into his hands?

"Sarmi," I called. She poked her head into the room an instant later.

"Yes, mistress?"

"What do you know of the *fuath*?"

"Not much, I'm afraid. However, I know of a few who aren't shy about asking. What would you like to know about them?"

"Everything."

Sarmi nodded. "Give me twelve hours," she said, and she disappeared from the room.

I put thoughts of the *fuath* out of my mind, and entered my bedroom. The books about the Wild Hunt Christopher had requested from our libraries had been sorted and delivered, along with a stack of paper, pens and ink, and an entire wooden desk and matching chair and footrest. The more I worked with Sarmi, the more I understood why Mum had found her indispensable.

I sat at the desk, leaned on my elbows and held my head in my hands. I hadn't even been Queen of Winter for a full month, and I was already close to losing my title, my power, and perhaps my life. Crom had not only defeated us, he'd nearly entombed us. What if he returned?

I heard the door open and close. Assuming it was Sarmi, I stayed where I was. A moment later Christopher entered the room.

"Hey." He sat on the desk next to my elbows, and stroked my hair. "You okay?"

"Just wondering if we've angered an ancient deity, and if that deity will exact his revenge in blood." I tossed back my hair and wiped my cheeks.

"You sound like Rina."

"Yes, well." I leaned back in my chair and regarded him. "You frequently say she's the most intelligent person you know. Perhaps if she'd come along with us she would have cautioned against antagonizing Crom in his home, where he's strongest."

He laughed softly. "That's where you're wrong. If Rina thought confronting Crom was the next step we needed to take she'd have led the charge herself. She's fearless, and I have the gray hairs to prove it."

"And you're the responsible one? Never done a rash thing in all your days?"

"You know me better than that."

I appreciated his attempts to cheer me. They almost worked. "I fear we've made a grave error."

"Everyone makes mistakes. What matters is how you fix them."

Christopher took my hands and I let him pull me upright—or did I? "How strong are you?" I asked.

He shrugged. "I'd say average adult male strength. Why?"

"More than average, I'd say." He was wearing a blue button down shirt and tan pants; such the professor, he was. I tugged the shirt up and out of his pants and started unbuttoning it from the bottom up, revealing the smooth planes of his abdomen. "Much more."

He put his hands on my hips and drew me closer. "How so?"

"Your mother." Having unbuttoned his shirt all the way, I slid my hands over his shoulders and onto his back. He was delightfully warm. "Volva's are known for both mental and physical strength, and resilience. And here you are, a scholar with the body of a warrior."

"I'm no warrior." He dipped his head so he could nuzzle my ear. I stretched my neck to the side, asking for kisses. He obliged. "You're the brawn and the beauty around here," he said, his warm breath awakening sensations across my skin.

"Does that make you the brains of our operation?"

"Nah. You're much smarter than me." Christopher untied my robe's belt and slipped his hands underneath the silk. "No idea why you keep me around."

"You do have one talent that I particularly enjoy." He raised his head, his brows pinched together.

"Just one?"

I burst into laughter. I hadn't realized how much I needed to laugh, but Christopher knew. He always knew.

"Yes. You have this uncanny ability to always give me exactly what I need, even when I don't know that I need it."

"Do I." He stood, then he lifted me against him with his hands underneath my thighs. I wrapped my legs around his waist and let him carry me to bed.

"I have an idea of what you need now."

"Show me."

***

Afterward, Christopher laid on his back with his arm around me, snug and safe. He stared at the patterns on the ceiling while my head rested on his shoulder and I made patterns of my own in his chest hair. "You really are quite strong," I murmured.

"Am I? I've always been athletic, but I've never considered myself to be particularly strong."

"You lift me as if I'm a feather, and we both know I'm much heavier than a human woman."

Christopher looked down at me. "Anya, you're not that heavy at all. In fact, you're pretty light. If I had to guess I'd say you weigh less than Rina."

"But, giants are denser than—"

And I shut my mouth.

"I'm sorry," I whispered. "I… I forgot."

My hands were trembling and the backs of my eyes burned, so I rolled away from Christopher and hid my face in the bedclothes. His arm snaked around my waist, keeping me close as I wept into the pillows.

"It's okay," he said. "It's still new, and now he's here. You must have all these emotions swirling around inside." He tightened his arms around me. "It's okay."

"Da almost died earlier," I choked out around my sobs. "First, he outright rescued Maelgwyn, then when the cave collapsed he pushed both of us to safety and the entire cavern landed on top of him. All of it! I was so mad at him for getting drunk and hounding Mum, and then for destroying my throne room, and then for smashing those foolish stones, but then he almost died." Christopher gently turned me to face him, and he wiped away my tears with his thumb. "What would I ever do without him?"

"You would go on," he replied. "You would remember him, and honor his memory by living. That's all we can do, when we lose someone."

I remembered that Christopher had lost both of his parents some time ago. "Is that what you did after your parents… After they were gone?"

"Eventually, but not at first. Rina was still very young, and I had to get myself named as her guardian so she wouldn't end up in the foster system."

"Foster system? What is that?"

"When a child loses their parents, if there isn't any family or a guardian able to care for them they could end up in a group home, or they might get adopted by strangers," he replied. "We didn't have any other family, and I was only twenty… But there was no way I was letting Rina end up living with a bunch of people we didn't even know. I promised her that as long as I was alive, I would take care of her."

"And look at the wonderful job you did."

"I'd do it all again, too. Gray hair be damned." He sobered, and said, "I hope nothing ever happens to Bod or Beira, but if something does I am not adopting Angus, or any of your brothers."

"Neither am I," I said quickly. "That lot can look after themselves." I settled against his chest, my ear over his heart.

Christopher resumed stroking my hair. "Do you think Angus stole Maelgwyn's crown?"

"It's certainly something he would do," I replied. "I suppose the better question is why would he take it? What would he do with it?"

"Would he give it back to Fionnlagh?"

I bit the inside of my mouth. The thought had occurred to me, too, since Angus had been present when the *fuath* had shared with us the untrue information that led us to Crom. "I don't see how he could. Fionnlagh remains frozen in the world's coldest ice."

"Good." Christopher kissed the top of my head. "I want you safe from him."

"Angus or Fionnlagh?"

"Both."

I repositioned myself so I was propped on my elbows above his chest, looking down at him. "Such the caretaker, you are. You've spent your life caring for your sister, then your students. Now, you're taking care of me."

"It's my job." He pulled me in for a kiss, then I settled the length of my body against his, my head tucked underneath his chin. "My number one job is to make sure you're happy, and safe."

I kissed his throat, and let my eyes close. "It seems we have the same job, because that is all I want for you."

"Good. I plan on doing it for a long, long time."

Chapter Twenty Two
Chris

We lazed about in bed for a while talking about everything and nothing, and I could have stayed there with Anya for the rest of the day. Or the week, or even forever. However, a seasonal deity's work is never done, and soon enough Sarmi knocked on our door to remind us of that.

"Enter," Anya called.

"Please tell me you're covered," Sarmi said through the door.

"Of course we are."

Sarmi opened the door, and scowled when she saw us in bed. Evidently, Sarmi's definition of "covered" meant by more than just sheets and blankets. She shook her head, then pushed a serving trolley laden with a pot of tea and snacks toward us.

"Thank you, Sarmi," Anya said. "How goes things in the rest of the palace?"

"Everything is coming together quite well, as always," Sarmi replied. "We've got the bulk of Bod's messes cleaned up, and the walls are shored up so nothing will topple them in the meantime. Just like the old days," she added with a chuckle.

"Is Da still here?" Anya asked. "And what of Maelgwyn?"

"Maelgwyn went home to your mam," Sarmi replied, her expression carefully blank. I wondered how she felt about her longtime mistress staying at the Unseelie Court instead of here at the Winter Palace. "As for Bod, he's gone off in search of Angus. When the rest of your brothers woke up and heard the news, they went in search of Bod. And before you ask," Sarmi added, spearing me with her gaze, "the Ninth have kept well to themselves. I've never seen a group of men who needed anything less than that lot."

"Legionnaires were trained to rely on themselves," I said. "Besides, Lucius adores you, and has instructed his men to not be a bother. He's complimented the efficient way you run the household several times."

Sarmi harrumphed, but she did slide an extra cookie onto my plate. "I'll leave you to your repast. Ring if you need anything."

As soon as Sarmi was out the door, Anya stole my extra cookie. "Hey!"

"Complementing Sarmi so she would bring you sweets is a ploy I perfected long ago," she said, then *she ate my cookie*. "We should bring our plates to the solarium. I've a bit of work to do."

"We can bring what's left," I grumbled.

We dressed and relocated to the sunroom, which boasted an entire wall of floor to ceiling windows. Even though it was an ideal place to set up a greenhouse there were very few plants in the room; Beira hadn't been one for houseplants, so Sarmi had limited them to a few potted citrus trees, and a very robust climbing red rose. I thought the rose was overgrown, but Sarmi claimed it was a rare specimen behaving exactly the way it should. What the sunroom had in abundance—aside from dried up rose petals—were several upholstered chaises and polished wood tables, all of them clustered around a large crystal globe.

Anya seated herself in front of the globe and drew it closer to her. She used the globe to monitor weather patterns, and to make sure winter was proceeding as it should. I had no idea how winter or any season should proceed, but I loved watching her work.

"Can you affect the weather everywhere?" I asked. "Make it snow in Jamaica, maybe?"

"I suppose, but to branch out beyond Scotland would be a wasted effort," she replied. "In hot climates, such as near the equator, any wintry weather I summoned wouldn't last long. Besides, if I did something so bold I could anger the local wardens, and that wouldn't do at all."

I paused with my teacup halfway to my mouth. "Wardens? That makes it sound like you keep the seasons locked away until you need them. Is… Is that how it works?"

She popped a tiny cake in her mouth and winked at me. "Is it?"

I wasn't falling for her teasing. I'd just ask Sarmi later, when Anya wasn't listening. Sarmi knew everything, except proper rose maintenance. "Then tell me, Warden

Anya, how goes winter in this neck of the woods?"

"Well, mostly."

"Just mostly?"

Anya waved her hand over the globe, and Scotland increased in size while the rest of the world shrank away. "There is one location on the eastern coast that refuses to cool down, and for the life of me I don't understand why."

"Where is this hot spot?"

"Crail."

"Oh." The exact place where my sister's house was located. I'm sure this recent development had nothing to do with the fact that the house was a gift from Fionnlagh. "What are you going to do about it?"

"I'm not sure. Before I do anything I would like to understand why it's staying so warm to begin with. It's possible that this is a known temperature anomaly."

"And if it's not?"

Anya blew out a breath, then she waved her hand over the globe and everything went back to its regular size. "Then, I don't know what it could be."

"Looks like we have a mystery to solve." I stood and rubbed my hands together. "Let's go check it out."

"What about Crom?"

"What about him? Oh, do you think he's the one heating up Crail?"

"I mean, what if he strikes back at us?"

"Oh. That." I sat heavily; from what Anya had told me Crom was more terrifying than Fionnlagh, stronger that the Bodach, and—based on his steady diet of sacrificial victims—more evil than Nicnevin. A trifecta of fun, then. "Do you think he will?"

"I've no idea." Anya leaned back on her chaise and rubbed her eyes. She looked like a heroine from a Gothic romance, and I loved it. "Gods below, I don't know anything today."

"Then let's figure it out." I got up and started pacing across the room; my mind always worked better when my body was in motion. It's how I got started playing basketball. "What do we know about Crom? He's powerful and awful, and if he attacks it will probably be with something earth-based. What do we have in the way of defenses?"

"That's the problem," Anya replied. "If Crom were to attack the Unseelie Court, Maelgwyn could easily stop him. The same would be true if he went after Beinn na Caillich, the Winter Palace, or the seat of anyone's power. But, large swathes of Elphame are currently undefended."

"Such as, the Seelie Court," I said, and she nodded.

"Exactly. Crom could decimate that portion of Elphame without breaking a sweat, assuming a being such as he does sweat."

I remembered what Rob told me about Elphame being full of innocent people. "All right, so what we need is to either find a power to match Crom, or someone to hold the throne in the Seelie Court against his possible attack. Let's go to Crail."

"Why Crail? Because of the anomaly?"

"Yes. Something tells me Nicnevin's at my sister's house."

Anya stood, took my hand, and blinked.

The next moment we were in Crail.

"What makes you think she's here?" Anya asked. She'd teleported us to the meadow that stretched behind the cottage, probably so we could attempt to sneak up on whatever or whomever was in there. The first thing I noticed was the mellow sea breeze.

"It really is warm." I looked down, but none of the wildflowers were blooming. That was a shame, since in summertime the meadow was covered in white and yellow and pink blooms. "Do you think the increase in temperature will harm the local ecosystem?"

"Christopher. Why do you suspect Nicnevin is here?"

"I've got a few reasons, actually. First of all, we have this unseasonable weather, though the warmth is nice."

Anya sniffed. "A snowfall would greatly improve this meadow."

"A snowfall would be beautiful. Also, Rob told me that work on the house is being done well, but slowly. So slowly he couldn't understand why such skilled craftsmen were behaving that way. Seems to me that someone doesn't want the gallowglass and the walker moving back into their house any time soon. That, and Nicnevin hates winter."

"Winter hates Nicnevin as well. This extended

summer could definitely point to her." Anya kissed my temple. "Appears you're the brainy one today. Shall we have a knock, see what she's up to?"

"Might as well." As we approached the back of the cottage, I saw flashes of bright wings flitting about the garden. "Want to grab Wyatt so he can be my bodyguard?"

"You will never let me live that down, will you?"

"Nope."

We skirted the walled garden, and approached the cottage's front entrance. Just as Rob had described, work had been done—and done well—but everything was unfinished; for instance, the front door was hung, but the trim wasn't up. The same was true for the windows, and while the majority of the walls had been repaired they didn't look up to keeping out a Scottish winter.

Huh. Maybe Nicnevin keeping the area warm was her misguided attempt to help.

We entered without knocking—I still sort of lived there, after all—and took in the common room. Drop cloths covered the floors, and plastic sheets hung over the bedroom and bathroom doors. Tools and makeshift tables were scattered about, along with boxes of tile and piles of lumber.

"Rob wasn't kidding about the slow work," I said. "They were supposed to install that tile a month ago."

"Notice the stairs," Anya said. They were perfect, from the polished wood bannister and spindles to the plush red carpet that lined the steps. It was a staircase fit for royalty, human or Seelie.

I sighed, and steeled myself for yet another encounter with my least favorite person. "I would rather talk to Fionnlagh than her."

Anya patted my arm. "I will keep her from harassing you too much. Remember, I'm now the more powerful of the two of us."

That did make me feel better. I rolled my shoulders, and said, "All right, beautiful. Let's see what the evil queen has to say for herself."

The heady scent of roses wafted down the stairs. "Smell that? She left us a trail."

Anya wrinkled her nose. "I prefer lavender."

"So do I."

We ascended the stairs, and learned that not only was the staircase complete, the upstairs hallway had also been carpeted and wallpapered. That meant that the stairs and second floor hall were the only refinished areas of the house. Interesting.

The rose scent led us to the master bedroom. There we found the Seelie Queen lounging on an absolutely enormous bed heaped with cushions and draped in yards of gauzy silk, reading a gossip magazine.

With a put upon sigh, Nicnevin said, "If you two are here you must need something. Desperately."

Chapter Twenty Three
Anya

There she was, the Seelie Queen we'd been searching for these past months reclined in comfort on someone else's bed. Nicnevin was wearing the sort of silken gown one would don to meet one's lover, and the silver bedside tray was laden with wineglasses and the remains of a rich meal. It was all I could do to keep from freezing her. "Are you enjoying yourself?" I demanded.

Nicnevin quirked a ginger brow, but otherwise didn't move. "I was. How is your first winter faring? Seems a bit warm in my opinion."

I clenched my fist and willed myself to stay calm. "Elphame needs you. You must leave this… this nest of yours and reclaim the Seelie throne."

"Or at least reign in your creepy stepchildren," Christopher added.

"Have the *fuath* been misbehaving?" she asked. "Surely you can handle them, Christopher. You are so good at handling things."

Christopher's lips flattened and he moved toward the bed with his hands poised as if to shake some sense into her. I placed my hand on his arm, halting him. "They sent us on a wild goose chase that ended up with Crom Cruach nearly killing me, and Maelgwyn, and my Da."

Nicnevin flicked down the corner of her magazine. "The Bodach is loose? Gods below, this is a crisis. What of those ruffian brothers of yours?"

"Yes, they are all free." I managed to keep my voice even. Barely. Meanwhile my fingernails dug into my palm so deeply I wondered if I'd bleed. "You don't seem surprised to hear Crom's name."

"Elphame stopped surprising me long ago." Nicnevin raised her magazine so it obscured her face. "Regardless of what gods you've angered, your brothers are the ones you should be worried about, not the *fuath*."

I snatched the magazine from her hands and flung it aside. "The *fuath* lied to us!"

"That's what they do." She calmly took another magazine from a pile on the bedside table and opened it. "They were born in pain and misery, and thus spread pain and misery wherever they go."

"They helped us defeat Fionnlagh," Christopher said. "When we told them he'd imprisoned you—" He glanced around the room. "Were you ever imprisoned?"

"I was, thank you for your concern," she replied. "From what I've gathered, when you froze the mighty king his *geas* over me was broken. I then retreated here," she gestured about the room, "in order to recover from that most harrowing ordeal."

"You seem to be recuperating well," I said, then I paused. "The *geas* bound you to this realm?" She nodded. "Where were you?"

"Tantallon Castle. It's where Fionnlagh puts all of his inconvenient people, lovers and otherwise," she added with a grimace.

"I'm sure you all had much to discuss," I said. "Now you must return to Elphame."

"Must?" Nicnevin put down her magazine and regarded me. "I don't believe I must do anything, and certainly not because you wish it."

"Careful," I said, frost accumulating on my palm. "I'm more powerful than you."

"Are you?" Nicnevin purred. "What will you do, o mighty queen? Freeze me like you froze my husband?"

"That's a great idea," Christopher said. "Let's freeze dry this one and stick her underneath the palace with Fionnlagh. Lovers reuniting is always so heartwarming."

"I'd rather die than spend another moment with him," Nicnevin snapped. "Which means no, I will not return to Elphame, not for you or anyone. Or anything," she added.

"If you return now, you will rule alone," I said. "The *fuath*, the Picts, and the full might of the Seelie Court will be yours alone."

"Perhaps for now, but what of when Fionnlagh returns?"

"He is frozen. The ice won't thaw for at least half a millennia. You will have a full five hundred years to build your power base before you need worry about him." Nicnevin remained silent, and I finally understood the emotion in her eyes: fear. The Seelie Queen, she who bowed to no man, was scared of her husband.

"Is five hundred years not enough?" I ventured. "I can keep him frozen for longer, if you like. It's no bother."

Nicnevin glared at me as one would regard a simpleton. "Let's strike a deal then, shall we? Prove to me that Fionnlagh is where you claim him to be, and offer me assurances that when he comes for me and everyone else he feels has wronged him, I will have your protection."

Christopher started to say that of course Fionnlagh remained imprisoned, but her words gave me pause. "Have you reason to believe he escaped?"

"I know my husband. It is only a matter of time before he frees himself, and he does have a mighty temper." Nicnevin sighed, her gaze resting on Faith's cradle in the corner of the room. "The reason I surrounded myself with warriors—the Picts, the *fuath*, and even the many gallowglasses that served me over the years—was not for power, but for protection. *My* protection. Fionnlagh's ego bruises easily and often, and he's not one to let go of a grudge."

"And now you're hiding from him in the gallowglass's home," I said. "We can protect you. Even if I cannot hide you at the Winter Palace, we have the might of the Unseelie behind us."

Nicnevin laughed, a hollow rattle that I'm sure mimicked the dry husk of her soul. "Beira and I, under the same roof? That would destroy Elphame as surely as Crom would." She sobered, and continued, "For now, I think it's best for all involved for me to remain hidden. My enemies far outnumber my friends, and if my enemies become yours it won't end well for any of us."

It was not the answer I'd hoped for, but I understood her point. "If we have no other options, we will come get you."

Nicnevin nodded. "So I gathered."

"We're also telling Rob and Rina you're staying here," Christopher said. "If you're lucky, Rina will only send you to Elphame."

"I look forward to weathering your sister's wrath. I do

hope she brings the child when she visits."

Christopher opened his mouth, no doubt to tell Nicnevin to have a care when she spoke of Faith. Instead of dealing with that shouting match, I took Christopher's hand, and blinked back to the solarium.

"She is the worst," he grumbled, "but, that was enlightening. Why did you want to know where Nicnevin was held?"

"We may need that knowledge later on." I went to my globe, and called up an image of Tantallon. Once, it had been an imposing fortress, but human folly had ruined it centuries ago. That begged the question of why the Seelie King frequented it, and what else he'd left in the castle for safekeeping.

"Karina has been to Tantallon, has she not?" I asked.

"I think so, back when she first met Rob."

"Did she tell you about it?"

"A bit. They almost drowned."

"They almost drowned inside a fortress, on land? Were the *fuath* present?"

"From what I recall, there was a ghost and Rina wanted to help it, so they went to a cave beneath the castle to check things out. One of the spirits wanted to capture Rob and turn him over to Nicnevin—this was back when he still bound to her and wore that collar. Rina and Rob ended up jumping into a well and were swept out to sea."

"Oh." I scrutinized the image of Tantallon, then I enlarged the image of the cave beneath. "You're telling me that this location—a location we have confirmed Fionnlagh has used to imprison people quite frequently—has an otherworldly way below?"

"I don't know if it's otherworldly."

"They survived, didn't they? What are the odds of that happening without magical assistance?"

"Pretty low, I guess. What does that mean?"

I tapped the globe's surface with my fingernail. "It means that we should have a look around Tantallon."

Chapter Twenty Four
Chris

Anya teleported us not to Tantallon itself, but to a rocky finger of land a few hundred yards away that faced the castle, and the sea cliffs the fortress sat upon. Even at that distance the sight of the castle, though ruined, was awe inspiring. Tantallon was constructed from a reddish stone, and had a tower sitting at each corner with a large gatehouse in the center, but those weren't the main defenses. That honor went to a massive curtain wall that separated the main structure from the headland, and from anyone or anything that considered invading. The other three sides of the castle were bordered by steep cliffs that dropped off to the sea. As defenses went, this place was nigh on impregnable.

"Tantallon reminds me of the Unseelie Court," I said, indicating the cliffs. "Maybe these are Maelgwyn's old stomping grounds."

"Perhaps they are," Anya said. "It must be lovely in summer."

"I can see why Fionnlagh likes to stash people here," I said. "If the curtain wall didn't keep others from finding you, the sea cliffs would."

"Or, perhaps they would force you to discover a more creative approach."

"How so?"

Anya gestured toward the area below the castle. Since it was low tide we could see whole of the promontory's cliffs and a fair amount of the beach below. "You could easily land an army at that beach. Equip the soldiers with ropes and pickaxes, send them up the cliff, and you could surprise the household as they slept."

I almost asked Anya how she'd come to such a conclusion, when I realized she was thinking not like the woman I met in New York, but as a queen ever ready to defend her home and people. "Is that what you'd do?"

"Of course not. I would freeze them out." She walked a little way down the beach for a different view. "That appears to be the cave Karina spoke of."

I followed her gaze, and saw the dark hollow below the castle. "I guess that's where we go in."

"So it appears." Anya took my hand, then paused. "All of this teleporting doesn't affect you in any way?"

"It's a little weird, being in one place and then at a completely different location a second later, but I don't seem to be having any side effects, bad or otherwise," I replied. When she smiled, I asked, "Should I be having side effects?"

She nodded. "Most mortals cannot bear teleporting often, never mind more than once a day. This unusual tolerance may be yet another trait you inherited from your mother."

"Maybe." I thought for a moment. "Rob has never mentioned any side effects from Rina's portals."

Anya laughed. By the time it faded she'd teleported us to mouth of the cave. "Robert is too wise to complain in Karina's hearing, and to stubborn to complain in anyone else's. Let's see what the Seelie bastard's left behind."

We entered the narrow opening with my super powered girlfriend leading the way; Anya may think I'm strong for a mortal, but she's easily as strong as a giant, maybe more so. Soon enough the passage opened into a large chamber of striated orange stone. I noticed an opening in the dead center of the floor.

"That must be the well," I said, recalling Rina's escape story. "It empties into a tunnel that connects to the Forth."

"Good to know." Anya walked along the edge of the chamber, examining the walls. "Karina said a ghost was in residence?"

"They were told it was the ghost of one of Fionnlagh's past lovers, but she turned into some type of monster. Regenerating limbs, and all that."

Anya paused. "Who told them?"

"There was a tour guide up top, who sent them after the ghost and then disappeared like the Cheshire Cat."

"Gods below. I understand Karina's natural curiosity, but how did Robert fall for such a tale?"

"Have you seen them together? He's been wrapped around her finger since day one." I looked around the chamber, which was quite well-lit for a room carved out of bare rock.

"Where is all of this light coming from?" I asked. "It should be much darker in here."

"I believe it's coming from the walls." Anya placed her hand flat against the rock. "It's warm. Perhaps the light is coming through them?"

I placed my hand on the cave wall next to hers. Instead of the rock being merely warm I could feel heat flowing through it. Pulsating, as if it was alive and blood coursed through its veins. "There's something behind the walls."

"What could be back there?" Anya ran her hands over the surface, then she backed up a step and regarded the wall. "It appears to be solid rock."

"It's a heartbeat." The words just tumbled out of my mouth, but as soon as I said them I was certain. "Someone's trapped back there."

"What if it's Karina's ghost?"

I shook my head. "It's not. If there's anything Elphame's taught me it's what monsters feel like. This isn't a monster. This… these are people."

"People," Anya repeated, then she gasped. "I only know of one group of individuals Fionnlagh went to great pains to hide."

I nodded. "How do we move this rock?"

Anya pushed up her sleeves. "Stand back."

I did as instructed, and watched as Anya created a ball of frost between her palms. Once she gauged it complete she flung it at the wall, then she raised her arms and the cold returned to her. Anya completed the cycle a few more times, and I realized that when she called back the frost the rock thawed, only to refreeze when she tossed it back. She threw and summoned back her enchanted snowball at the walls over and over until the rock couldn't bear the constant freezing and thawing, and wide crack appeared.

I ran to the crack and peered inside. "There's light and heat back there!"

"Grab the edges," Anya ordered. "Peel away the surface!"

"I can't rip apart solid rock!"

"It's not rock. It's a spell."

We each grabbed an edge and pulled. The rock crumpled in my hands like wrapping paper. Anya and I peeled and tore away the entire back of the cave wall, and revealed a hidden room. It looked like a movie set depicting the inside of a genie's bottle.

The room was circular, with a shallow bench that ran the length of the room. The bench and floor were covered with plush velvet cushions in bright jewel tones, and sheer fabric hangings further divided area into smaller rooms. Other than the bright fabrics and cushions, the room appeared to be empty.

"Curiouser and curiouser," I said, then something moved on the bench. I stepped closer, and saw a child lying underneath a blanket, her eyes closed. "Anya, there's someone in here."

Anya was at my side in an instant. "She's asleep," she said, then she looked farther into the room. "There are more."

I crouched down and looked over the sleeping girl. She was breathing, and didn't appear harmed in any way. "Are the rest sleeping, too?"

"Yes. They've been asleep for centuries, I'd wager." Anya picked her way toward the back of the room, then she pulled aside one of the curtains. "Christopher, there's a baby."

I approached Anya, and saw a baby nestled in a cradle, wrapped in turquoise blankets. She looked to be a few months older than Faith, and had round pink cheeks, dark curling hair, and a white flower clutched in her chubby little hand.

The baby clutched a daisy.

"These are Maelgwyn's children," I said. "Anya, we found them!"

"I'll get him," Anya said, then she was gone. An instant later she returned with Maelgwyn on her arm.

"Anya, Christopher, what—" Maelgwyn's gaze fell onto Daisy. He fell to his knees and touched her hand.

"Daisy?" He smoothed back her dark hair. The baby blinked herself awake, and smiled at her father. Maelgwyn picked her up carefully, as if he was worried that touching her might make her disappear. Daisy gurgled a smile, and he hugged his daughter for the first time in centuries.

"How did you find her?" he asked, his face buried in

Daisy's hair.

"You'll have to thank Nicnevin," Anya said. "She told us that this cave is where Fionnlagh likes to hide those he finds problematic. Christopher and I thought we'd best have a look."

Throughout the room, the rest of the inhabitants stirred in varying stages of wakefulness. "Maelgwyn, the rest are waking up."

"The rest?" He looked up, tears coursing down his face. "They're all here?"

"See for yourself."

Maelgwyn went to each in turn, reuniting with his long-lost children one by one. There were eleven kids in all, ranging in age from a few months to early teens. Throughout it all he never set Daisy down, not even for a moment.

"Eleven children," I said, counting them as Maelgwyn made his way around the room. "Six boys and five girls. You will have the most epic sleepovers," I added, bumping Anya with my shoulder.

"I never realized there were so many, or that they were so young," Anya said. "I wonder if Mum not telling Maelgwyn about me wasn't just about Da. Perhaps the wounds from losing his other children were still too fresh, and she worried he couldn't bear it."

"For two women who embody winter you're both rather warm-hearted."

"We will both do anything for those we care about. In that way we're the same."

"You're like your mother in many good ways." I draped my arm around Anya's shoulders. "We did a good thing today, beautiful."

She leaned her head against my shoulder. "We certainly did."

Chapter Twenty Five
Anya

A few hours after my and Christopher's wonderful discovery of Maelgwyn's missing children, all of us were back at the Unseelie Court. The children's arrival had caused the most tumultuous uproar, and what joyful chaos it was. The court staff—many of whom had served Maelgwyn since his days as the Summer King—leapt into action, and in short order had converted the antechamber of his private rooms into the most well-appointed and largest nursery I'd ever set eyes on. Mum oversaw everything, moving from one of my siblings to the next as she made sure they were warm, and fed, and had everything they could possibly need.

Siblings. I had eleven new siblings.

"Just when you thought you had the market cornered on brothers, here comes a whole new set of them," Christopher said.

"And sisters," I added. "I'd always thought Karina would be my only sister. How wonderful it is to be wrong, at least about this."

Christopher glanced at me. "You consider Rina your sister?"

"Of course. Shouldn't I?"

"I think it's great, since she feels the same way." He grinned, and added, "Bet you never thought you'd have a walker and a gallowglass in your family."

"I never thought any of this was possible." Ever since the males in my family had been exiled it had only been Mum and me. I'd grown so accustomed to being a family of two I'd resigned myself to living my life as an only child. But Mum, she never gave up, and even though her methods weren't always noble she'd spent every moment since Da and my brothers' imprisonment trying to free them.

Maelgwyn had never given up on his children, either. His struggle had been longer, and lonelier, but at last they were united again. Perhaps he and Mum were quite well-suited for each other, after all.

"Anya, Christopher," Maelgwyn called as he

approached us. Daisy was still in his arms, and I wondered if he would ever put her down. "You must have Karina and Robert visit, and soon. They must meet everyone! Faith and Daisy will be wonderful friends, I'm sure of it! And Anya, you must bring all of your brothers, too. They will all be grand friends."

"I have no doubt they will," I said. "They will be as pleased as I am to have eleven new siblings."

"And you make an even twelve." Maelgwyn cupped the back of my head and kissed my forehead. He'd never before shown me such affection, and I wondered if he kept himself distant to deal with his pain over losing his children so long ago.

"Anya, my dear heart," he continued, "none of this would have been possible without you. My biggest regret shall ever be not being there for you to watch you grow. Thank you, for bringing my babies home."

"It was the least I could do," I said, tears pricking my eyes. "And now we can watch the rest of them grow. All is as it should be."

He smiled at me. "Yes, I believe it is. Our family is together, and we will never be parted again."

Mum called Maelgwyn to her side, and he left us to see what she needed. Once he was out of earshot, Christopher said, "None of them have his eyes, except you."

"Is that so unusual?" It was true, only I shared Maelgwyn's iridescent gray eyes. Then again…

"These aren't all of his children," I said. "He's had scores over the centuries, but these eleven were the ones who hadn't grown to adulthood, and the only ones who still lived under is roof when Da attacked him… and they were the one who most needed his protection. Fionnlagh deliberately targeted the weakest members of Maelgwyn's family for his revenge."

"I know he's your uncle, but Fionnlagh really is an asshole," Christopher said, and I did not disagree. "Does everyone in this batch have the same mother?"

"I… don't know." I'd never once heard of Maelgwyn having a lover. The Unseelie King was famously solitary. "Whoever bore them did so a long time ago. This lot was born when Maelgwyn was still the Summer King, long before I came along."

"Was Beira their mother?"

"No," I replied, then I caught myself watching her as she moved from one child to the next, doting on each of them as she'd once doted on me. "She couldn't be. Could she?"

"All I know is that around here, anything's possible." Christopher frowned, then he withdrew the *aquila* from his chest pocket. It hummed and quivered as if an electric current ran through it. "And Lucius wants my attention."

Lucius wouldn't summon Christopher unless it was important. "I'll tell Maelgwyn we're leaving," I said, then I made my way across the room toward my parents.

My parents!

I paused in the center of the room and turned in a slow circle. I was surrounded by family, more family than I ever hoped to have. I felt safe, and loved, and happy. I was content.

I caught Christopher's gaze, he who was such a very big part of my contentment. He cocked his head to the side, wondering what I was doing. I smiled and shrugged, and continued on my path.

"Mum," I said. She looked up from her charge— Nuala, a sweet girl only a few years older than Daisy—and gave me an exasperated smile.

"Well, now, this is not how I was expecting to spend my day," she said, surveying the children. "Anya, you have made your father very, very happy."

"And you?" I ventured.

"I am happy," she said. She smiled, but as per usual admitted to nothing. "I am honored to help Maelgwyn and his children get to know each other again. And for you to acquaint yourself with your siblings," she added.

"As am I, but that will have to begin another time. We must return home. The Ninth has news for Christopher."

"Perhaps they've finally located Nicnevin."

"Oh, we found her," I said. "She's at the gallowglass's home in Crail. Could you tell Maelgwyn we'll return as soon as we can?"

Mum nodded. "That I shall."

Chapter Twenty Six
Chris

When Anya and I arrived at the Winter Palace, Lucius was waiting for us next to the main entrance. His second in command, Titus, was standing at attention at Lucius's side. They were both dressed for battle and armed to the teeth.

"Let's hear the bad news," I said, since Lucius never summoned me for anything else.

"Angus and the rest of Domina's brothers have returned," he replied without preamble; one of the things I appreciated most about Lucius was his ability to quickly pare a situation down to its salient points. "They have disavowed all knowledge of the whereabouts of the Stag Lord's crown."

"Interesting. Do we believe they don't have it?" I asked Anya.

She shrugged. "While Angus is perfectly capable of sneaking into Maelgwyn's treasury and running off with the crown, we've no proof he did so. I will take him at his word unless I learn otherwise."

"If you believe him then I do, too." I turned back to Lucius. "You wouldn't be in full armor juts to tell us that."

"We have captured one of the *fuath*," Lucius, the master of burying the lead, said. "It was skulking about the palace, no doubt spying for its master, whomever that may be."

"However did you manage to catch it?" Anya asked.

"The Ninth are no strangers to monsters, Domina," Lucius replied. "We dealt with the *fuath* often while stationed at the Seelie Court, and we know their tricks. Come, I will take you to it." Lucius frowned, and added, "We were forced to trap it in your solarium. They don't do well with bright light, and we had few options for containment."

"Quick thinking is as valuable a weapon as a sharp sword," Anya said, and Lucius's shoulders relaxed. I wondered if Nicnevin had ever had him punished for entering her private space uninvited. "You three go on. I'll collect Angus and meet you at the solarium."

Anya went in search of her brother, and I followed

Lucius and Titus into the royal apartment and toward the sunroom. They'd cornered the *fuath* into the only pocket of shadow it could find in the bright, airy room, right behind Anya's crystal globe.

"You said it was spying?" I asked from the doorway. I had no intention of getting any closer to the creature than I absolutely had to.

"It was in a dark patch of shadow inside the stable," Titus replied. "We surrounded it, and drove it to this room. It can only move through shadows, and is thus currently incapacitated."

"Good work." Before I could say more, I heard Anya and Angus coming up the stairs.

"And all the bairns were asleep?" Angus said.

"That they were, eleven of the sweetest babes you ever did see," Anya replied.

"Five more sisters," Angus grumbled. "Getting to be a sorority around here."

"Imagine how I felt growing up with all of you," Anya countered. "I suspect you'll meet them soon. Mum and Maelgwyn are caring for them now."

Angus grunted. "I wonder what Da will have to say about that."

I was wondering that, too; Beira seemed rather comfortable caring for Maelgwyn's children, and if I had to guess she now had many more reasons to stay at the Unseelie Court. I was also wondering if the Winter Palace could withstand Bod hearing what could potentially be bad news. If what he'd done to the throne room was indicative of what could happen to the rest of the structure, Bod could level the palace in a day.

"Any news on the crown?" I asked Angus, once they stepped into the sunroom.

"No, and why does everyone thing I have the manky old thing?" Angus countered. "None of us brothers want anything to do with that Seelie mess."

"We may have a solution for the Seelie mess, as you put it," I said. "We found Nicnevin."

"Where is Domina?" Lucius demanded.

The *fuath* appeared an inch in front of my face. I looked toward the floor; it had skipped across Lucius's shadow and was now standing in mine. "Yes, where is Mama?"

To stare into the face of a *fuath* is to know true fear. I glanced at Lucius, and he nodded. "Tell it, if you wish. The *fuath* have no reason to harm Domina."

Not that I would mind Nicnevin being taught a lesson, but I also didn't want to inadvertently send trouble her way. I have a sense of responsibility, even if the Seelie Queen doesn't. "She's at my sister's house, in Crail."

The *fuath* dissipated. "It could have left at any time," Anya said. "Why did it wait around?"

"Probably not for anything good," I replied. "Where's Bod?"

We all looked at Angus, who shrugged. "I thought he was with you."

"I am sure he will be back soon enough," Anya said. "If for no other reason than to test Sarmi's latest batch of ale. I'm going to have another look at what Da did to the throne room, and repair what I can."

"Good luck." I turned to Lucius. "Will you and the rest of the Ninth go to Nicnevin?"

"Is she safe?" Lucius asked. "Besieged in any way?"

"Not in the slightest. In fact, she is rather comfortable. She seems to be on a vacation, of sorts."

"Then we shall await her summons. We remain under your command, Dominus."

"Maybe I'll command you to call me Chris."

A woman's scream tore the air. Anya. Before I could call out to her or even move, she blinked to me, grabbed my hands, then teleported us to the throne room.

"What happened?" I looked around, and noticed we were standing on the edge of the very large, very deep hole Bod had punched into the floor. "Whoa."

"Christopher!" Anya pointed into the hole. "Look!"

I did. "I don't see anything but darkness."

"That's just it. Fionnlagh's gone!"

Chapter Twenty Seven
Anya

"How did this happen?" Christopher crouched down at the edge of the hole, peering into the darkness. "You froze him, and Rina put him in as deep as he could go."

"However it happened, happen it did." I linked my hands behind my neck and stared at the ceiling. It bore a second gaping hole, where Mum's prized possession—the chandelier she'd crafted with her own hands—had once hung.

"Why would Da have taken out his anger on the throne room's floor, of all places?" I wondered out loud. "I hardly remember him ever setting foot in here, yet when Mum didn't return home with him, he came to the exact spot where Fionnlagh was imprisoned..." I squeezed my eyes shut as I came to an awful, inevitable conclusion, one that made my heart ache.

"Christopher." He looked up at me, and the sight of his big summer blue eyes was the only thing helping me hold myself together. "Do you think..."

I cleared my throat, and began again. "Did Da free him on purpose?"

"No," Angus roared, as he rushed into the room. "No he did not! Da would never..." He swallowed, probably remembering a lifetime of Da's foolish, failed schemes. "He didn't, Anya. We'll prove he didn't."

"Doesn't Bod hate Fionnlagh as much as the rest of us do?" Christopher asked. "It's not like they were buddies. Why would he want to free a man he despises?"

"He has no love for the Seelie, that's for certain," I said. "But, there is the matter of Mum."

"You think Beira freed Fionnlagh?" Christopher asked.

"Not that," I said. "Da will do anything to gain Mum's favor. Each and every ill-thought plan of his had the sole purpose of increasing his standing in Mum's eyes."

"But, how would freeing Fionnlagh impress her?" Christopher asked. "He was already punished."

A shred of memory came to the surface of my mind.

"When we went in search of Crom, Da said that when he was in the ground he could hear the old ones whispering to him."

"Aye, that's true enough," Angus said. "Once you learn how to listen, you can catch all sorts of secrets from below."

"From below." As I stared into the icy chasm that had once held my worst enemy, I only saw Da. Maelgwyn and I had followed him around Ireland, where he'd known exactly where the well that led to Crom's lair was located. Once we were inside that lair Da had known exactly when to push us out of the way so we wouldn't be hurt by the cave's collapse. How could Da have known each and every one of Crom's actions before they happened, unless Crom had warned him ahead of time?

Unless Da and Crom were working together.

I also knew that by claiming Fionnlagh's court, Da would feel himself equal to Maelgwyn, and therefore once again worthy of Mum. All of Da's schemes, from the time I'd been born bearing another man's eyes until now, had been to bring Da up to the Seelie—or the Unseelie—level. He must have felt he'd won after beating Maelgwyn nearly to death, but then Fionnlagh rose to power. Da sought to unseat him, and got himself and my brothers stuck in a hole in the ground as punishment.

And now, Da thought he'd finally found a way to best Fionnlagh once and for all.

"Da has thrown in with Crom." A hot tear slipped down my cheek. I dashed it away. "I don't know how Fionnlagh fits in to the equation, but Da has played us all for fools."

"Maybe he means to reinstall Fionnlagh and become part of the Seelie Court," Christopher suggested, but Angus shook his head.

"Da's not much for sharing, and neither is Fionnlagh," Angus said. "If anything he's struck a deal with Crom and using is Fionnlagh as some sort of prize."

"We never did learn how Fionnlagh became so powerful," I said. "Perhaps Da figured it out, and wants the same for himself?"

"Anya! Angus!"

Mum appeared behind us. She was wearing her usual

deep red gown, but the hem of her dress was splashed with something darker. "What is it?" I asked.

"The *fuath* are swarming the Unseelie Court," she replied. "The shadow beasts are weaving in and out of the palace." She paused, and added, "They're searching for the children."

I turned to Angus. "Maelgwyn's children are my half siblings."

"That means they're our family, too. I'll round up the lads and get them over, quick as I can."

I nodded. "Christopher, the *aquila*."

He held out the standard. I grabbed it with both hands, and blinked.

A moment later Christopher, Lucius, and I were standing in the midst of Maelgwyn's apartments. It was pure chaos, with both servants and soldiers wielding all manner of weapons against the smoke beasts that were the *fuath*; some wielded swords, while others held torches aloft while they flung handfuls of salt into the shadows.

"Where are they coming from?" I demanded.

"Not sure," Maelgwyn replied. "My magic is mostly keeping them away from the children. What I don't understand is why they're attacking."

"I fear that's my fault," I said. "Christopher's legion captured a *fuath* spying at the palace. Later, I was telling Angus about the children, and it must have overheard us." I set my hand on Maelgwyn's forearm. "My brother swears he didn't take your crown, and I believe him."

Maelgwyn sighed. "Which means Bod most likely has my crown, and he has betrayed us yet again."

"I am so sorry," I began, but Maelgwyn made a cutting motion with his hand.

"His actions reflect only upon himself," Maelgwyn said. "Come, and let us see to this latest batch of demons. We'll figure out how to deal with Bod once the *fuath* are under control."

"My lord," Lucius said, stepping forward. "My men and I have some experience subduing this type of creature. By your leave, we would lend help."

Maelgwyn nodded. "Please, do so."

Lucius turned to Christopher, who held out the *aquila*

at arm's length. A moment later a dozen legionnaires appeared. While Christopher and the Ninth organized their attack on the *fuath*, Mum reappeared.

"Beira," Maelgwyn greeted, then he frowned. "Why are you all bloody?"

I looked closer at the stains on Mum's hem. They were indeed blood stains. Before I could ask her if she was hurt, Angus arrived.

"Anya, there's something you need to know," he began, then he turned to Maelgwyn. "Cheers on finding your bairns. I don't have your crown."

"Thank you, and so I've been told," Maelgwyn replied. "Is the reason behind your arrival also why Beira is covered in blood?"

"Doubtful," Angus replied. "Da's attacking the Seelie Court."

I felt as if the floor had gone out from under me. "Is Fionnlagh with him?"

"Fionnlagh is free?" Maelgwyn demanded.

"Aye, but he's not the one attacking the court with Da," Angus replied. "Crom is."

***

While the Ninth dealt with the *fuath*, the rest of us retreated to the apartment's inner chambers. Thankfully the children were already safe inside with their nursemaids, and once the rest of my brothers arrived they set about amusing the babes. Satisfied that the children of all ages were occupied, the rest of us gathered near the library.

"What does Da hope to accomplish with all this?" I asked. "He can't rule the Seelie Court. He's not fae."

"Neither was Fionnlagh, but that never stopped him," Maelgwyn said. "This is typical behavior for Bod, all of this sound and glory to create a show in hopes of returning to Beira's good graces."

Mum sniffed. "As if I ever wanted him to do any of those things. I've no love for the Seelie or its court. I could care less if the place burned to the ground."

"But, what if they do just that?" Christopher asked. "If Crom and Bod actually burn down the Seelie, what will that mean for the rest of Elphame?"

"He couldn't mean to destroy it," I began, but even as I said the words I knew I was wrong. "But then, why would he involve Crom, if not to have that beast destroy the Seelie for him?"

"What Bod wants—what he has always wanted, ever since the day Anya was born—was to go back to the way things were," Mum said. "Before the days of Seelie and Unseelie. He wants a Summer King and a Winter Queen to rule Elphame, as we once did."

"And I'm certain he does not want me to reprise my role as Summer King, which means after the Seelie fall—and fall they will—we will be the next target." Maelgwyn rubbed his eyes. "This is Bod's worst scheme yet. Angus, have you any idea what defenses remain at the Seelie Court?"

"They're pretty light. What with the Ninth here chasing after the *fuath*, only Conall and the rest of the Picts are left."

"Gods below, Crom will chew them up and spit them out." I closed my eyes and took a breath.

"Christopher, tell Lucius to split his men," I began. "Some will remain here in order to contain the *fuath*. The rest will come with us to defend the Seelie Court from Crom Cruach, and the Bodach."

"You're going into battle against them? Against him?"

"Yes. I am going into battle against Da, may all the gods help me."

Chapter Twenty Eight
Chris

Lucius left half of the legionnaires behind to deal with the *fuath* rampaging through the Unseelie Court. I worried that wouldn't be enough to protect the children, but Lucius claimed that since the *fuath* drew their power from water, without a convenient source they were unable to cause any true harm beyond their considerable annoyance. I made sure to remember that.

Anya and Maelgwyn teleported the three of us and the rest of the Ninth in one go, bringing us to a paved road that led straight to the Seelie Court. I worried that such a massive power output would weaken them, but Anya seemed fine. Maelgwyn had already been exhausted from watching his eleven kids, and after the jump he looked so weak I worried a strong wind could topple him. Just as I was about to ask Lucius to assign a few of the legionnaires to guard Maelgwyn, Angus and the brothers appeared. They'd left behind their human guises and appeared as true giants, all of them ten feet tall and wide as a truck.

"Da," they bellowed, beating their chests. "Da, Da, Da!"

"Are they with us, or not?" I asked Anya.

"We're here to get Da away from the Seelie, and Crom," Angus, who had come up behind me, declared. He was bigger than the rest of his brothers by half, and his voice was deep enough to shake a mountain down to its roots. "No good ever came from dealing with the Seelie, and Crom's a right mess."

Anya nodded. "You lot approach first, try to get Da's attention and then get him to safety. Christopher, have the Ninth back them up."

I extended the *aquila* at arm's length. As the standard lengthened from four inches to five feet, I swung it toward Lucius.

"You heard the lady," I said. "Back up those giants!"

Lucius grimaced at my command, then he shouted for the legionnaires to march. As the giants and then Romans filed past us, I asked Anya, "Shouldn't we be in front?"

"The boys should absolutely take the lead, at least for now," she replied. "If Da really has allied himself with Crom, the two of them would be almost unstoppable. The only person who could possibly convince Da to put this madness aside is Angus."

"Not you?"

She glanced at Maelgwyn. "Once, perhaps I could have gotten through to him. Now, I am not sure how he feels."

"He loves you, as he's always loved you," Maelgwyn said. "Never doubt that."

Anya squared her shoulders. "Hopefully he remembers that, today of all days."

We fell into step behind the Ninth, and I checked out the surroundings. I'd never been to the Seelie lands before, save for the time I'd spent enthralled to Nicnevin; not only had I not been in my right mind, I'd never once stepped outside of her den. I didn't even know if it was in the Seelie portion of Elphame, or somewhere else entirely. The less I remembered about that short, awful time, the better.

The portion of Elphame we were now traversing was so beautiful it looked as if it was right out of a storybook. Lush meadows rolled away from either side of the road we were stomping down, the road itself being paved with smooth gray stones. I made a mental note to ask Lucius if the Ninth had built one of the famed Roman roads in Elphame. The meadow on the left was filled with red poppies in full bloom, while the right side blazed with thousands of nodding daffodils. What I assumed was the Seelie Court sparkled in the distance, a crystal and white castle surrounded by Elphame's version of a city. Our magical destination coupled with the wide, paved road made me feel like I was off to see the wizard.

Based on Anya's description of Crom, I did not want to meet this wizard.

After we'd marched in silence for a few minutes, posts set on either side of the road came into view. They reminded me of the telephone poles that had lined the street I grew up on, which of course they weren't. As we got closer I realized they were gibbets, and that each one of them had a headless body hanging from its crossbeam.

"Who are…were these people?" I asked. "Guards?"

"Observe the clothing, the weaponry," Maelgwyn said. "It seems Crom has removed the Picts from the defenses."

"The fact that he strung up each man fully armed must mean Crom brought an army of his own," Anya said. "No one's looted the swords, or shields."

"It also means the court is now defenseless against Crom," I said.

"If Crom is there, few could have stood against him," Maelgwyn said. "Even our shared might may not mean victory."

I swallowed the lump in my throat, and hoped Maelgwyn was exaggerating.

We kept on, me trying and failing to not scrutinize every Pict we passed. I'd only ever met three of them, Conall and his two commanders, and I didn't recognize them on any of the gibbets. Then again, it's hard to recognize someone without their head.

Soon enough, Anya's brothers resumed shouting Bod's name. "They must have found Da," Anya said.

I held the *aquila* aloft, and the legionnaires parted to allow us to pass. Angus was standing in front of the Seelie's gates, hands on his hips while his brothers raged and shouted for their father to join them.

"Are they yelling for Bod to come out, or stay in?" I asked.

"Look," Maelgwyn said, nodding toward an area just beyond the gates. In the center of the courtyard stood a creature made of mud and nightmares, his skin cracked like a dry lakebed, with those cracks revealing a bloody red glow beneath the surface. I knew without asking the creature was Crom Cruach.

Next to Crom was the Bodach, spine straight and wearing Maelgwyn's missing antlered crown atop his head. Angus hadn't taken it after all. In front of Crom knelt Fionnlagh, the once proud Seelie King.

"What have they done to him," Anya whispered. Fionnlagh was covered in dark bruises and smears of blood, and the skin beneath his wounds was ashen. Bod's ruse of being distraught over Beira had all been for the sole purpose of beating a hole down to Fionnlagh's prison in the ice, and dragging him out. Based on Fionnlagh's pale skin and stiff posture wondered if he'd even fully thawed out.

"Da," Anya called. "What are you playing at?"

"I play at nothing," Bod bellowed. "The Seelie and their ilk have wronged us for centuries! I mean to have my retribution."

"Their ilk?" Maelgwyn repeated. "Do you mean to come after me next? And after me, who then? How many more will need to suffer to repair your wounded ego, Bod? Will you take your anger out on Anya, too? She is half Unseelie." When Bod spluttered, Maelgwyn added, "No matter who feels your vengeance, it won't make Beira love you again."

"Beira has always loved me," Bod shrieked. "You were just a dalliance! A mistake!"

Anya gasped, and Bod realized what he'd said. "I didn't mean—"

"Enough," Crom said, his voice rumbling across the countryside. "Your family and its squabbles bore me. The Seelie Court is mine. I care not what happens to the rest of Elphame, so long as you leave me be." He bared his cracked, muddy teeth. "I'll take more when I'm ready."

"Will you?" Anya asked. "You forget, we stand in your way."

Crom thrust his hand onto Fionnlagh's head, gripping his cranium like a vise. With a single grunt and turn he ripped the head from his shoulders.

"Watch closely, for this will be your fate." Crom held the Seelie King's head aloft, heedless of the gore than dripped down his arm, then he flung it at Anya.

Angus caught the head mid-flight, and threw it back. "You do not throw things at our sister," Angus growled, "and you do not get to claim this or any other part of Elphame. Crawl back into the sewer where you belong!"

Fionnlagh's head came to rest at Crom's feet. Bod snatched up the head as two of the *fuath* dragged Fionnlagh's body deeper into the courtyard.

"We never learned where the Seelie power originated," I said.

"Does that matter right now?" Anya asked.

"Since Bod is taking what's left of Fionnlagh out of the line of fire, I'd say it does." Before I could send some legionnaires after Fionnlagh's remains, Crom bellowed and struck the ground. A score of giants made of rock rose up from the dirt and formed a line between our forces and Crom.

"The twelve disciples," Maelgwyn said. "The very ones we spoke with at *Magh Slécht*."

"There are more than twelve," I said, then twenty more erupted from the ground. "Way more."

Maelgwyn nodded. "So there are."

"It seems Bod's had his own agenda all along." I glanced at Anya. "I'm sorry."

She rolled her shoulders. "We will deal with Crom, then I will deal with Da." Anya grabbed a charm off her bracelet and threw it into the air. It came apart, and by the time the pieces hit the ground they had transformed into another group of giants, none other than Long Meg and her daughters.

"These giants are beholden to me, Crom," Anya yelled. "Meg, Bod's not on our side!"

Meg cracked her knuckles, a horrible, sickening sound. "What of Angus and the boys?"

"We're with you, Meg." Angus took his place next to Meg. "Just like old times, eh?"

She grinned. "Just like."

Meg bellowed a war cry and launched herself at the disciples. Angus and the rest followed, chunks of stone flying as the giants beat the disciples apart with their bare hands. When they weren't making any headway, I realized something.

"The disciples are regenerating!" Even as the giants beat apart their bodies and limbs, the disciples drew stone and earth up from the ground they were standing on. The giants would beat their hands to pulp before the disciples went down. "We need to find another way!"

"The *fuath*," Anya shrieked. The black smoke monsters coalesced around the giants until we couldn't see them. Lucius gave the order to contain. The legionnaires surrounded the *fuath* and confined them, much like how they'd surrounded Bod when he'd beat open the floor at the

Winter Palace.

But, there were too many *fuath* for the Ninth to handle, and they kept escaping. We needed the legion to back up the giants, but they couldn't do that if they were busy chasing down smoke demons. In the midst of wondering what the hell I should do, I felt a triangular piece of metal in my pocket.

The absinthe spoon.

I held the spoon aloft, and shouted, "*Elding!*"

Lightning struck the spoon. Amazingly, it didn't kill me.

Even more amazing, the lightning branched out and struck down the *fuath*, obliterating each and every one of them.

"What is that?" Anya demanded. "How did you do that?"

"It's a spoon," I said, staring at the item in my hand. It had been struck by lightning, yet it wasn't even warm. "Remy gave it to me, at the bar."

"Did he?" Anya said. "Did he also tell you to say *elding*?"

"I don't even know what that means."

"It's the Norse word for lightning," Maelgwyn said. "A bit of your mother coming through, eh?"

"I guess so." I looked toward Lucius. He was rallying the legionnaires to strike at the disciples. I raised the *aquila*, and Lucius held his sword aloft in response.

"We'll rout the stone creatures," Lucius shouted. "Go, handle the beast!"

Anya tied back her long yellow hair. "I will beat this monster back into the mud he spawned from."

I rolled my shoulders. "Let's do it."

Chapter Twenty Nine
Anya

I watched as the disciples struggled against the Ninth, but gained no purchase. The legionnaires claimed to have much experience against monsters, and they clearly held the upper hand. While the some of the disciples floundered against the legion, the rest battled the giants, both my brothers and Long Meg's crew. Every single one of those giants was part of my family. Even though I wasn't a giant's daughter, I was a sister to giants. A cousin.

I won't let one man destroy my family, no matter how much I love him. But before I stopped him, I needed to fully understand his intentions.

I searched the battle until I found Da, who was uncharacteristically avoiding the fray. Odd for a bruiser like him, who'd rather knock heads than do almost anything else. He was standing over Fionnlagh's body, tearing through his clothing as if searching for something. What could be so important about Fionnlagh's remains? I recalled what Christopher said, that we still didn't know where the Seelie power originated.

Da met my gaze across the battle. He knew the answer, I was certain of it.

I blinked to Da, and recoiled at the gore soaking his clothes and the ground around his feet. He'd split Fionnlagh's corpse from neck to groin and splayed him open, baring organs and bone to the chill air.

"When did you begin desecrating the dead?" I demanded.

"I am not desecrating anything," Da snapped. "I thought Fionnlagh might have hid the key to his power inside his body."

I looked down at the bloody, butchered mess that had been the Seelie King. "Is that why you tried to pummel your way down to him in the ice, to look for an object he might not even have? Why not just ask someone for help instead of sneaking about?"

"I did ask for help," Da said. "I went to Beira, and she

refused."

"Mum refused you, so you went to Crom?" A disciple's stone arms shattered near our feet, the arrow-like shrapnel narrowly missing Da and me. I grabbed Da's arm and pulled him farther away from the fighting. "Did it ever occur to you that Mum's no longer as strong as she once was? She likely cannot assist you the way you needed her to."

"Beira's not lost one iota of strength," Da said. "She may have you and that Udane fooled, but she has never fooled me." Da pulled me closer, his black eyes boring into mine. "Never, not for one blessed moment."

Mum is still powerful? I thought about all the things she could still do, and all of the magic I'd seen her work with my own two eyes. There was also all the magic she'd worked without me being present, such as repairing not only the entirety of the Winter Palace on her own, but rebuilding the enchanted paths that led from the palace into Elphame and the mortal realm.

"If she's so powerful why am I the Queen of Winter?" I demanded. Another rocky piece of disciple shattered next to us. As much as I needed these answers, they could wait. "Never mind her. You think you found where Fionnlagh obtained his power?"

"Remember when I took you to Iona?" he asked, and I nodded. "When the world began, it started out as a single stone. Eventually an ash tree grew upon the stone, and that was the beginning. The stone and tree both still exist, and it's said that they remain on Iona."

I glanced toward the battle. Lucius was rallying his men yet again, and the giants were battered and bloody. We needed to end this altercation before more ended up like Fionnlagh. "Go on," I urged.

"After I rightly trounced Udane, his family scattered to the four winds," Da continued. "His only living brother, Fionn, retreated to Iona. Less that a turn of the seasons passed before Fionnlagh emerged, fair to glowing with the power he'd obtained." Da leaned closer, and said, "No one understood how he'd transformed himself from a powerless sot to a mighty warrior in so short a time, but I did. I remembered. I believe when Fionn was on Iona he found either the stone, or maybe a bit of the sacred ash tree, and swallowed it so no one else could duplicate his efforts. There's no other way to explain how he became so strong in such a short time."

"And how is Crom involved?"

"I heard Crom whisper in the earth, wondering where in the nine realms the Seelie might had originated. I whispered back that the power is in the *dahm coroin*, and Crom agreed to help me claim the Seelie lands in exchange for the crown. I once thought Fionnlagh had put a portion of the stone or tree in the crown, but it seems I was wrong. Not the first time that happened." Da regarded Fionnlagh's mutilated body and frowned. "It wasn't inside him, either. I've no idea where he stashed it."

I drew back. "It won't be long before Crom knows the truth. He'll kill you for this!"

Da shrugged. "Many have tried to end me, and they all failed. Crom's welcome to have a go." Da looked down at the body, and tried to shake the blood from his hands. "There's neither stone nor tree in this fool's corpse. Let's handle Crom and get our people out of here."

I nodded, not in the least bit comfortable with Da's frank assessment of things, but understanding that we must deal with one catastrophe at a time. However, now that Fionnlagh was well and truly gone the Seelie Court was more vulnerable than it had ever been.

"After Crom, what of the Seelie?" I asked. "You can't mean to reinstall Nicnevin."

"All the realms are better off without that scheming viper in play," Da replied. "You could lead the court."

"Me? But I'm winter!"

Da faced me, and in the depth of his dark eyes I saw the sweet man he'd been, the caring father who would move mountains just to make me smile. He'd done so many, many times. "Is that all you are?"

A massive piece of the courtyard's wall crashed in front of us. Da pushed me behind him, and turned toward the beast who had thrown it. Crom.

"You do not harm my lass," Da bellowed, then he launched himself at Crom. The monster drew upon the earth he stood on and increased his size, but Da was a giant. When he wished it he was taller than the highest mountains on earth or Elphame. Crom could have grown until his head brushed the stars, and Da would have matched him inch for inch, and blow for blow.

Only, Da didn't do that. He remained man sized and attached himself to Crom's shoulder, then started tearing Crom apart with his bare hands. Chunks of the beast—stone and mud and stinking, green-tinged flesh—fell haphazardly around us, striking friend and foe equally.

I surveyed the battle. Christopher led the Ninth Legion at Lucius's side, his standard aloft and proud. They harried and harassed the disciples, while my brothers and Meg beat as many of the stone men down to pebbles as they could get their hands on.

"Angus," I shouted. My eldest, sneakiest brother was at my side in an instant. "Get them to lay off the disciples. It's Crom we need to rout."

"We can't rout him," Angus said. "Crom's a true earth god. His power comes from the dirt we're standing on."

Frost grew in my hands. "Then I will separate him from the dirt."

I threw the frost at Crom's feet. A layer of ice built up between him and the ground, limiting his ability to regenerate. I hoped.

"Get Maelgwyn," I said. "And a few of our brothers."

"On it," Angus said. The Unseelie King was the first to arrive.

"Separating Crom from his power source," Maelgwyn observed. "My daughter is brilliant."

"We need to get Da off his back, literally," I added, since Da was still ripping Crom apart, one handful at a time, "and send Crom back to the crypt where we found him."

"He will likely regenerate there."

"Yes, but he will be there and not here. Hopefully it will take him a while to recover, and by the time he reemerges we'll better understand how to resist him."

Maelgwyn nodded. "What do you need me to do?"

"When Da breaks contact with Crom we will send him back to his lair."

Angus arrived with three of our brothers. "You lot, crawl up Crom's back and knock Da loose," I said. "When Da complains tell him I said it's for his own good."

My brothers attacked Crom like a gang of thugs, going in for cheap shots and sucker punches and scurrying off before the much-larger beast could retaliate. They weren't able to crawl up his body as I'd ordered, but while they harried our foe I grew the layer of ice beneath his feet, thickening it layer by layer until Crom had no way to pull strength from Elphame's soil.

"He's shrinking," Maelgwyn said, then he yelled, "Bod, let go!"

For the first and possibly only time in his life, Da did as he was told. As soon as he hit the ground Maelgwyn and I linked hands, created a portal, and pushed Crom out of Elphame and back to that dark cave beneath the holy well and its graveyard. I hoped he would stay down there for a long, long time.

"That's my lass," Da bellowed. "A finer Queen of Winter there never was! Don't tell your mother," he added.

"I won't," I promised. "Get over here, you big lug!"

Da's face split into a grin, and I felt at ease for the first time in days. We'd overcome the beast, and all was well. Da took a step toward us, slipped on the ice and landed on his backside.

"Did you have to make the ice so slippery?" he demanded, laughing. Before I could respond the ground opened up behind the layer of ice and Crom's head, now big as a hillock, emerged.

In one bite, Crom swallowed Da whole, then the ground swallowed them both.

"Da!"

I ran to where he'd last been, slipping on my own ice and falling hard. I shoved my hands into the mud where Crom had dragged away my Da. "Da!"

"Blink to him," Angus said, dropping to his knees beside me.

Maelgwyn grabbed my hands. "We go now!"

"The cave," I said, and we blinked.

A moment later we were back.

"It's warded against us," Maelgwyn said.

"Wards have never stopped you," Angus said. "You can blink to anyone living, anywhere!"

I thought of Da, held the image of him, the feeling of

him, in the forefront of my mind.

I closed my eyes.

I opened them. I hadn't moved.

"Anya," Angus shrieked. "Go get him!"

"I... can't."

Angus's face fell, then his whole body collapsed against the mud. Christopher ran to me; he was streaked in mud and ash, but appeared unhurt.

"Anya, what happened?" He dropped the *aquila* and held my face with his hands. "The disciples disappeared right after Crom." He glanced around. "Did we win?"

"Crom... Crom took Da," I replied. "I can't blink to him."

"What does that mean?" Christopher asked.

"It means he's not alive," Maelgwyn said as he set his hand on my shoulder. "Anya, I am so sorry."

My Da was gone.

I clenched my fist, frost spiraling outward.

Crom would pay for this.

Chapter Thirty
Chris

We tried everything we knew, but no one could locate the Bodach, or Crom Cruach. We feared the former was dead. As for the latter, none of us were foolish enough to hope he was gone. Since Crom was a true chthonic deity, I wondered if he could die, or if he was one of the few truly immortal beings.

Anya, Maelgwyn, and Rina had all tried to portal to Bod, and none of them had been successful. Even Beira had tried her hand at locating them, though instead of teleporting she'd sat crouched over the solarium's globe for hours, gesturing wildly and muttering incantations. I didn't know if she was searching for Bod or Crom, and didn't ask.

Two days after Bod's disappearance I ended up in Glasgow, while Anya remained in the Winter Palace. We'd decided that the best course of action was to divide and conquer, so while she continued to search Elphame I told Rina and Rob the awful truth: we needed Nicnevin to reclaim the Seelie throne and rebuild the court, the sooner the better.

"What it all comes down to is that Bod thought Fionnlagh had some sort of object that gave him his strength," I explained. "He told Anya a story about a stone and a tree on Iona."

Rob grunted. "He was referrin' to the sacred ash?"

I spread my palms. "Maybe. Do you know where that is?"

"Is it Yggsdrasil?" Rina asked. When Rob and I both stared at her, she continued, "You know, the world tree? The one Chris and I visited?"

"I guess it could be," I muttered. Trust Rina to see the obvious while we all ran around like chickens with our heads cut off. "Regardless—"

"That's what he always says when I'm right and he's irritated," Rina interjected.

"If Crom found whatever Fionnlagh supposedly had, the incredibly powerful bad deity could become even more powerful," I finished. "And possibly more bad."

Rina rolled her eyes. "Nice grammar, Mr. Professor."

Rob grunted again. "Ye say Nicnevin is holed up in our home, relaxin' in our bed?"

"Last we knew, yes."

"Verra well." He stood and summoned his sword. "I shall do me best to persuade her, and after she is out o' the cottage I will burn that cursed place to the ground."

"Probably for the best," I said. Gifts from the Seelie always bit you in the ass, sooner or later. Since the cottage was a gift from Fionnlagh himself it probably had an extra layer of evil built into it.

"Are we quite certain the king is dead?" Rob asked.

"I watched as Crom manually decapitated Fionnlagh."

"Still. Can no' be too sure with that one." Rob extended his hand to Rina. "Are ye coming with me, love?"

"I feel a lot better," she replied, referring to her recent sickness. "Might as well go talk to Nicnevin and feel like crap again. Chris, can you stay and watch Faith?"

"Avoid confronting Nicnevin while hanging out with my favorite girl? Sounds like heaven. Be careful."

"We will." Rina took Rob's hand, and they portaled out.

I flopped back onto the couch. Since Faith was sleeping and Colleen was out the flat was quiet, which was good. I didn't know if I could handle any extra noise. The thoughts rushing through my head were more than enough.

Across the room, something sparkled. I got up to investigate, and learned that the shining object was the bottle of well water the Norns had given to Rina. The light had caught the stones that were affixed to the bottle's neck just right, and had turned it into a mini light show.

I held the bottle in my hand, testing its weight. It seemed like Rina and I had gone to the Norns for help such a long time ago, even though it hadn't been more than a few days. I remembered the central Norn explaining which stones corresponded to the past, present, and future, and how to invoke a vision from each.

Visions brought on by enchanted water were about the only way we hadn't tried to locate Bod.

Why hadn't I thought of this before? Oh, because I'd never before been tasked with locating a missing giant, or had a bottle of enchanted well water on my hands. Growing up in New Jersey hadn't prepared me in the slightest for where my life had taken me.

I grabbed my phone to call Rina and ask her to send me to the Winter Palace so I could get my own bottle of magic water... and didn't call. Not only was I supposed to be watching Faith, I was already holding a bottle of the same well water in my hand.

I decided to take a sip. I didn't think I would drink it all, and even if I did I had a backup supply at home. If I did consume all of Rina's water I would just give her the other bottle.

So. Past or future? Since we needed to know what Crom had done with Bod, I pressed my thumb over the blue stone, closed my eyes, and drank.

Colors swirled in my mind's eye, then the coalesced into a room. A room I had been in before, I was sure of it. A few more details settled into place, and I realized where I was: the room I had grown up in. I checked the calendar on the wall, and realized this moment was from almost thirty years ago, long before Rina had been born. I heard shouting coming from the first floor, and went to investigate.

I followed the voices toward Mom's studio. At some point I realized the voices belonged to my parents, which was weird. I couldn't remember either one of them ever raising their voice, and I'd never once seen them argue, much less shout at each other. I made it to the studio's doorway, and froze.

Mom was sitting on the floor, hunched over and bawling her eyes out. Dad was pacing on the far side of the room, clearly agitated. He spun around on Mom and she shrank back, raising her arms to protect her head.

Had he hit her?

I ran to Mom, but in the vision I was little more than a toddler and no defense against a grown man. Mom saw me and snatched me into her arms, holding me so tightly I could hardly breathe.

"I won't let it happen to you," she said, rocking back and forth as her tears wet my cheeks, my hair. "I won't let her kill you."

I snapped back into my present self, shaking and

confused. I glared at the bottle in my hand, and wondered how accurate these visions were. I had no memory of my father raising a hand toward Mom or anyone, but why had she been so upset? Why had she recoiled at his approach? What the hell had gone on in my house back then?

As much as I liked to remember my parents, and especially my father, in the best light possible, there was no way I could have known everything that went on when I was so young. I also remembered Mom's frequent panic attacks, and wondered if that was why I'd stumbled in on. Now I knew her panic attacks were part of her foresight, and that she'd seen a future where a woman kills me.

That must have been the moment I walked in on. But, why that moment? How was anyone helped by me seeing that? One thing was certain, that vision wouldn't help anyone now. Perhaps I should try the water again, but not to see the past.

Seeing the past had only led to more confusion. Let's find out what the future holds.

I pressed my thumb over the purple stone, uncorked the bottle again, and took a sip. While I'd immediately been thrown into visons of the past, this time nothing happened. Wondering if I needed to wait for a time in between sips of the water, I set the bottle back in its spot on the bookcase, and reclaimed my place on the couch. I'd no sooner settled onto the cushions when the vision took hold of me.

A woman was standing with her back to me. She had long brown hair, which meant it wasn't Mom or Anya. I felt future me pleading with the woman, and her reticence to do what I was asking. Without turning she extended her arm toward me, and I fell through a portal. No, not a portal; unlike a portal the darkness thickened around me until I couldn't hear or feel anything else, and I could barely see At the last moment, the woman turned and I saw her face.

Rina.

I finally understood Mom's prophecy. My sister is the one that kills me.

My sister sends me to the underworld, and I beg her to do it.

My phone rang in my pocket, nearly giving me a heart attack. I checked the screen; Rina was calling. She was a born texter, and never called unless it was something truly important. My mind still reeling from the vision, I accepted the call.

"Yeah?"

"Chris! Nicnevin's been murdered!"

<<<end>>>

Anya and Chris's story continues in ***Elphame's Queen***, available here. Keep reading for a preview!

Want to keep up on my latest releases and be the first to hear about new stories? Join my mailing list here.

Glossary

Angus – the eldest of Beira and the Bodach's sons.

Anya Darach – Queen of Winter. Daughter of Cailleach Bheur/Beira and Maelgwyn, the Unseelie King.

Beinn na Caillich – a hill west of Broadford on the Isle of Skye. Its name is translated into English as Hill of the Old Woman.

Bodach [pɔt̪əx] – a trickster or bogeyman figure in Gaelic folklore and mythology. Husband of Beira.

Cailleach Bheur/Beira [kall-EE burr/BEE-ruh] – Celtic weather deity. Personification of winter. Mother of Anya.

Carson University – an institution of higher learning in Manhattan that studies sciences, liberal arts, and theoretical magic. Both Christopher and Karina Stewart have attended and taught there.

Christopher Stewart – an Elizabethan scholar and bestselling author, and older brother of Karina.

Colleen Worley – administrative assistant for the earth sciences division at Carson University. Karina Stewart's best friend.

Cornucopia]kôrn(y)ə'kōpēə] – a symbol of plenty consisting of a goat's horn overflowing with flowers, fruit, and corn.

Crom Cruach – a pagan god of pre-Christian Ireland.

Demeter [dɪ-MEE-tər] — in Greek mythology, Demeter is the goddess of the harvest and agriculture, who presided over grains and the fertility of the earth.

Dob's Linn – a site near Moffat, Scotland. It is the location of the Global Boundary Stratotype Section and Point which marks the boundary between the Ordovician and Silurian periods.

Doon Hill – a hill near Aberfoyle, Scotland that some believe to be a gateway to Elphame. Some believe that Robert Kirk is still imprisoned in the Minister's Pine at the crest of the hill.

Elphame [el-faym] – Fairlyand; abode of the fairies.

Fairy ointment – an ointment applied to a mortal's eyes that allows them to see fairies in their true form.

Faith Elizabeth Stewart Kirk – daughter of Karina Stwart and Robert Kirk.

Fionnlagh [fin-lay] – the Seelie King.

Fuath [fuə] – malevolent water spirits. Their name literally means "hate" in Gaelic.

Gallowglass [gal-oh-glas, -glahs] – a heavily armed mercenary soldier. In Elphame, the gallowglass is the Seelie Queen's personal assassin.

Geas [geSH] – (in Irish folklore) an obligation or prohibition magically imposed on a person.

Glamour [glam-er] – an illusion that conceals flaws or distractions.

Good People – a euphemism for fairies.

Hades [hay-DEEZ] — the ancient Greek chthonic god of the underworld, which eventually took his name.

Karina Stewart – an American geology studying at Carson University. Younger sister of Chris, mother of Faith.

The only living walker in the mortal realm.

Ken [ken] – knowledge, understanding, or cognizance.

Kirk [kurk] – a church.

Long Meg and her Daughters - a Bronze Age stone circle near Penrith in Cumbria, North West England.

Maelgwyn – the Unseelie King. Formerly Udane, the Summer King.

Magh Slécht – a historic plain in Ireland.

Nemeton [neh-*meh*-ton] – places sacred to the old Celtic religion, primarily trees but also including temples and shrines.

Nicnevin [nik-*neh*-van] – the Seelie Queen.

Ninth Legion - a legion of the Imperial Roman army that existed from the 1st century BC until at least AD 120.

Norns - creatures in Norse mythology responsible for tending Yggsdrasil and the fate of humans.

Persephone [per-SEH-fə-nee] — goddess of the underworld, springtime, flowers, and vegetation.

Picts - a group of Celtic-speaking peoples who lived in Scotland until about the tenth century AD.

Robert Kirk – currently the gallowglass. Before that, he was a minister, Gaelic scholar, and folklorist, best known for writing *The Secret Commonwealth of Elves, Fauns, and Fairies.* Father of Faith.

Sarmi – caretaker of the Winter Palace.

Seelie Court – the home of the light or good fairies.

Tantallon Castle – a semi-ruined mid-14th-century fortress in East Lothian, Scotland. It sits atop a promontory opposite the Bass Rock, looking out onto the Firth of Forth.

Teind [tend] – a tribute due to be paid by the fairies to the devil every seven years.

Transmutation Regulations – regulation passed during the Industrial Revolution limiting the practice of alchemy in the US.

Udane – the Summer King. He was dethroned by the Bodach.

Urdarbrunnr [urd-AR-brunner] - the well lies beneath the world tree, Yggdrasil.

Volva/volv – an individual said to have the ability to foretell future occurrences.

Wight [wahyt] – a small, winged fairy commonly found in gardens.

Yggsdrasil - an immense ash tree that is center to the cosmos.

WINTER'S QUEEN TRILOGY BOOK THREE

ELPHAME'S QUEEN

JENNIFER ALLIS PROVOST

Chapter One
Anya

"I need to show you something."

I looked up from my globe and saw Karina standing in my solarium. Karina, my lover's sister. Karina, the only living walker. Karina, the only one I knew of who'd bested the Seelie, a host of Greek gods, and, most impressively, my mother. I wondered if someday she'd best me.

"All right." I stood, and took her hand. Then we blinked to a murder scene.

"Gods below, what happened here?" We were standing in a human bedroom, and the occupant of the bed had gone to their final slumber. The bed, once hung with pale silk curtains, was soaked in the same red that splashed the walls and stained the carpet. Whoever was in that bed had not gone quietly.

"Where are we? Who is that?" I stepped back from the bed and saw Robert Kirk, the gallowglass himself, leaning on the doorframe. "Did you kill this person?"

"No," he replied. "As for where we are, we're in Crail. This is my home."

Memories of the last time I'd been in Crail flooded my mind. Christopher and I had been searching for clues about a weather anomaly, and we'd found—

"Nicnevin," I gasped, clapping my hand over my mouth. Nicnevin had been in hiding in Robert and Karina's home, and had been the source of the weather anomaly. Had been.

This was Robert and Karina's bedroom. This was the last place I'd seen Nicnevin alive.

"What happened?" I reached toward the body, toward Nicnevin's rosy gold hair that I'd always admired, but had never admitted to anyone. No longer was her hair the rich hue of sunsets and ripe peaches. Now it was the red of an abattoir.

"We don't know," Karina replied. "Robert and I came here to tell Nicnevin to get out of hiding and go back to the Seelie Court, and we found her." Karina paused, her throat working. "I called Chris, and he said you needed to know as soon as possible. And here we are."

"Yes. Here we are." I paced around the perimeter of

the bed and back again. She was dead from all angles. "Christopher and I saw her—spoke to her—only three days ago."

"And that was the last time ye set eyes on her?" Robert asked.

"Are you accusing me of murder?" I demanded.

"Do not put words in me mouth," he snapped. "I've a dead woman in me bed. It's my right to be askin' questions."

I glared at Robert, insolent man that he was, but he was correct. "I won't insult your intelligence by asking who wanted Nicnevin dead," I began; that list was long, indeed. "Who could have accomplished this?"

"Any number of beings," Robert replied. "Accordin' to Christopher, he told one o' the fuath that Nicnevin was holed up here. Those beasts whisper amongst themselves, and anyone willin' to take the time can learn to listen."

Da heard the old ones whispering from beneath. "Do we think it was Crom? He is the most likely suspect."

"Is he?" Robert countered. "From what I was told o' the battle, he may already think he won."

An image of my Da being consumed whole by Crom's massive head flitted behind my eyes. "Well and so, Crom is my main focus now, as is finding my Da."

Karina touched my hand. "Have you learned anything?"

"No," I whispered, ignoring the pressure behind my eyes, the pain like glass in my throat. "Neither I nor Mum can find a single trace of him."

Karina's gentle touch became her fingers grasping mine. "We'll find him. I promise."

And what if there's nothing to find but a body? I'd asked Mum the very same question. Her response was that if nothing more remained of the Bodach than his corpse, she would drag it to the center of Elphame and light the biggest funeral pyre anyone in any world has ever seen.

I didn't want a pyre. I wanted my Da.

"We will," I said. Based on Karina's frown, I didn't sound all that convincing. "We will," I repeated. "As for Nicnevin, there's nothing more we can do for her, except find out who did this."

"Aye," Robert said. "Can ye freeze her for a time?"

"You want to preserve the body?"

"Only for a day or so. We do need to get the workmen paid and let go, and I do no' want them askin' questions I'd rather no' answer. There is also the matter o' relocatin' the wights."

"I will bring them to the Unseelie Court," I said. Before Maelgwyn ruled the Unseelie he was the Summer King, and the wights had tended his gardens. I imagine them returning to him would be a homecoming for all involved.

Maelgwyn was also my true father, a fact that until recently had been hidden from all but my mother and my da.

I shook my head, then I spied a cradle in the corner of the room. "Where is Faith?"

"In Glasgow," Karina replied. "Chris is watching her."

"We should go to them." I raised my hand, and a layer of ice grew around Nicnevin's corpse. "Whoever did this to Nicnevin is not one to be trifled with. I don't want to leave our vulnerable unprotected." The body dealt with, I glanced around the room. "Is there anything from here I can help you bring to the flat?"

"I'll no' have items tainted by death near me bairn, no' if I can help it," Robert said, then he wrapped his arm around Karina's shoulders. "As far as I'm concerned it can all burn."

I tightened my grip on Karina's hand and made ready to blink to Glasgow. "Then burn it shall."

<<◇>>

Continue the story here.

Is this your first time meeting Chris and Anya? Turn the page for a preview of Gallowglass, the book that started it all.

JENNIFER ALLIS PROVOST

GALLOWGLASS SERIES: BOOK I

GALLOWGLASS

Chapter One
Karina

"I can't believe you're dragging me to another old rock."

I glared at Chris. Why had I brought him along, again? "It's not an old rock. It's a church. And since we're in Scotland, it's called a kirk." I would have said more, but I needed to concentrate. This driving on the wrong side of the road business was for the birds.

"Kirk," Chris repeated, rolling the word around in his mouth. "And, what are 'kirks' made of?"

I scowled at him, almost veered into a ditch, and jerked the car back onto the road. I'd grown up in northern New Jersey just over the water from New York, the Mecca of public transportation. I'd done more driving during these last two weeks in the United Kingdom than I'd done in my entire life. "Chris, do you have to be such a jerk all the time?"

"Rina, do you have to be such a bad driver?"

"Stop drinking all that complimentary Scotch, and you can do the driving."

"When in Rome."

He had a point. Nearly every place we'd visited in Scotland had either presented us with a few samples of the local whisky, or boasted a friendly proprietor with a flask at the ready. Add these samples to all the pubs we'd visited, and the many pints we'd downed, and my liver was starting to ache.

"Besides," Chris continued, "if I was driving, you wouldn't get to drag me to every known fairy sighting in the UK."

"You liked Stirling," I reminded him. During our tour of Stirling Castle's grounds Chris had made full use of that Shakespeare degree by randomly quoting the Scottish play, despite the guide's many reminders that *MacBeth* was a work of fiction. After the third time he shouted "Out, out, damn spot!" I was worried she'd deck him.

As for me, I was working toward a Ph D in geology at Carson, just a few buildings over from where Chris lectured about dead Elizabethans. Since I was technically in the UK to research my thesis I was mostly interested in Stirling Castle's location on the Stirling Sill, a quartz-rich expanse of bedrock that ranged throughout the countryside. Though the ghost stories were cool, too.

I'd always been interested in supernatural occurrences, which was the main reason I'd applied to Carson. It was one of the few North American schools that studied mystical subjects as well as the mundane. I'd ended up majoring in geology and minoring in alchemy; both subjects concerned the earth and how its elements worked together, though it was hard to do any real alchemical work in the states since the transmutation regulations had gone into effect over one hundred years ago. Back when railroad barons had still been a thing, some politician had gotten the idea that alchemists would go around transmuting all the base metals into gold, thus using up all the iron and subsequently bankrupt the industry. My advisor speculated that the politician had tried transmuting metals into gold himself and failed, and had a case of sour grapes. All I knew was that if it really was that easy to create gold from things like iron filings and aluminum foil, instant noodles wouldn't be my go-to dinner.

When the packet about the research grant had arrived in my mail slot, I knew it was the perfect opportunity learn more about my minor, and fine-tune my thesis. That, and putting an ocean between mine and Chris's problems was about the only thing keeping us sane.

My brother didn't believe in anything that he couldn't see and touch and smell, never mind that his department chair was a scholar so old he'd studied under Aristotle. That was the rumor, anyway. I'd always found it ironic that the least magical guy in the world taught at the most renowned magical university on the east coast. Chris was of the opinion that all magic had died out centuries ago, and magical creatures along with it. Most shared that viewpoint, even those enrolled in alchemy and other metaphysical courses, which is why I kept most of my ideas to myself. I didn't need some nonbeliever casting a critical eye on my work. My work just needed to get done.

"At least real people lived at Stirling," Chris said as we pulled into the car park. "What sort of imaginary creatures inhabit this kirk?"

"No imaginary creatures." Not letting yourself be baited is a crucial survival tool for younger sisters. I pulled up the emergency brake, pocketed the keys, and jammed my water bottle into my daypack. "There was a reverend here in the seventeenth century called Robert Kirk, and he had dealings with the local fairies and elves. I guess this place is something of a *nemeton*," I said as we got out of the rental.

"*Nemeton?*"

"You know, a magical place alongside a church," I explained. Chris gave me a look over the roof of the car, raising a single eyebrow. That had always irritated me, since my own eyebrows refused to act independently. Chris must have some mutant extra muscle on one side of his head. My brother is a freak. "Anyway, the reverend wrote a book telling everyone their secrets, and it angered the fairies so they imprisoned him in the tree at the top of Doon Hill, just past the kirk. They still call the tree the Minister's Pine."

"Anyone can write a book," Chris grumbled. "I've written several."

I bit my lip; Chris had just enough midgrade liquor in him to be itching for a fight, and anything I said about his crumbling literary career, good or bad, would add fuel to the fire. After a few moments of silence, I said, "The walk starts with that bridge."

Chris and I started walking toward the stone bridge that spanned the River Forth. "Did you get a pamphlet about this place?" he asked.

"Yeah." I rooted around in my daypack, and pulled out the wad of information supplied by Spiritual Sights of the UK, the tour group my research grant had booked on my behalf. I was glad that I'd opted for the cheaper, self-guided package, and hadn't saddled a hapless tour guide with my brother's foul attitude for the duration of the tour. That sort of torment was reserved for family.

I pulled out the slightly rumpled pamphlet and handed it over. Chris opened it, scanning the paragraphs with an English professor's ease. "The reverend wasn't taken by fairies," Chris said. "He had a stroke while he was walking around the hill."

"You know where the term stroke comes from?" Without waiting for his smart-ass reply, I continued, "It was thought that a fairy stroked your cheek. That's why only one side was paralyzed."

"Thank God for modern medicine," Chris muttered. We reached the remains of the kirk, and headed toward the cemetery. Chris might think I was a loon, but he readily agreed that gravestones were cool. After we poked around for a few minutes, he announced, "Look, your man's buried right here. Case closed."

I walked over to where Chris was standing, and gazed at the minister's grave. It was a headstone coupled with a long rectangular slab that was set flush to the earth. The slab was engraved with a shield, and the inscription, *Hic Pultis Ill Evangeli Promulgator Accuratus et Linguae Hiberniae Lumen M. Robertus Kirk Aberfoile Pastor Obiit 14 Maii 1692 Aetat 48.*

"Can't these people write in English," I muttered. "What is that, French?"

"Latin. It says, 'Here lies the accurate promulgator of the Gospels and light...no, *luminary* of the Hibernian tongue, Robert Kirk, pastor of Aberfoyle, who died May 14, 1692, aged 48'," Chris translated. I guess it hadn't been a waste of his time to take eight years of Latin. "Do you know why they called him a 'luminary'?"

"He was some sort of language expert, and translated things like the Bible and the Book of Psalms from Latin into Gaelic," I replied. "I think he was the first to do so." Chris grunted; while he would never lower himself to read a book about fairies, he maintained healthy respect for his fellow scholars. After a suitable moment of silence, I suggested we climb the fairy hill.

"We're here, so we might as well," I said when Chris whined. "Besides, the walk will burn off some of that booze."

Chris grumbled as he followed me toward the hill. After a far longer and more difficult climb than I'd anticipated we stood at the top of Doon Hill, gazing at the Minister's Pine.

The tree was, in a word, magnificent. It was old and stately, like a Scottish version of Yggsdrasil, and wishes, scrawled on white or colored bits of cloth, were tied to the branches and tacked to the wide trunk. More offerings were nestled around the gnarly old roots, and shiny coins and colorful bottle caps were jammed into the bark.

"Some walk," I grumbled, digging in my pack for my water bottle. The water was warm, but it was better than nothing.

"So, they say the preacher's still in here, huh?" Chris leaned close to the trunk, and picked at a coin. "Why hasn't anyone tried to chop it down, set the poor guy loose?"

I shrugged. "To keep from angering the fairies?"

Chris barked a laugh. "Yeah. Or, they don't want to kill this golden goose of a tourist trap." I glanced around at the packed dirt path and discarded crisp packets; Disneyland, this was not. "This stuff is all so lame, Rina. Honestly, I don't know what you see in all these bedtime stories."

I fingered one of the cloth prayers, scrawled in a child's hand on a red strip of cloth; it read 'save my Mum'. "They remind us of where we came from, where we're going. They're comforting."

Another barking laugh. I suspected that Chris had had more complimentary whisky than he'd let on. "Comforting? That's your explanation for all of this nonsense—that it's *comforting*?"

"Of course," I said, trying to keep my voice even. Chris would sober up soon enough, and my normal brother would be returned to me. I hoped. "Why would people keep doing these things," I gestured at the tree, all of the flapping bits of cloth prayers and the offerings scattered about, "if no one ever got anything out of it?"

Chris looked from me to the tree, and back at me. "If all this goddamn magic shit is real, then why is my life over?" he ground out. "You think I didn't pray for an answer? For Olivia to come back to me? I did. Every single day, I did. You know what I got?" His voice cracked, and he looked toward the horizon. "Nothing. Because there's nothing to get."

He stalked down the hill, muttering away about the uselessness of magic and prayers. I watched him until he disappeared around a curve, then I turned back to the tree.

"Don't worry," I said, patting the rough bark. "I believe in you, Reverend Kirk. I know what really happened. And I'd rescue you if I could."

Chapter Two
Chris

I walked down the hill toward the rental car, mad at myself for lashing out at Rina, mad that she'd brought me to this God awful tourist trap, mad about so many things.

I was sick of being an angry jerk. My situation was the fault of exactly one person, and one person only: Olivia.

Olivia, whom I'd loved more than I thought I could love someone.

Olivia, who'd filed a lawsuit against me and was slowly, methodically ruining my life.

I tripped over a rock, and caught myself against a tree. Once I was steady I grabbed the rock and flung it as far as I could, and watched it drop soundlessly into the brush. Just like my life, the rock went out with a whimper rather than a roar. Shit. I'd do anything for a good roar.

I leaned against the tree, and gave myself a little pity party. In the past month I'd failed as an author, teacher, and man, and I just couldn't wait to find out what else life had in store for me. All the whisky in Scotland couldn't make me forget how I'd screwed up, nor could it help me fix things.

I heard Rina on the path behind me, and felt like an even bigger jerk. Rina had just had her own bout of life kicking her in the arse, and was she wallowing like a pathetic sot? No, she was out, working hard on her degree and moving forward. Rina was the one person who'd never doubted me, and the only one who had always had my back. If it wasn't for her, I don't know if I would have survived Olivia leaving me, and the rest of the fallout.

I straightened up and ground the heel of my hand against my eyes, not that I'd been crying. I'd moved past tears some weeks ago. I wanted to be strong for Rina, not some loser whose life was crumbling to bits. She's always been there for me, and I would be there for her.

I needed to be there for her, if for no other reason than to not fail again.

"Hey," Rina said, when she saw me after she rounded the bend in the trail. "You all right?"

"Yeah," I replied. "Just catching my breath." Rina

eyed me, but said nothing. I hated that she'd been reduced to taking care of me, when I should be the one guiding her. "Would you like to get some lunch? My treat, even though you dragged me to another lame pile of rocks," I added.

Rina's face broke into a smile; she'd never been offended by my teasing, not when we were kids, and not now that we were adults. "I do like lunch. And I saw a really cute pub when we passed through Aberfoyle."

I nodded, then we resumed walking toward the car park. "Cute pub it is."

Chapter Three
Karina

We drove away from the latest lame pile of rocks, as Chris had so eloquently put it, and went straight to the center of the village. Since the pub I'd wanted to go to had a window display of fairies dancing in a ring, I passed it and parked near the next, smaller pub. After how upset Chris had gotten at the kirk, and the last thing I wanted was to get into another argument. Besides, the poor guy had been through enough.

The pub was a seat yourself affair, so we picked a table near the bar. We'd just gotten settled when our waitress arrived.

"Welcome, welcome," she said as she set down menus. "Drinks to start?"

"Beer, a big one," Chris said.

"I'll have tea," I said. "What kind of soup do you have?"

"Today's is a cullen skink."

"Um." I glanced at the menu. "That's fish, right?"

The server smiled. "Aye, 'tis fish. A bowl with some bread and butter then?" I nodded, and she glanced at Chris. "And for you?"

"May I get a sandwich, roast beef or something like that? And a whisky with the beer," he added.

"O' course ye may." She gathered up our menus, and we stared out the window at the car park. When our drinks were delivered we silently tended them, me stirring my tea and Chris downing his whisky. As I watched my brother wallow in alcohol and despair, my heart cracked a little further. It killed me to see him like this; it killed me even more that there wasn't anything I could do for him, short of turning back time, and I'd watched way too many science fiction movies to think that that would end well. I'd probably step on a butterfly and ruin the world.

"What are you going to do when we get back home?" I ventured.

"What can I do?" he countered, staring into his beer. "I've lost my job, I've lost my reputation... Hell, I'm about to lose my home." He uttered one of those short, barking laughs. "Maybe I'll burn all the copies of my books and set up shop in the shipping boxes. Maybe the garbage men will pick me up, throw me in a trash compactor, and put me out of my misery."

"You don't know what's going to happen," I reminded him. "The case is still ongoing. If you get the plagiarism charges dropped all of this could go away."

Chris narrowed his eyes over the top of his pint. "This will *never* go away," he said. "She's been on talk shows, telling them about how we researched the manuscript together, telling them about us." He slammed his glass onto the table, beer sloshing up and over the edge, and held his head in his hands. "Us. Out of all of this, I wish there was still an us. I miss Olivia so goddamned much."

And now we were on to the waterworks portion of our day. Since Chris had been hit with the plagiarism suit by his ex-fiancée's lawyer, his days have gone thusly:

1. Wake up, ready to take on the world and prove my innocence!
2. My professional credentials will see me through!
3. I can't believe Olivia would do such a thing. What did I ever see in her?
4. My colleagues hate me. My friends won't speak to me. I am ruined, both professionally and personally.
5. Why can't Olivia just love me again?

Ah, Olivia. While I'd never disliked her, I had always suspected that there was a bit more to her than she let on. She had met Chris while he was in the midst of writing his third novel, *Bones of the Bard*, the New York Times bestseller that had made him a household name. It was a masterpiece of historical fiction, weaving together the known facts of Shakespeare's life along with several other Elizabethan writers, and some rather scandalous court intrigue. Olivia had stood by Chris while he struggled with the first draft of the novel, through rejection slip after rejection slip, while those first few reviews trickled in, and during the book's steep, quick climb up the bestseller list, where it had remained for nearly a year.

The day Chris had received a *two hundred and fifty thousand dollar* advance for his next book, Olivia's agent cum lawyer filed a lawsuit stating that Chris had plagiarized one of her manuscripts. We hadn't even known that she'd written a book. The fact that Olivia had met Chris while she had been a student in Chris's sophomore literature course was not helping matters.

The fact that Chris was actively trying to drown himself in all forms of booze also wasn't helping matters.

"Are ye all right, lad?" the server asked as she placed Chris's plate in front of him. It was filled with his sandwich, and a side order of neeps and tatties, which was what us Americans called mashed turnips and potatoes. I hoped all that protein and starch would sober him up a bit.

"He's fine," I answered. "Just been out in the sun a bit too long." I gave her my brightest smile, the one that had always worked wonders on grumpy professors and misbehaving customers alike. In addition to being a grad student, I'd held my own fair share of waitressing jobs.

My smile still had it, and the server looked sympathetically at Chris, and patted his arm before she set my soup before me. Before I started on my soup I pulled out my field notebook.

"You took notes at the hill?" Chris asked.

"I take notes everywhere," I replied, adjusting my glasses on the bridge of my nose. Sometimes Chris was proud of me working toward my doctorate in geology. Other times, I think he wished I'd chosen a major that didn't involve me being filthy all the time. Shakespearean professors do prefer having presentable siblings.

"Tell me again how you got your benefactors to buy into your hare-brained thesis?"

I ignored the jibe, but answered the question. "Probably because it's never been researched before." My "hare-brained thesis" was about the rock types and layers found in and around ley lines that passed through historically significant spiritual sites. Ley lines had been studied plenty—Carson even offered a dowsing certificate—but no one had ever studied the bedrock beneath the lines.

It is a known fact that certain types of stone, such as limestone and quartz, vibrate on specific frequencies which can be measured with an oscillator, which is why they're used in things like wristwatches. My theory was that areas said to contain spiritual phenomena were constructed of and on a similar type of stone, thus resulting in locations across the globe having accumulated similar magical attributions over the years. Basically, I thought ghosts were an expression of a location's natural vibrational capacity.

Chris snorted. "Why don't you interview some of those archeoastronomy and ley line experts on that television show?" he pressed. "You know, the ones that talk about ancient aliens?"

I glared at him; I knew exactly what show Chris was referring to, and it was atrocious. If you're going to claim to be a scholar, the least you can do is comb your hair. "My work has nothing to do with aliens, ancient or otherwise," I snapped. "There is a scientific foundation for what I'm doing. Telluric currents, for instance." He raised that eyebrow again, so I explained, "Telluric currents are natural energy currents running throughout the earth. Look it up."

"I don't need to look up," he grumbled. Satisfied that I'd won that little bout, I turned my attention back to my notes. No matter what Chris said, this "hare-brained theory" of mine had gotten me this research grant across the pond that we were both enjoying. Therefore, someone other than I thought it held water. That was good.

I penciled in a few notes while I nibbled at my bread, then I glanced at my phone. It was still early afternoon, and I was hoping we could stop by the Trossachs Discovery Center after lunch. If I'd read the map correctly, there was a walking trail that was adjacent to the Highland Boundary Fault. Walking trails with nearby fault lines were just the kinds of things that make geologists happy.

Satisfied with that day's notes, I reached into my pack for my favorite pen. When I couldn't find it, I upended the entire daypack onto the table, and noticed I was missing a few other items as well: a brush, a battered hair clip that had traveled to many dusty sites with me, and a lump of rose quartz.

My heart thudded as I searched for these items. Most—well, all—of them were easily replaceable, but the rose quartz had been a gift from Jared. I'd carried it around since I was a freshman at Carson University, and even though I'd resolved to cut all ties with Jared, I couldn't bring myself to get rid of the stone. Despite what had happened with Jared and me, the quartz had become my talisman.

I searched my memory, trying to recall the last time I'd held it, when I remembered reaching into my pack at the top of Doon Hill.

"I have to go back to the kirk," I said suddenly, sweeping everything back into my pack. "I think I dropped my lucky quartz."

"Jared's rock?" Chris smirked, and I glared at him. We had an understanding, my brother and I: as long as he didn't mention Jared, I wouldn't mention Olivia. If we didn't keep to the agreement we were both liable to weep our way across the countryside.

"Yes," I replied. "Will you be all right on your own for half an hour or so?"

Chris drained his pint, and waved to the server for a refill. "I'll manage."

***

I sped back to the ruined kirk, my knuckles white as I gripped the wheel. The real reason I didn't get on Chris about his constant mooning over Olivia was that at least he and Olivia had had something. I'd had nothing with Jared. No it hadn't quite been nothing, but it may as well have been. One thing that Chris and I had both learned on this trip is that an ocean is not nearly enough distance to outrun your past.

I parked in the kirk's tourist lot, leapt out of the rental and ran across the bridge and up the fairy hill, startling some of the local wildlife along the way. When I reached the Minister's Pine I was panting, my heart pounding as sweat poured down my back.

I had to find that quartz. I just had to.

I dropped to my knees and felt around near the base of the tree. I found my brush rather quickly, along with my hairclip and the stupidly expensive Mont Blanc pen that my advisor had given me when I earned my masters degree. But the quartz, the quartz wasn't anywhere. The bits of lunch I'd had turned to lead in my stomach; if the quartz was gone, then it was really, truly over.

"Lookin' for this, are ye now?"

I turned toward the voice, blinked, and pushed my glasses up to my forehead. Yeah, he was really there. Standing in front of me was a tall man in what I assumed was period dress. Instead of a kilt—we American girls tend to think that all Scotsmen run around in kilts, no matter the occasion; sadly, this is not the case—he was wearing a padded brown leather coat topped with chain mail, along with matching brown pants and well-worn leather boots. A helmet was tucked under his arm, and I could see the hilt of a claymore, one of those medieval broadswords that were so heavy you had to swing it with two hands, poking up over his shoulder. A shield rested next to the sword's hilt, its curved edge just visible above the man's shoulder.

I hadn't realized they did reenactments at Doon Hill, and I made a mental note to check the brochure for show times. I also noticed that the actor had his hand extended, with my lump of rose quartz sitting on his open palm.

"Yes!" I got to my feet, and grabbed the stone. "Thank you," I said once I remembered my manners, stroking the stone with my thumb. The man looked at me intently, his expression wavering somewhere between confusion and curiosity. "What made you think it was mine?"

"Saw ye drop it, I did," he replied.

"And you've been waiting here since then?"

"I knew ye would be back for me."

I blinked, since I must have misunderstood his accent. What I'd heard as 'me' must have really been 'it'. Accents do tend to garble words. "I really appreciate you waiting for me. Thank you," I said, extending my hand.

He eyed my hand, dark brows low over his blue eyes. Then he grasped my fingers and brought them toward his mouth.

"What are you doing?" I snapped, snatching my hand away.

"I thought ye wanted me to kiss your hand," he explained.

"I wanted to *shake* your hand!" He looked befuddled rather than offended, so I attributed this to yet another cultural misunderstanding. It was becoming quite the list. "Well, regardless, thank you. I'm Rina."

"Rina," he repeated, that Scottish brogue of his making my nickname sound positively decadent. "'Tis quite an unusual name."

"It's short for Karina," I explained. "Karina Siobhan Stewart," I added, wondering why I'd felt compelled to give him my full name. Historically I'd only been called Karina Siobhan when I was in trouble.

"And I am Robert Kirk," he said, extending his hand. This guy was way deep in character, like method actor deep. I shook his hand, and we both smiled.

"Good to meet you, Mr. Kirk."

"Reverend Kirk," he corrected.

"My apologies, Reverend Kirk." These reenactors sure liked to stick to their roles, though I'd never expected to see a reverend wearing chain mail. We stood there for a moment, holding hands and grinning like a couple of fools, and I took the time to really look at him. He was older than me, probably a bit older than Chris too, with dark, tousled hair, chiseled features, and a roguish glint in his blue eyes. They had obviously picked reenactors that would appeal to the ladies.

"Do no' fash, Karina lass, no offense was taken," he murmured, and my cheeks were suddenly hot. I took back my hand, barely resisting the urge to fan myself.

"I should be going," I said. "My brother's waiting for me." I scanned the area around the Minister's Pine, ascertained that I'd left nothing else of import behind, and turned toward the path. A hand on my arm stopped me.

"Ye canna leave me here," the reenactor said. "Ye must take me with ye."

"What? No!" I faced him, planting my feet before him and whipping out my cell phone. "I don't know what goes on here in Scotland, but I'm an American citizen. Stay back, or I'll call 911." I didn't even know if they had 911 in Scotland. Would I have to call Scotland Yard instead? I hoped my phone had some kind of app for international emergencies. I waved my phone in what I hoped was a menacing manner, and Robert—or whatever his name was—eyed it as if it would bite him.

"Put away your tricks, lass," he said. "It was ye what called me here in the first place."

I shook my head. "This is an act, right? Reverend Kirk, freed at long last from the Minister's Pine?"

"'Tis no act, lass. Would that it were." He stepped closer, and took my hands in both of his. Robert's hands were warm and callused, and, despite all this nonsense, comforting. "I am Robert Kirk himself, and ye have freed me no from just a tree, but from Elphame, and the Seelie Queen herself."

"Elphame?" I asked.

"Aye," he replied. "Some refer to it as the Fairy Realm."

I leaned against the Minister's Pine. He claimed he was from Elphame. Of course he was. How did I always attract the weirdos?

It was generally agreed that when magic left the world, it was because the fairy realm had closed its doors to humans. Some claimed that human industrialization, and its rampant use of iron, had caused the fae to retreat, while others claimed the global shift from pagan to monotheistic faiths was the culprit. No matter which theory you favored, the end result was the same; there was no new magic. For hundreds of years humans had made do with a few crumbling artifacts and enchanted items, but those items were wearing out too. It was as if magic had a half-life, and we'd long since passed the middle point.

"You can't be from Elphame," I said. "It's closed. It's been closed for centuries."

"Has it, now? I will say this, when I was a boy the land was thick with magic. Ye could hardly walk the roads without encountering one o' the Good People."

"When you were a boy," I repeated, then I remembered that Robert Kirk had lived in the seventeenth century. Magic hadn't started disappearing until a century later. "Still, it's closed now."

"Just because a door has been closed, does no' mean it canna be reopened."

I slid down to the ground and Robert sat beside me, both of us leaning against the tree he'd recently emerged from.

Wait, when did I start believing him?

"So, um, you think all of this is real?" I ventured, gesturing around the clearing. "The legend and all?"

Robert smiled wanly. "Ye have heard o' me, then?"

"They say you told the world of the fairies' secrets, so they imprisoned you in a tree."

"That is no the whole of the tale." Robert closed his eyes as he leaned his head back against the trunk. "I did have dealings with the Good People, but it was no them who abducted me."

"Then who did?"

"'Twas Nicnevin, the Seelie Queen herself."

My jaw dropped, and if I hadn't already been on the ground I would have fallen. As it was, my arm went out from under me, and my shoulder bumped into Robert. "Are ye all right, lass?" Robert asked.

"Yes," I lied. There was nothing all right about this. "Why did the queen take you?"

"She fancied me," he replied. "Offered me an apple, ye ken. I said no, it angered her, she cursed me. And here we are today."

I looked up at him. He still had his head tipped back against the tree, his eyes closed. "That sounds like the ridiculously oversimplified version."

At that, he opened his eyes and speared me with his gaze. "Would ye be likin' all the details, then, lass?"

I swallowed. "Um, maybe not just yet." My gaze moved from Robert's face to the quartz in my hand. "What makes you think I freed you?"

"Ye made contact wi' the tree, wishin' to rescue me. Wishes are powerful things, ye ken." Robert leaned over and touched the quartz. "Then ye dropped your stone, and a door opened for me. I ha' been waitin' for ye ever since."

"Wishes are powerful things," I repeated. "Why do you want to leave with me? You don't even know me."

"I know ye freed me, and that is no small thing," Robert replied. "I also know that as soon as Nicneven kens I've left me post, she will send her creatures to retrieve me."

"Creatures?"

"Aye. And I do no' want to be here when they arrive."

I took a deep breath and got to my feet, Robert following suit. Once we were standing I looked into his clear blue eyes, his guileless face, and sighed. He was either telling the truth, or he was the greatest actor in the world. Or I was the world's biggest idiot; the jury was still out on that.

"Well, let's go."

"Go?" he repeated hopefully.

"If you're telling the truth—and I'm not saying that you are—I can't just leave you here. And, if you're not telling the truth, I'll drop you at the nearest police station," I added, trying to act tough in front of the armored man with the sword.

Robert inclined his head, and took both of my hands in his. "Lass, soon enough ye will ken that I only speak what's true." He once again brought my knuckles to his lips; this time, I let him kiss me. It was nice, having one's hand kissed by a dark, handsome man. "Karina Siobhan Stewart, I am now your charge, and I shall follow your every command."

"Okay. Um." I looked him over and issued my first command. "First of all, you can't tromp around Aberfoyle wearing chain mail. You're going to have to take off your armor."

<<◇>>

Continue the story here.

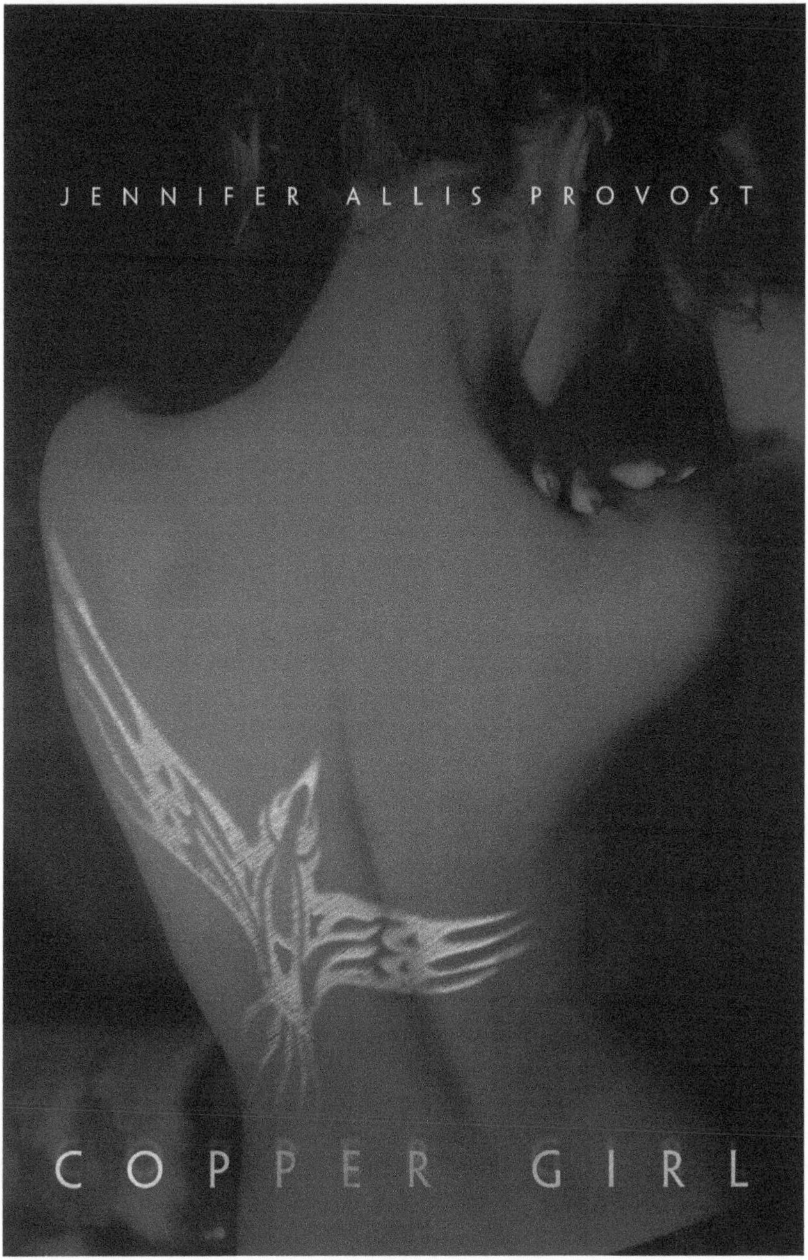
JENNIFER ALLIS PROVOST
COPPER GIRL

Chapter 1

It seemed like a good idea at the time.

My office, like most modern offices, cranked the air conditioning down to Arctic proportions during the summer months. Consequently, we workers arrived in the morning dressed in sandals and sleeveless tops, donned heavy sweaters upon reaching our desks, and ended up shivering by noon. Ironically, when our workday ended we were hit by a wall of oppressive heat the moment we stepped outside the main doors. No, this wasn't a flawed system in the slightest.

That day, I wasn't having it. I conceived the grand idea of spending my lunch hour outside, away from the icy wind stiffening my fingers and chilling my neck. After I unwound myself from the afghan I kept in my desk (and only used in the summer months), I gathered up my lunch and my phone, and headed out for an impromptu picnic in my car.

What I hadn't considered was that the office runs the air conditioning so high because it was, well, *hot* outside. Very hot, in fact. So hot that the cheese was melting in my sandwich and the lettuce looked like something that had washed ashore months, maybe even years, ago. I was parked in the shade and had taken down my car's convertible top, but I still couldn't manage to get comfortable. I'd already shed my sandals and cardigan, which left me wearing my sundress and...

Dare I?

I glanced around the parking lot of Real Estate Evaluation Services, the 'go-to firm for all your commercial real estate needs', according to the brochures. No one, human or drone, was taking a noontime stroll, and by virtue of my being on the far side of the lot, no cars were near mine. Most of my coworkers didn't even have cars, so the lot was rarely more than half full. What was more, from where I sat, I couldn't even see the office.

I dared.

I took a deep breath and channeled my inner wild woman, then leaned the seat back and slipped off my panties. Removing that small bit of cotton made an incredible difference, and the heat became somewhat bearable. Enjoyable, even. Was that a breeze?

Ignoring my decrepit sandwich, I fully reclined the seat, set the alarm on my phone, and closed my eyes. A nap. Now *that* would make today bearable.

Suddenly, he is there.
Here.

Kissing me, holding me.

I know I'm dreaming, because he's perfect. His lips are soft but insistent, his hands gentle. I glide my fingers across his back, feeling thick cords of muscle, before sinking my fingers into his hair. It's superfine, like cobwebs, and when I crack an eyelid, I learn that it's silver. Not gray or white, but the elegant hue of antique candlesticks and fine flatware. Cool.

I squeeze my eyes shut again, not wanting the dream to end any sooner than it has to. He kisses me once more, and I can't help melting against him. His hand travels up my leg, up past my hip... shit! No panties!

I try twisting away, but he already knows. I feel his mouth stretch into a smile, and he moves to nuzzle my neck. "What's your name?" he murmurs.

"Sara," I reply. "Yours?"

"Micah." By now, his hands have traveled to my waist, and he slides one around to stroke the small of my back. "Why did you summon me, Sara?"

"I didn't," I protest. "I don't know how." I would say more, but he nibbles a trail from my neck to my shoulder, and pushes my dress to the side. Me, I let him.

Micah raises his head, and I get a good look at him for the first time. His eyes are large and dark gray, like thunderheads, his features chiseled into warm caramel skin, and his unruly mop of silver hair seems to float around his head. He wears an odd, buff-colored leather shirt, made all the odder in this heat, and matching leather pants and boots. Boots?

"You did summon me," he insists. "My Sara, you must tell me why."

"Does it matter?" I ask. I pull him back to me, kissing him with a passion I've never felt with anyone during my waking hours. Micah kisses me back, fingers deftly unbuttoning my dress while his other hand rubs my lower back. I've never felt so free, so alive, as I do in Micah's embrace, and I have no intention of rushing this. None at all.

My phone screamed for attention, thus ending the best dream that had ever been dreamed. Ever. I fumbled to silence it then shook myself back to reality. I still felt warm and glowy from the dream, almost after-glowy. It wasn't until I stretched and got tangled in my clothing that I noticed anything amiss.

The straps of my dress had slid down around my elbows, and the dress itself was unbuttoned to my waist. What's more, my bra was all askew and a nipple was dangerously close to freedom. I shot a quick glance around the parking lot as I fixed my clothing;

luckily, there was no one around, either of the human or robotic drone persuasion. I hoped no one had gotten an eyeful of me fondling myself in my sleep.

Some dream. Soon enough, I got the top half of my dress squared away and reached into the passenger seat, only to come up empty. My panties were gone.

Great. Either one of my coworkers had found me sleeping and stolen them, or a randy squirrel had absconded with my delicates. Hoping for the latter, I stuffed my feet back into my sandals and returned to the office and an ever-growing mound of paperwork.

Speaking of the mound, there was a fresh sheaf of reports on my desk, ready for sorting. My title, if it can be called such, is Quarterly Report Collator. *This impressive moniker means that I have the ability—no, make that the responsibility— to place various documents and reports in their proper order, usually alphabetical, but I've been known to utilize ascending numbers when the occasion warrants, a feat those who get paid far more than I cannot seem to manage. As long as they keep paying me, I'm fine with my place on the food chain, low though it may be. It sure beats the alternative, a luxurious but caged life as a sellout government shill, performing spells on command as if they were parlor tricks. My family may have lost much, but we still have some pride left.*

I dove right into the heap of reports, for once appreciating the mindless work, since it gave me the mental space to dwell on my dream lover. Why would a man in my dream claim that I'd summoned him? And what was with his getup? Micah had looked like he should be playing the part of a swashbuckling hero in a trashy romance novel, not hanging around in the parking lot of a midsized corporation specializing in commercial real estate acquisitions and liquidations.

And his name: Micah. I was certain that I'd never heard it before, which puzzled me. If I were going to create a dream lover, wouldn't I give him a regular name like Tom, or Joe? A name I was at least familiar with?

I swiveled in my chair and called up my search engine. We are not, under any circumstances, supposed to use this bit of technology that is standard issue with each and every one of our ergonomically correct workstations. I'm not quite sure what the punishment for internet usage is, but I've always imagined ninjas dropping out of the ceiling and hauling me off to their lair. After enduring a mild torture session, I'm given a cup of hot sake and sent on my way.

I could have waited until I got home. I have a nicer computer and better, faster internet access than the office does, but

I couldn't wait. Not while the image of Micah's thundercloud eyes still burned in my memory, inciting not-safe-for-work thoughts.

I typed in *Micah: define,* and the results page immediately listed a bunch of Biblical references. Mmm, not exactly helpful. I clicked around for a while until I found one of those sites that specialized in the meaning of names. It read:

Micah (mī ' kə) he who resembles God.

Huh. My dream man was certainly attractive, but I didn't know if I'd go so far as to call him a god. Then I remembered that there was also stone called mica, which also seemed like an unlikely source for me to pull a name from. In the midst of typing *mica: stone,* I was interrupted.

"Hey, beautiful."

I glanced up and saw Floyd, the office sleaze, hovering at the edge of my cubicle. This day kept getting better and better. I clicked off the browser and nonchalantly swiveled away from the keyboard. To throw the ninjas off my trail, of course. "You and Juliana heading over to The Room tonight?" he asked.

The Room is a local hangout, stocked with stale beer and watered-down liquor, not to mention a floor that has never, ever been mopped. Not. Even. Once. But it's cheap and close to the office, so we all go. Since I had first started working at REES, I'd been a regular. "We haven't discussed it."

"Everyone's going," Floyd pressed. "C'mon, I'll buy you a drink. You like gin and tonic, right?"

I heaved the stack of reports from my lap to my desk and uncrossed my legs, squarely planting my feet in order to deliver the Keep Away From Me speech to Floyd yet again, when I remembered my lack of undergarments. Quickly, I snatched my afghan from where I'd tossed it before lunch and spread it across my lower body like a shield.

"Whatever," I mumbled, which Floyd counted as a victory.

"See you there," he drawled. *I hate him.*

I spent the rest of my shift with my thighs clamped together, having mild anxiety attacks whenever I stood. Or sat. Or reached for anything. Needless to say, by the end of the day I was more than ready for something eye-wateringly alcoholic. Juliana, my best friend and REES' office manager, was game, as she usually was, and we made it to The Room in time for happy hour. Normally, I feel like I'm in her shadow, what with her long, dark hair, matching eyes, and the body of a pre-war pinup girl, but tonight I didn't care. Right about now, a little overshadowing was just what the doctor ordered.

After a few bowls of pretzels, and more than a few cocktails, I confessed my *al fresco* state, to which Juliana and I clinked glasses and downed a few shots in honor of my missing panties. Floyd, the scum, welshed on his promise of gin and tonic. *I really do hate him.*

Chapter 2

Happy hour turned into last call, and Juliana gladly accepted my offer of crashing on my couch. We were forever staying over at one another's apartments, since we lived on opposite sides of town. Not to mention the fact that Juliana didn't own a car and public transportation was both expensive and unreliable. If you counted on the bus schedule, you might get caught out after curfew, and Peacekeepers, our friendly neighborhood government goons, weren't known for their understanding natures. Since neither Juliana nor I wanted to pay the late penalty, whoever's place was closer to the side of town we ended up on invariably became our resting place for the evening. Since I lived closest to The Room, I played hostess more often.

While Juliana settled herself on the couch, I grabbed a quick shower, only to end up standing before my closet, dripping wet, overthinking what I would wear to bed. Like it mattered, right? Normally, I'm a tank top and shorts girl, but there was this cute, pale lavender silk, just sexy enough nightie that hung out in the back of my closet. I'd bought it almost a year ago for a boyfriend who hadn't lasted long enough to see it. His loss, really.

I unceremoniously dropped my robe and slipped the nightie over my head. The lace bodice was so revealing I was practically topless, and the short skirt floated over my hips. As I pulled on the matching panties, I deliberately did not question why I'd decided on this outfit. Then I flipped off the air conditioner *(whenever it runs while I sleep I get a headache)*, opened the window, and climbed into bed. In no time, I was asleep.

I felt him before I saw him, his firm body pressed against mine, his lips caressing the back of my neck. *Micah.* I rolled over to face him. Even in the darkness of my room I could see he was still in that weird brown getup, boots and all, but I didn't care. Hopefully, it would be gone soon.

"Micah," I murmured, savoring his name on my tongue. "You're here."

"I heard your call, my Sara," he murmured. "You're wearing more here," he continued, tracing the edge of my panties, "but less here." His deft fingers danced across my lacy bodice.

"Do you like it?"

"I do." Micah hooked a finger inside my panties and drew them lower. "I most certainly do." We remained wrapped in each other for long, blissful moments, until he spoke again. "I am so glad you called me again, my Sara."

"Why do you keep saying that?" I asked. Yes, I argued with a dream. I am a psychology student's dream thesis. Ha ha. Dream. "You're not even real."

At that, Micah raised his head. "I am as real as you are," he replied, somewhat indignantly. "Twice now, you have called me to your dream."

What? No, no, no, no, that's not good. Not good, not good at all. "That's not possible," I whispered.

"It is more than possible, my Sara. It has come to pass." Serious now, Micah sat up and took my hands. "I have watched you often, gazing toward the entrance to my lands. I've always felt your power. Still, until earlier today, I had no idea that you are a Dreamwalker, as I am."

He said it. He just had to say it. "Don't say that!" Micah looked hurt and confused, so I amended, "If anyone hears you, there'll be questions." I glanced toward the open window, but I neither saw nor heard a drone whizzing by.

Micah nodded, but his brow remained furrowed. "As you wish."

"I still don't understand," I continued, moving to sit up. "You say I was looking toward your lands, but I don't even know where you're from."

"Where you put your mechanical for the day," he replied as he tucked a lock of hair behind my ear. "The trees you favor mark the entrance to my domain."

Once I figured out that 'mechanical' meant 'car', I considered where I parked in the office lot. I'd always chosen to leave my convertible in the back of the lot, mainly because it was a nice car and most of my coworkers, like most everyone else these days, were dirt poor. I didn't want to answer any questions about how I could afford such a nice vehicle if I didn't have to.

But Micah was right in that I'd always favored one particular spot. It was situated in front of two pine trees, their massive trunks wound together like a lovers' embrace. I'd never seen anything like it, certainly not in such big trees, and they'd captivated me from the moment I saw them. And yes, I gazed at them often.

"The pine trees?" I asked. Micah smiled when he nodded. But that didn't answer my questions, since they weren't in front of a door or path. There wasn't even anything behind them, except the electric fence separating REES from the property next door.

Suddenly, my eyes widened in shock and recognition and I grabbed a handful of his silvery hair, exposing a set of pointed ears. "You're an elf!"

"Micah Silverstrand, Lord of the Whispering Dell," he replied, with a polite nod. Rubbing my temples, I considered my situation. I was in a dream that wasn't a dream, sitting in bed with a man whom I'd thought was a mere figment of my imagination, but who happened to be some sort of royal elf. And a Dreamwalker. Like me. Maybe—hopefully—I was just really drunk.

But... I can't explain it, but as I looked at this elf, with his silver eyes and fluffy hair, he was more real to me than anyone else I'd ever known.

"I'm sorry, Micah," I said at length. "I didn't know I could call anyone this way. Nothing like this has ever happened to me before."

At that, his pale brows nearly touched. "When you offered a token and lay nearly bare before me, I assumed you wanted me." Token? Oh, right, panties. "And tonight, you have bathed for me, attired yourself as a queen, and have allowed me egress to your chamber. What else was I to think?" I stared from the open window to my silk nightie. Why *had* I put this on? Had I been calling him, subconsciously? Could I even do that? I didn't know. But I couldn't do it again. Not unless I wanted to end up like Max.

Micah was still speaking, so I met his gaze. "When I learned that you are of metal, as I am, our attraction became clear." *Crap. He knows I'm an Elemental, too?*

Of metal. *There are two ways one can learn the workings of magic: years and years of rigorous study, or by simply being born to it. If you're born into a magical bloodline, you're said to be touched by an element, either earth, air, fire, water, or metal. The nature of your element is passed from father to child, just like a surname. Once in a while, someone is born touched by more than one element, but that's awfully rare.*

You also take on the characteristics of your chosen element, or rather, the element that's chosen you. For instance, those touched by fire tend to be quick to anger, and those of earth are stubborn but loyal. I've never met anyone who admitted to being touched by water, but I've always imagined them as cowardly. And air? Who knows what they're like? Flighty, perhaps?

I've always been glad that my family's line is of metal. It means I'm strong, both physically and mentally, and courageous. I'm loyal, like those of earth, but not quite so stubborn. And... and that's all I really know, because we haven't been allowed to speak of magic since the wars ended, and magic was outlawed.

I was young when the wars had begun, but from what I remembered, the news reports all said that the wars had started when those who'd been born without magic became jealous of

Elementals' innate abilities. So, the learned magicians got together with the Mundane humans and started up their own civil rights movement, claiming that they should be considered equal to the Elementals. The problem was, they weren't equal. They never, ever would be, being that it took months, or years, for a Mundane to learn even simple spells, like the casting of a fey stone. When the Elementals brought up this small but important fact, all hell had broken loose. Literally.

Still, there had been no war or outright rebellion. The learned magicians may have been collectively outraged, but they grudgingly accepted their place, and the Mundane humans—those who did not study magic—were content with things as they were. Then, a Fire Elemental conceived of a way to sell fey stones to the masses. Normally a fey stone will only burn in the presence of its caster, but this enterprising individual spent decades studying the spell and determined which materials would cause the light to burn for years. It was a brilliant invention, one that could save the average family hundreds, or maybe thousands, in electricity. Just imagine, a never-ending light bulb.

The Mundane CEO of the power company had not been pleased by this development.

The wars had lasted almost three years, but we weren't discouraged. We—the Elementals—knew that we were stronger, and we'd never had any doubt that we'd prevail. Then, the unthinkable happened. We lost.

To this day, no one knows how. Oh, there's lots of speculation, but the real reasons remain somewhat elusive. The schoolbooks say that many of the war mages realized the error of their ways and immolated themselves. Yes, they used the word immolate, and that, right there, is a clue that it's all propaganda. Other sources claim that Elementals don't mesh well with those of opposing natures, and infighting was what did us in. That supposed infighting was also the impetus for creating the Peacekeepers, a squad of government goons specially outfitted to make Elemental lives miserable.

Well, no matter which version they hand out in their propaganda, the end result was the same: the Council of Elementals disappeared, and without their leadership, we lost.

My dad was on that council.

Once the Mundanes claimed victory, we assumed that life would pretty much return to normal, but we were so, so wrong. Instead of just declaring themselves equal to the Elementals, the learned magicians were outlawed, along with all other 'unlicensed magic.' In essence, without a special dispensation from the government *(who toss spells around like cheap confetti)* you could be thrown in prison for something as innocuous as conjuring up a bit of heat to warm your coffee.

We never found out what happened to Dad.

I'd spent most of my life trying to pass for ordinary. I tried to act like a Mundane human, someone who didn't understand magic. I never talked about it, never thought about it, and never, ever practiced it. So, how did Micah know?

"Of metal?" I asked, tentatively.

"I was certain when I felt your mark." Huh. No one mentioned marks, either. I usually kept mine covered, but those who saw it either thought it was a tramp stamp, or refused to let on that they recognized the signs of magic. "Copper, yes?"

"Copper," I affirmed, my voice now hardly a whisper. "You could tell just by feeling it?"

"By your hair," he replied. I protested that I dyed my hair, but he looked pointedly at my hips. Oh, right. "May I see it? Your mark, I mean."

I didn't see any reason why he couldn't, since he'd pretty much seen the rest of me. I turned around and lifted my nightie, exposing the mark across my lower back that forever named me as a member of the Raven clan, one of the most powerful bloodlines in history. Well, before magic was outlawed; now we were just... regular. And watched. My mark was copper colored, and took the shape of a raven with its wings outstretched, the tips of the feathers reaching my sides. My sister, Sadie, bore a nearly identical mark. I didn't remember what Max's mark had looked like.

Micah traced the edges of the raven, his light touch sending shivers through my body. I remembered how he'd massaged my back during our earlier encounter, how I'd instantly become a molten heap of need. "Is everyone's mark so sensitive?" I asked.

"Some, but not all," he replied, his fingers now stroking my spine, near the raven's maw. "Fire marks may burn you if you touch them, and those of stone feel hardly anything at all."

"Do you have a mark?" I asked, peeking over my shoulder. Again, Micah smiled at me.

"I do." He pulled off his leather shirt, revealing wiry muscle sheathed in warm, caramel skin. Before I could truly appreciate the most attractive male chest I'd ever encountered, he turned his back and I saw his mark. It was shining, metallic silver, just as mine was copper. It swept across his back like filigree wings emanating from his spine, arching over his shoulder blades in a graceful fall that reached below his waist.

"You... you're silver," I murmured, my eyes flitting from his mark to his hair. "Just like I'm copper, you're silver." Micah murmured some sort of an agreement, but I barely heard him.

Hesitantly, I touched his back, his mark glinting in the near-dark. His flesh was warm and inviting, almost hot where it was incised with silver. "Oh, Micah. I've never seen anything like it."

"Many thanks, my Sara." His muscles tensed, and I wondered if touching his mark was having the same effect on him as when he'd touched mine. I dropped my hands, and he turned to face me. "Forgive me, if I've misinterpreted your actions."

"I didn't know what I was doing, calling you," I admitted. "But I am that glad you came back to me." At that, he kissed me— hard—and pushed me onto my back. I didn't resist, far from it. I welcomed him.

"Wait," I breathed. "Will I ever see you while we're awake?"

"You wish to?"

I nodded. "More than anything."

"Hold me tightly, my Sara." I did, and the air thickened and rippled around us. Once again, I heard street noises, the radio blaring one floor up, and I could smell the alley. I'd been so thoroughly enchanted by Micah, I hadn't noticed the lack of the usual annoyances. But now that I was awake, they had returned, and there was a half-naked man in my bed.

I screamed, my wakeful self having no idea who Micah was or why he was here. Ever practical, Micah kissed me, effectively smothering my cries and jogging my memory at the same time. He knew he'd succeeded when I stopped screaming and kissed him back.

"I'm sorry," I whispered, still trembling. "It was so sudden!"

"It is hard to pull yourself to wakefulness so quickly," he murmured. "You behaved much better than I did my first time."

"I did?" He nodded, and wiped away tears I hadn't noticed. "Thank you."

"For what, my Sara?"

I didn't get to answer. My screams must have woken Juliana, and she was banging on my door. "I'm fine!" I yelled. "Just a nightmare."

"Open up!" Now, she was jiggling the handle. Luckily, I always locked my door, a habit left over from sleeping in the dorms, but she was insistent. Once she had decided on doing something, nothing could stop her.

"She can't find you here," I whispered. "They'll kill you if they find you." Micah nodded, and in the next moment, he was gone. I don't mean he left by way of the window, which I assumed was how he got in; he was here, and then he wasn't. I blinked but was quickly dragged out of my amazement by Juliana's banging and yelling. I pulled on my robe and threw open the door.

"You're gonna wake the neighbors," I admonished.

"The way you screamed, I thought one of them was murdering you," she countered.

"Aw. My Juliana in shining armor." She responded with an artful sneer, and we were back to normal.

"It's almost six, anyway. I'll make some coffee."

I nodded and shut the door to dress. Not only did I not want to explain my silk nightie to Juliana, but I figured I might as well get ready now. There wouldn't be any more sleep for me at the moment. After I picked out a pair of jeans and a shirt, I took off my robe and almost screamed again. He had taken my panties!

Continue the story here.

About the Author

Jennifer Allis Provost is a native New Englander who lives in a sprawling colonial along with her beautiful and precocious twins, a dog, a parrot, a junkyard cat, and a wonderful husband who never forgets to buy ice cream. As a child, she read anything and everything she could get her hands on, including a set of encyclopedias, but fantasy was always her favorite. She spends her days drinking vast amounts of coffee, arguing with her computer, and avoiding any and all domestic behavior.

Find her on the web here:
http://authorjenniferallisprovost.com/

Friend her on Facebook:
http://www.facebook.com/jennallis

Follow her on Twitter: @parthalan

Other books by Jennifer Allis Provost:

The Copper Legacy, a four book urban fantasy:
Copper Girl
Copper Ravens
Copper Veins
Copper Princess

A duology based in the Copper world:
Redemption
Salvation

Gallowglass, an urban fantasy set in Scotland and New York:
Gallowglass
Walker
Homecoming

The Winter's Queen Trilogy, featuring characters from Gallowglass
Touch of Frost
Giant's Daughter
Elphame's Queen

The Chronicles of Parthalan, a six volume epic fantasy:
Heir to the Sun
The Virgin Queen
Rise of the Deva'shi
Golem

Elfsong
Blood Prince

Changes, a contemporary romance:
Changing Teams
Changing Scenes
Changing Fate
Changing Dates

Lightning Source UK Ltd.
Milton Keynes UK
UKHW010710310821
389774UK00001B/136